HARD TRADE

A RINEHART SUSPENSE NOVEL

OTHER JACOB ASCH NOVELS BY ARTHUR LYONS

A RINEHART SUSPENSE NOVEL

HARD TRADE

Arthur Lyons

HOLT, RINEHART AND WINSTON
New York

Published by Holt, Rinehart and Winston,
383 Madison Avenue, New York, New York 10017.

Published simultaneously in Canada by Holt, Rinehart
and Winston of Canada, Limited.

Library of Congress Cataloging in Publication Data
Lyons, Arthur.
Hard trade.
(A Rinehart suspense novel)
1. Title.
PS3562.Y446H3   813'.54   80-19679
ISBN 0-03-053621-9

FIRST EDITION

Designer: *Lucy Castelluccio*
Printed in the United States of America
1   3   5   7   9   10   8   6   4   2

HARD TRADE

A RINEHART SUSPENSE NOVEL

One

The woman was a Munchkin. In three-inch Wedgies, she stood no more than five-one, which would have made her four-ten in her Supp-hosed feet, and her tiny, childlike body seemed lost in the baggy wool skirt and jacket she was wearing.

She stood just inside the doors of the restaurant, eagerly scanning the faces of the people waiting in the foyer, as if we were all new arrivals on Fantasy Island, and I knew immediately she had to be the one. Even if she had not told me she would be wearing gray, I would have known. The heavy-breathing, leggy blondes all went to Spade and Marlowe; I wound up with the refugees from Barnum and Bailey.

She stood there for a few seconds longer, then took a deep breath and moved reluctantly toward the reservation desk as if being forced to run a gauntlet. She had just made it to the desk when I stepped up behind her. "Miss Calabrese?"

She turned, startled.

"I'm Jacob Asch," I said, smiling reassuringly.

"Oh. Hello." Her hunched shoulders relaxed a little and she offered her hand, which was warm and unpleasantly moist. "I'm sorry I'm late. I got caught in the traffic. I hope you haven't been waiting too long."

There was nothing childlike about her face, nor anything

1

particularly distinctive about it. The lines around her mouth and the corners of her eyes read around thirty-five. She had an olive complexion and shiny, black, shoulder-length hair that ran straight across her forehead in bangs. Her nose was a bit too wide for her heart-shaped face, and she had a tiny pucker of a mouth darkly daubed with lipstick. Her brown eyes were wide-set and held the look of being startled, even after she had found out who I was.

"Not long at all," I told her. "Shall we sit down?"

She smiled nervously. "Fine."

I turned to the blonde beach-bunny hostess behind the desk and said: "You have my name—Asch."

The girl consulted her seating chart and told her assistant, another beach-bunny clone, to take us to table forty-two, wherever that was. We were led through a cocktail lounge filled with backgammon tables and stuffed leather couches, into a brick-walled dining room, where we were dropped into a dimly lit corner booth. It was only 11:40, but the place was already filling up with people trying to get a jump on the lunch crush.

A cocktail waitress came over and I ordered a Bloody Mary. When I asked her if she wanted a drink, Sylvia Calabrese shook her head ruefully. "Oh, no, thank you. I rarely drink, and never this early." When the waitress had gone, she said: "I hope this place wasn't too far out of your way."

"No."

"I suggested it because I had some business to take care of near here. That's why I was late. It took a little longer than I anticipated."

Her eyes refused to focus on my face while she talked, jumping back and forth from my chest to a spot somewhere over my head. The effect was disconcerting.

"What business are you in, Miss Calabrese?"

"I'm not in any business," she said quickly. "That is to say, I don't work. The business I had to take care of was personal."

Her saying she didn't work made me search her hands for a wedding ring. I didn't see one. "It *is* Miss Calabrese?"

"Miss," she said, smiling diffidently. "Actually, that's the reason I wanted to talk to you. I—"

She was interrupted by the waitress coming back with the Bloody Mary. I thought she would get into it when the waitress left again, but almost immediately another waitress was on top of the table, asking if we would like to order. Just to get that out of the way, I gave the menu a quick perusal and ordered the seafood salad. She ordered the same.

"Now," I said, trying to get eye contact, "what were you saying?"

For a heartbeat or two, I managed to grab her gaze, but then she looked away again and said: "Forgive me if I seem nervous, Mr. Asch. I . . . it's just that all this is so . . . well . . . strange to me. I've never done anything like it before."

I sipped my Bloody Mary. "Don't worry about it. The seafood salad is good here. I've had it before."

"I didn't mean *that*," she said seriously. "I meant hiring a private detective."

"Don't let that worry you, either," I told her. "You haven't hired one yet."

Her eyes widened and she blinked. "Pardon me?"

I shrugged. "After talking to me, you may not want to hire me. You may not like what I have to say. Then again, I may not like what you have to say. After all, you haven't told me what you want done."

She leaned forward. "Oh, I'm sure I'll like you. You seem like a very nice man."

There did not seem to be much to say to that, so I came back: "Then there's the matter of my fee—"

"Money is no object," she jumped in. "It's just that I have to be sure you are discreet. It's a very . . . delicate matter."

"You said on the phone that I'd been recommended to you, Miss Calabrese. May I ask by whom?"

Her eyes went from the ceiling to the tablecloth. She began fidgeting with the fork and said softly: "To tell you the truth, Mr. Asch, I lied. I picked your name out of the phone book. From the Yellow Pages. That's a bad way to choose somebody to handle a confidential matter, isn't it?"

"It could be, I suppose."

"I just didn't know anybody who'd ever dealt with a private detective before."

We were back to that again. I wondered if she was ever going to start talking about it. I took a good gulp of my Mary. I had a feeling I was going to need it. Maybe another one, too. "Are you really sure you want to deal with one now?"

"I *have* to," she said, her eyes imploring my collar button. "You see, I'm going to be married next month."

"Congratulations."

"Thank you. I just hope it's not premature."

"Why do you say that?"

"That's what I want to hire you to find out," she said in a tremulous voice. "I—I have to find out if Merle loves me."

"Merle?" I said.

"Merle Hoffman. My fiancé."

"Ah." I drained the vodka and tomato juice from my glass and signaled the waitress for another one. Her eye I could catch. She acknowledged me with a nod and went to the bar, and I turned my attention back to Sylvia Calabrese. Feeling like Dear Abby, I asked: "And what would make you think he doesn't love you?"

"He *says* he does and I want to believe him. I want to believe him more than anything in the world. But I have to be sure. You see, Mr. Asch, recently I came into an inheritance. Quite a sizable inheritance. I have to be sure that it's me Merle wants and not my money."

"Why would you think he's after your money?"

She began fidgeting with the silverware on the table in front of her. "Last week, I got a phone call. From a man. He

4

wouldn't tell me his name but said he was 'a friend.' He told me Merle is just marrying me for my money because he owes a lot of people money. He wouldn't say who the people were, but I assumed they were gamblers. He also said that all the time he's been seeing me, Merle's been seeing other women.

"Well, at the time I thought it was just some sort of sick joke and I hung up on him. There is so much sickness in the world nowadays. I never even mentioned it to Merle. As a matter of fact, I went over to Merle's office at the dump. I thought I'd surprise him and take him out to lunch—"

"The dump?"

She nodded her black bangs. "Merle is a sanitation engineer for the county. His office is at the Piedras Canyon landfill." She hesitated, and her face contorted painfully. "That's when I saw it."

"*It?*"

"Him. Them. Merle and a young girl. I was just parking my car when they came out of the office. They were laughing and she had hold of his arm. They got into his car and drove off without seeing me. I stayed in the car. I didn't know what to do. I wanted to follow him, but I couldn't. I just couldn't. It was like I was paralyzed. Maybe I was afraid of what I'd find out."

"Sometimes things look bad when they're really not," I offered. "Maybe it was just one of the girls from his office. It could have been just an innocent lunch."

"Don't you think that's just what I wanted to believe?" she asked earnestly. "That night, when we were out, I told Merle I'd tried to reach him at the office all afternoon, but that he hadn't been there. You know what he said? That he'd had an inspection to do on a dump site and he hadn't gotten back into the office until four-thirty. You don't take innocent four-and-a-half-hour lunches with your secretaries."

"It may not have been a lie. Maybe he went to lunch, then went out to his inspection site."

5

Her hand scampered across the table like a bug and covered mine. "Don't you see? That's what I have to find out. I have to know if Merle is lying to me. This is the most important step in my life. I have to make sure it's the right one." She sighed and leaned back. Her face grew taut, then seemed to shrivel. She stared at the napkin in her lap. "All I've ever really wanted out of life was to get married and raise a family with someone who really loves me. But pretty soon, I'll be too old to have children. All of my friends are married, or have been, and I'm thirty-three years old and I've never even been asked." There was genuine anguish in her voice, and she gave me a prolonged look for the first time. She leaned toward me, her eyes misty. "You know something, Mr. Asch? Except for Merle, I've never even dated anyone steadily. Do you know what it's like sitting home night after night watching television while everyone else you know is going out and having fun?" She paused and covered her eyes self-consciously with her hands. She spoke through them: "When Merle came along, I'd given up hoping. I never thought anyone would ever love me. But I'd rather go on like this than be tricked. I have the right not to be made a fool of on top of everything, don't I?"

In the face of her emotional outburst, I felt nonplussed and a trifle guilty. Even though I had long ago come to the conclusion that all of my own love affairs were destined to turn into baked Alaska, at least I had had a shot at it, and would probably have a few more. Sylvia Calabrese deserved one, too. Everybody did. I just hoped I would not be taking it away from her.

The salads arrived, filling in the momentary awkward silence that hung over the table. For something to do, I dug into mine. She didn't even look at hers. She remained with her eyes closed in an apparent effort to regain her composure. Finally she opened them and daubed at their corners with a napkin. "I'm sorry."

"Don't worry about it. What exactly do you want me to find out?"

"Everything," she said, sniffling. "If there are other women. If he really does owe money and to whom. And I want pictures."

I looked the question, rather than asked it. She answered it anyway: "If it's true, I want to see it. I don't want him to be able to deny it. I want him to hold the proof in his hand and explain it to me. He owes me that much."

The tone of her voice kept wavering between the desire to believe in the man's innocence and the certainty of his guilt. She was obviously trying to defuse the future by expecting the worst.

"My fees are two hundred a day plus expenses," I said. "Plus fifteen cents a mile."

"I said I don't care about the money."

I nodded and took out a small spiral notebook, flipped it open to a clean page, and began jotting down her answers to my questions.

Merle Stanley Hoffman, age thirty-seven. Occupation: sanitation engineer for the County of Los Angeles. Residence: 456 White Oak, Apt. 345, Encino. Automobile: 1979 Mercury Montego, dark brown, beige top, license number 127 TRD. I asked if she had a picture, and she pulled a 5 by 7 color snapshot from her purse and handed it to me.

The man in the picture looked tall, too tall for her. He was standing outside a trailer building in work denims, talking to another man, who had his back to the camera. He had a full, craggy face with large eyes and a thick, reddish mustache that umbrellaed a wide white smile. His hair was blond, combed straight back from a high tanned forehead. He was well muscled and his bulk visibly stretched the chest and arms of the white T-shirt he was wearing.

"He looks like he works out."

Her eyes flickered away. "Yes. I suppose."

7

The picture was slightly blurred and it seemed like a strange sort of a snapshot to be giving me. It looked as if it had been snapped candidly. I'd expected something more posed. "This is the only picture you have?"

She touched her neck, gently. "Yes. I mean, I have others; but not with me. That's the only one I brought."

I stared at the shot, trying to picture her with the man. He was too rough-looking to be termed handsome, but the physical unlikelihood of the match only increased the possible truth of her suspicions. But then maybe Hoffman had a thing for trolls. "Can I keep this for a while?"

"I'll want it back," she said anxiously.

"No problem. I'll just need it for a couple of days until I make him."

"Make him?"

I took a forkful of salad. "Get him matched up with his picture."

"Oh."

"It might be a good idea if you tell Hoffman you'll be out of town for a few days. If he's going to do anything, he'll be more likely to do it if he thinks you won't be around to find out about it."

"Yes. I see. That's a good idea. I'll phone him this afternoon."

Through a mouthful of shrimp and lettuce, I said: "How do I get in touch with you?"

"My number is 445-7780. That's an answering service. You can leave a message there and I'll get back to you. I'm seldom at home."

"Where is home?"

She cleared her throat. "Pardon me?"

"Your home address?"

"What do you need that for?"

"My files."

She did not answer immediately. "Five Seventy-two Pickfair Lane, Beverly Hills.

I knew the neighborhood. It was up in the canyons. Half the houses up there could have looked natural with moats around them. While I wrote the address down, she leaned forward and said anxiously: "I don't want you trying to contact me there, though."

"Why?"

"I haven't been in California that long," she said, not looking at me. "I only moved here a few months ago from North Dakota, right after my daddy died. I've been staying with my great-aunt until I get a place of my own. That's her house."

"And you don't want her to know you've hired a private detective."

She touched my arm with a tiny hand. "She wouldn't understand. Aunt Becky is kind of funny. I love her, but she has certain ideas about things and you can't talk her out of them. She doesn't approve of Merle. She's done everything she can to break us up. If she ever found out about this, it would just be adding fuel to the fire."

"Why doesn't she like Merle?"

Her eyes danced away. "She thinks he's after the money Daddy left me."

"What business was your father in?"

"Feed yards," she said. "That was in North Dakota, near Bismarck. I was raised on the farm."

I did my best to ignore all the possible wisecracks that last one offered. "I'll need a retainer," I said, wiping my mouth with a napkin. "Five hundred dollars."

Without flinching, she took a leather wallet from her purse and counted out five crisp one-hundred-dollar bills. There were at least five more like them inside. I took the money, somewhat surprised, and asked: "Do you usually carry that much cash around?"

"Most of the time," she said, smiling sheepishly. "I have this quirk. I always pay for things in cash if I can. I got it from Daddy. He always taught me that credit was an insidious plot by bankers to work the public into a state of enforced servitude. He drilled that into my head when I was a child: 'If you don't have enough money to pay for something, save up until you do.' I guess it always stuck. I've never even owned a credit card."

I pocketed the money and made her out a receipt, then leaned back and went to work on the rest of my salad. Marlowe and Spade could keep the breathless blondes, I thought. They were nothing but trouble anyway. I'd take the Munchkins any day. There were no legs to get distracted by and I didn't even have to wait for the check to clear.

Two

On the way home I stopped at the office of Associated Credit Bureaus and ran credit checks on both Merle Hoffman and Sylvia Calabrese.

Hoffman's credit seemed in pretty good shape. Only one outstanding bank loan appeared on the printout, a car loan for $5,500, but he evidently had no problems making the payments. There were several trade items listed, but no slow pays or skips. There were no legal items, so apparently he had not been sued for anything since 1968, which was as far back as the sheet went. Of course, all that was on the surface. He could have been in hock up to his eyeballs—to friends, gamblers—and it would never appear on paper. There was also the possibility that he was perfectly solvent but tired of making the car payment every month and was out for the big score, in the form of Sylvia Calabrese's inheritance.

That inheritance did not appear anywhere in Associated Credit's computers. There was nothing on Sylvia Calabrese—nothing at all—which was what happened to you when you listened to your daddy and paid for everything in cash. You became a nonentity, you did not exist. But those five one-hundred bills in my wallet existed, and that was all the corroborating evidence I needed.

I nearly tripped over the pair of roller skates as I stepped

11

inside the door of my apartment. "What the hell are these things?"

Mary Kay Blane looked up from the dishes she was washing in the sink. She was dressed in jogging shorts and a baggy sweatshirt and managed to look quite good in them.

"Roller skates," she said, poker-faced. "What do they look like?"

"They look quite a bit like roller skates," I said. "What are they doing here?"

"I have to teach a roller disco class tonight on the promenade."

"Roller disco? What happened to the Tai Chi or whatever you were teaching?"

"You have to go with the times," she said. Not wanting to get into any long discussion about that, I simply nodded.

Mary Kay Blane was a twenty-seven-year-old, very attractive UCLA graduate student who lived in a nearby shack on the Venice canals with a current boyfriend and a six-year-old daughter from a previous marriage, and who cleaned my apartment once a week to help finance her quest for an M.A. in English lit. She had been referred to me three months ago when I'd moved to Marina del Rey by Jim Gordon, a Deputy D.A. friend of mine from Organized Crime–Narcotics who had assured me that even though she was a "Commie," she was a "damn good housekeeper." "The Red Tornado," he'd christened her.

Mary Kay was not really a Commie. She embraced what might be termed *creative radicalism*, and her belief system would have been a challenge for any political scientist to compartmentalize. She belonged to the Student Cadre of the Socialist Workers Party, the Militant Feminist League, the United Peace Party, and the Lesbian Women's League. And she was not even a lesbian. But whatever her opinions lacked in coherence she made up for by the intensity with which she held them.

12

One of her beliefs was that crime was an aberrational product of our cities, caused by the unnatural squeezing and crowding in the human zoo, and if you were to tear down the cities and replace them with parks, crime would cease to exist. Prisons also only added to the aberrational cycle and should be torn down and all the people in them freed.

Which was why Jim made it a condition of his referral that I never reveal to Mary Kay what he did for a living. He'd told her he was a lawyer and he was afraid that if she found out he put people in prison instead of getting them out, she would break all his crockery and split.

I went to the refrigerator and took out a package of cheese and some bread and started to make a sandwich.

"That bread has preservatives in it," she said, watching me.

Mary Kay was, among all the other things, an organic militant. Paraquat was the ultimate capitalist plot, hatched by the imperialist oil companies to deaden the minds of the working masses and supporters of the ERA.

"I know," I said. "I'm getting old and I need all the preservatives I can get."

"That cheese has gum in it, too. You can see the way it bends. See on the package? It says 'cheese food.' It's got so many additives in it, they can't even call it cheese, they've got to call it 'cheese food.'"

"Yeah, well, scientists have proven that the number one cure for hunger is food, Mary Kay. That's why I eat it, because it's food. If it said 'cheese clay' on there, I probably wouldn't attempt it."

"Go ahead and joke about it," she said warningly, "but you're just poisoning yourself. You're just killing yourself slowly."

"And an agonizing death it will be. Acute cheese poisoning is the worst way of going. I've seen a couple go that way. They never stopped screaming. It was horrible."

"Make jokes about it," she said, brushing a strand of blond hair from her forehead with the back of her hand. "It's all right with me. You're the one who's going to die."

I finished brown-bagging the two sandwiches and went into the bedroom and changed into a T-shirt and jeans. I pulled the camera case down from the closet shelf and sat on the edge of the bed while I loaded the Nikon FTN with high-speed recording film and cleaned the 300 mm telephoto lens. I put the camera case back, and after making sure Mary Kay wasn't looking, I fished my manicuring kit down from the shelf and rummaged through it until I found the unmarked bottle of black beauties.

The first day Mary Kay had come to my place to clean, she had cleaned out my medicine cabinet, and I don't just mean dust. She had thrown away every bottle of prescription and patented medicine in there, replacing them all the following week with little green bottles of herbs and ginseng. Fortunately, Jim had warned me what was coming prior to her arrival and what I'd left her was mainly decoy stuff. The good stuff I'd hidden.

I shook out one of the black capsules—a little Indianapolis 500-type speed to help me make it through the night, just in case it turned out to be a long one—and put it in my pocket, along with a tin of aspirin, then put the kit back. Mary Kay was just finishing up the dishes when I came back out into the kitchen. She eyed the camera bag and asked: "You leaving?"

I nodded. "I've got a job."

"What kind of job?"

"We just got the inside word that Standard Oil is dumping oil into the ocean at night and Ralph Nader called me up to get pictures of it."

"Very funny," she said.

"It's just a sordid little job," I said. "I have to follow a guy around for a while. His fiancée is rich and she wants to know

14

how he spends his free time before he starts spending her money."

"If she settled down in her own space and let him occupy his, she wouldn't have to worry about it."

"It's not the space she's worried about, it's what he's doing inside it."

"That's sick," she said. "You're going to get sick being around it, too."

"I'm already too far gone for it to matter. Terminal cheese-food poisoning, remember?"

I picked up the brown bag on the drainboard, and she said icily: "What about my money?"

"Oh, right." I took a twenty out of my wallet and put it on the counter.

"You owe me another eight dollars and fourteen cents on top of that."

"What for?"

"I had to buy some things. Laundry soap and furniture polish."

"*Eight bucks* for laundry soap and furniture polish?"

"It's organic," she said, and turned away.

Along with my aspirin, Mary Kay had also thrown out every can and package of household cleaner I had in the apartment. The soap had not been biodegradable and aerosol cans were wreaking havoc with the ozone layer. Jim had not warned me about that.

I took out another eight bucks and said, "Can I owe you the fourteen cents? I don't have any change."

She gave me a distrustful look. "You can leave it for me tomorrow. I can't finish everything tonight. I've got to get to my roller disco class."

"Tell me something," I said. "You charging for this instruction?"

She looked at me as if I'd just gone screaming yellow bonkers. "Of course."

15

"Doesn't that make you a war-mongering capitalist?"

"I consider my fee a contribution," she said in an aloof tone. "My master's will better arm me to work for the cause of freeing the minds of the masses."

"A master's in Chaucerian lit should really do a lot for the struggle," I agreed.

She didn't act as if she had heard that. She seemed more interested in the bag in my hand. "I'm going to stop by the health food store and pick up some things for you. You need food with some nutritional value."

"I don't think I could afford it," I said, thinking of the eight bucks.

"You can't afford not to. That crap you eat is killing you right now."

"I thought the cramp in my leg this morning was a charley horse. It must have been rigor mortis."

Again it went sailing right by her. Mary Kay was on a different wavelength from the rest of us. As I picked up the camera case, she said: "You know, people think that just because something is good for you, it has to taste bad."

"Hmm," I said.

"That isn't true at all."

"I know," I said and went to the door.

When I got there, she called: "In case I don't see you tomorrow, don't forget my fourteen cents."

"I couldn't do that," I said. "I'd feel as if I was setting the class struggle back twenty years."

Three

The Piedras Canyon landfill, known officially as Landfill Number Eight, was situated in the middle of the Sepulveda Pass, on the terraced side of a hill overlooking the San Diego Freeway. The sign at the bottom of the concrete road that wound steeply up the hill said that the gates closed at 5 P.M. It was twenty-to when I parked below on Sepulveda Boulevard and walked through them.

A constant parade of huge trucks, county and private, rumbled up the road past me like a procession of elephants holding each other's tails. Intimidated, I walked as far over on the dirt shoulder as I could to keep from being inadvertently flattened. A strong wind blew off the top of the mountain, carrying a perfume blend of rotten garbage and chaparral, along with the dry smell of dust being swirled up from the road surface by the trucks.

A breath-shortening way up the hill, the road leveled and widened into a concrete plateau. In the middle was a weigh station, with the trucks backed up at the kiosk there, waiting to pay for the right to dump their loads. A string of trailer offices stood off against the scruffy side of the mountain. A sign above one of the doors said: ENGINEER. There was no-

17

body outside the trailers. I got just close enough to make sure that Hoffman's Merc was among the half-dozen cars parked there, then went back down the hill.

At 5:10, the Merc drove through the gates and turned left on Sepulveda. Traffic on the freeway was bumper to bumper, and Hoffman passed the on ramp without even slowing up, apparently deciding to stay on Sepulveda over the pass. The grade made it easy to keep him in sight, and I maintained a comfortable distance.

From the top of the pass, the lights of the San Fernando Valley wavered miragelike before fading into the haze of dusty smog that hugged the distant foothills, and then they disappeared completely as we wound through the canyon to the valley floor. At Ventura Boulevard he made a left, and because of heavier traffic and more traffic lights, I had to close the gap between us to make sure I didn't lose him.

At White Oak he signaled and hung a right, and at the second block he turned into the underground parking lot of an apartment complex called the Oak Knoll. I took a look at the place as I drove by.

It was one of those four-hundred-unit, five-story, rambling stucco monsters that served doughnuts in the rec room every Sunday morning and was usually inhabited by single stockbrokers who drove Porsches and legal secretaries who drove 280 Z's.

The only parking space I could find was a block away, but I could still see the driveway well enough. I took out a cheese sandwich and shoved a Randy Newman tape into the cassette deck. The sandwich was stale and so was Newman. Probably just the mood I was in. I rewrapped the uneaten portion of the sandwich and poured myself a thermos capful of coffee.

By 7:30 the coffee was starting to work on the brain center that controlled my bladder and I drove up to the corner gas station seeking relief. That took a total of nine minutes and cost me my parking spot. I found another one a half-block down and settled into it.

By 9:15, Hoffman still had not showed himself outside the Oak Knoll. Chances were that if he had not left by then, he would not be leaving at all. I decided to check the garage, just to make sure he had not left while I was on my pit stop.

The wrought-iron gate across the driveway was electronically controlled by a box into which coded plastic cards were inserted. Sometimes regular credit cards would trip those things, sometimes not. I gave it a try. My Union Oil and MasterCard didn't work, but my Shell did.

The space allotted to Hoffman's apartment was down on the end. The Mercury was not in it. Nothing was in it. I checked around to make sure he had not parked in someone else's space, then went back to my own car, muttering obscenities. At least I hadn't taken the speed. I would have been up all night muttering.

I was in position below the dump by 11:00 the next morning. At 11:30, Hoffman left in a car with three men from the office. They drove to the Velvet Turtle on Sawtelle, where I watched them eat lunch from my position at the bar. They were back on the job by 1:15.

That night, he did not go out at all. I watched the apartment until 2:00 A.M., then drove home, stuporously staring through the fine morning mist that clouded my windshield.

The third day was a repeat of the first two and by lunch of the fourth I was starting to think that Sylvia Calabrese was simply suffering from a case of prenuptial paranoia. The routine was taking its toll on my body. The speed was having a limited effect now, and sitting below the dump, I kept dozing off in the late afternoon warmth that filled the car. If Sylvia Calabrese wanted the surveillance continued, I was going to have to get another operative, and that would run into bucks.

I was fighting to keep my eyelids open, thinking I'd have to call her to find out what she wanted to do, when I saw the

Mercury drive through the gates and turn up Sepulveda. Since it was Friday, I thought at first that Hoffman was probably going home early, but then he turned onto Mulholland and I changed my mind.

We crossed the freeway and drove into the hills. As the road wound into the mountains, houses hung over it, precariously perched on stilt legs like hang gliders just waiting for the next good quake to take off. Then came a sign, SKYCREST ESTATES, and Hoffman turned.

The street was called Mirabelle Canyon Road. It was wide and straight and lined on both sides with pink and white flowers, but two feet on either side of the flowers the shoulder of the road crumbled into dirt and rocks and fell into a dry arroyo. The flowers had obviously been strewn along the roadside as an enticement for those seeking the cluster of condominiums that sat on the graded ridge about three-quarters of a mile above us. That was where I figured Hoffman was going. I figured wrong.

I was lagging behind him about a quarter of a mile when, just below the condos, Hoffman pulled over and parked. I had no cover, but I had no choice, either. I pulled over, too.

The street was steep and I had to wedge my tires into the curb to prevent the car from rolling back down the hill. When I was sure I was going to stay put, I picked up my binoculars from the front seat and looked through the windshield.

Hoffman was out of his car standing at the driver's window of a black Buick Electra that was parked in front of him. I tried to see the license number, but the Mercury was blocking my view. The other person was making no move to get out of the car. I could not see if it was a man or a woman.

Hoffman was talking to the driver of the Buick, and while he talked, he pointed. First he pointed up at the condo development, then he turned and pointed down the slope. I was immediately afraid he had spotted me, but then I realized he was pointing at something below me, on the left. I stuck my head out of the car window to see what it was, but there didn't seem to be anything, just the eroded sides of the arroyo and some ugly barren dirt plateaus baking brownly in the sun a few hundred yards below.

Hoffman wound up his lecture and got back into his car, and both cars turned around and started back down the hill. I flattened out on the front seat and waited until I heard them swish past, then bolted upright and fastened my binocs on the back of the Electra. The license number was A 38, which meant that the car belonged to the state assemblyman from the thirty-eighth district, whoever he was.

The two of them were still together when they crossed the freeway and headed south on Sepulveda. At Sunset, they turned right, toward the Palisades. The landscape turned verdant, with manicured hedges and lawns and trees providing plumage for the monumental houses that flanked the boulevard. We dipped and swept along a series of curves, and then the two cars ahead turned right.

The road steepened immediately, and the houses and trees began to thin and give way to scrub bush and sage. We were high enough to see the ocean. It lay flat and blue beyond the hills like a painting, and even though I couldn't smell it I could feel it in the air.

At the top of the rise, the cars pulled over, and this time both drivers stepped out. I stayed in my car again and reached for the binoculars.

The driver of the Electra was a man. He seemed to be fairly tall and lean and had dark hair, but he kept his back toward me and I could not get a good look at his face. The two men walked to the edge of the road and Hoffman began pointing and talking again, this time across a sage-covered canyon to a barren hillside where a corps of bulldozers and cats were busy shoving around loads of dirt. It must have been some sort of public works project, because all the vehicles belonged to the county. Maybe Hoffman was feeding the assemblyman ammunition for his next appearance at the Rotary Club luncheon, showing him how his constituents' money was being spent.

Whatever information Hoffman was trying to feed him, the assemblyman did not seem to be going for it. He kept shaking his head, which seemed to be making Hoffman mad. Then, suddenly, Hoffman began to wave his arms emphatically and shout at the man. At least he looked like he was shouting. Whatever might have drifted down to me was drowned out by the chugging of the bulldozers.

Hoffman continued his harangue for a minute or two more, then stalked off to his car. I could not take the chance he wouldn't recognize my car this time, so I started my engine and made a quick U to get down the hill ahead of him. At the first safe side street, I pulled in and waited.

The Buick went by first. I let both cars go, then followed.

They went back the way they had come, until they got to the freeway. There the Electra headed south, while Hoffman continued along Sunset heading east. He still was not going home.

We drove past the Bel-Air gates and UCLA, past the palm-treed palaces and colonial facades of Beverly Hills to Doheny Drive, where he made a right. At Beverly Boulevard, he made a left, and four blocks later he signaled and turned left into a parking lot adjacent to a block of red brick storefronts. I parked at a meter on the other side of the street.

There were four stores in the block, all of them dealing in furniture, carpets, drapes, or just plain advice for those contemplating a change in interiors. The fancy gold letters that spelled out the names of the stores also spelled out the message that any advice given would hardly be plain and most certainly be expensive.

The store Hoffman went into was called Dunland and had a black-and-white Art Deco awning out front. I waited until he was inside, then got out of the car on the passenger's side and put a quarter in the meter. I had used up only about seven cents' worth when the door of the store opened and Hoffman came out accompanied by a silver-haired man dressed in faded Levi's and a denim shirt.

Hoffman waited while the man locked the front door, then they walked to the parking lot together, talking animatedly. The other man got into a maroon Jag XJ. He drove off and turned right onto Beverly Boulevard as Hoffman followed in his car.

I was facing the wrong way, of course. I pulled out into the traffic, nearly sideswiping an oncoming car whose driver had great reflexes but, from the brief glimpse I got, a lousy temper, and hung a left on two wheels at the next corner. I turned around and punched it and managed to get back on track just in time to catch the tail of Hoffman's car disappearing on Doheny. By the time I made the corner I was quite a ways back, but the grade was uphill and I saw the Jag turning right on Sunset.

Traffic crawled. It was after 6:00 and many of the neatly awninged shops along the Strip had been closed for the day, but its restaurants were open and busy, and the sidewalks were filled to capacity with young people tripping out on the monstrous billboards that towered above the street hyping the latest rock album sensation, or just plain tripping out. In front of a health food restaurant whose open-air patio was packed with a crowd dining on alfalfa sprouts and mungbean meat loaf, the XJ turned left and headed into the Hollywood hills.

Hoffman must have been attracted to this kind of street. It twisted and turned and grew offshoots every twenty-five yards in an effort to lose me, but I stuck. Walls enclosed both sides of the road, and driveways swept through high gates up to cupolaed French châteaus and tile-roofed Spanish haciendas, their windows glowing in the twilight.

The taillights ahead of me kept spiraling upward, and then there was a sudden flash of red brake lights and they turned into a driveway. I drove past and turned around and cruised by slowly.

The house did not have a wall. It stuck out of the side of the hill like the white hull of an old battleship. It was streamline moderne, the kind of architecture that was in vogue in Hollywood in the 1930s: a multilayered stucco box with rounded glass brick corners and a low tower growing out of its center. A curved porch ran around the outside, surrounded by a stainless-steel ship's railing. The garage was to the right of the house at the end of a long asphalt driveway. The cars were parked there in tandem. I killed my engine and sat back to wait.

A little over an hour later, Hoffman and the silver-haired man came out of the house and got into their cars. Hoffman backed out of the driveway to let the Jaguar out, then pulled his own car back in and got into the XJ. I let them get halfway down the hill before I turned on my lights and followed.

I thought I had lost them twice on Sunset, but then I caught sight of them turning on Highland and followed them to Hollywood Boulevard.

If Hollywood used to manufacture dreams, all it manufactured now were heroin dreams and Laverne and Shirley nightmares. The glamor had long ago evaporated, like the bubbles from a glass of champagne that had been left out too long, and the brass-bordered stars embedded in its sidewalks were the only sediment remaining. The theater marquees that did not have triple X's on them looked tired, the gray stone buildings that lined the boulevard looked as if they had a four-day stubble of beard, and the sunken-cheeked, sallow-complexioned, quick-eyed inhabitants of its street corners lived only with the hope of *not* being discovered—by the police.

At Las Palmas, the Jag turned and pulled over to the curb

in front of the Gold Cup coffee shop. The Gold Cup was a well-known gathering spot for boulevard gays, and a group of them stood out front parading their wares in leather and drag. I pulled around the XJ and parked down the street in a loading zone. The Jag drove by a few minutes later. I got only a quick glimpse as it passed, but the long-haired boy in the back seat did not look as if he could have been much more than eighteen.

At Selma, they made a right and slowed down to cruising speed. This was part of a four-block area in Hollywood known as the Meat Rack, a place where chickenhawks came to fulfill their secret pedophilic desires and young male hustlers came to peddle their orifices for whatever the traffic would bear.

It was still early and pickings were rather sparse, and the cars that were out trolling jockeyed around one another, trying to get position on the few kids on the street. The drivers were not overcoated, drooling geeks one might expect to see lurking around playgrounds with lollipops in their hands. In fact, tomorrow morning they would be unidentifiable—doctors, lawyers, happily married Xerox executives, sanitation engineers. The only thing that gave them away tonight was the intent expressions on their faces and their slow-motion Johnny Rutherford driving technique.

Up the block, a black Grand Prix and a Mustang II were dueling for post position on a young boy with long blond hair who was standing on the curb eyeing traffic and suggestively massaging the crotch of his skintight jeans. The Grand Prix won the duel through sheer muscle and the Mustang peeled noisily around him on frustrated tires. The blond boy was bent down, checking out the driver of the Pontiac, when the Jag pulled up behind and stopped. I yanked the wheel and pulled over a few cars back.

The kid Hoffman and his cruising mate had picked up stuck his head out of the window and yelled: "Tony!"

The blond boy looked up, said something to the man in the Grand Prix, and went over to the Jaguar. The Grand Prix stayed where it was.

"Say, mister, which way you goin'?"

I looked up at the voice on the passenger side of my car. It belonged to a slim, dark teenager with black hair that kept falling into his eyes. "The opposite direction," I said, and turned my attention back to the XJ. The blond kid was talking to Hoffman.

"No kiddin'," the hustler at the window went on. "I'll go just as far as you want to take me."

The kid was subtle. Like the crescent moon on an outhouse door.

"Forget it."

He saw the camera on the front seat. "You into photography? I've done some modeling before."

The blond kid was getting into the Jaguar.

"Really, mister, I'm just going down the Strip—"

"Beat it, huh, kid?" I immediately regretted my choice of words. He must have thought I was talking in code, too, because he reached for the door handle. The Jag drove away and I pulled out with it. My would-be passenger still had hold of the door handle and he yelled something at me as he was ripped into the street, but I couldn't catch what it was.

The Jag drove back down Sunset, toward the Strip. The patio of the restaurant was still packed when we turned to go up the hill. I doused my lights down the street from the house and pulled up on the other side just as the four of them were walking up the porch to the front door. I snapped off four pictures, rapid-fire, before they got inside.

What the hell, I thought, if business got really bad I could always open a portrait studio. Jacob Asch Photography, Specializing in Pederasts, Sodomites, and Close Encounters of the Third Grade. I marked down the time in my notebook—8:55—and settled down to wait.

L.A. smoldered below, a grid of blue and green and yellow

lights, and I thought how beautiful it looked from up here. It would have been even more beautiful from an airplane. The farther away from the streets you got, the better they looked. It was easier to forget what was going on on them.

Between nine and two-something, when I finally dozed off, a couple dozen cars came up the hill, but none of them stopped at the house. At 7:20 A.M., I was awakened by the cheerful chirping of birds and the sound of a car starting. I raised my head stiffly to see Hoffman's car backing out of the driveway. The two boys were with him in the front seat.

I followed them back into Hollywood, where Hoffman dropped the boys off at a Howard Johnson's on the corner of Vine. They waved good-bye to him and went inside, and he took off up Vine, toward the freeway. I guessed he was going home and let him go.

I parked down the street and tried to fight off sleep, holding my eyes on the entrance of the restaurant. The boulevard was stretching and yawning and the stars embedded in the sidewalks glittered weakly in the morning light. The few people out, looking as if they had never been to bed, moved like ragged shadows along the street. A girl with disheveled hair and the nodding-out eyes of a hype stopped outside my car and peered at me queerly through the window, then wiped her running nose on the sleeve of her moth-eaten sweater and shuffled away.

Fifteen minutes later, the two came out of the Howard Johnson's, said good-bye to each other, and separated. I had to choose one or the other. I chose the blond kid. At least I knew his first name.

He started walking south on Vine. I followed slowly, pulling over when I started to get too close.

He crossed Sunset, then at La Mirada turned right. About half a block down, he turned into a peeling stucco bungalow court with an Islamic arch over its entryway and two dried-out palm trees in its front yard.

There was no space on the street, so I double-parked and

hurried to the archway in time to see him unlocking one of the apartment doors. When he was inside, I went to the door and checked the number, then went to the mailboxes. The name on the box was Bellonte, but that meant nothing. If the kid was like seventy-five percent of the hustlers on the Boulevard, he was a runaway and would not be using his real name. Besides, he wouldn't be living alone. There would probably be four others sharing the room with him, and any one of them could be named Bellonte.

I went back out to the street and took down the address. The flaking sign there said the name of the place was the Valentino Arms. Very romantic. I wondered if the Great Valentino ever charged for his services. Probably. After all, this *was* Hollywood.

Four

My body got up by itself after about four hours sleep, leaving my mind still in bed. That was the speed that was still rushing around in my bloodstream like a drill sergeant, shouting all my organs awake. I careened into the bathroom where I showered and shaved and tried to brush the taste of last night out of my mouth, then went into the kitchen and put on a strong pot of coffee.

I was getting too old for these all-night vigils. My eyes felt as if they were sinking into my head, and my hands were shaking from time-released explosions of amphetamine. I sat over my fourth cup of coffee and called Sylvia Calabrese's answering service and left a message for her to call me back, then made myself four scrambled eggs and a muffin and sat around the apartment.

She still had not called me back by 4:30. I decided to hell with it, I'd give it one more night and call it quits. I had already found out what she wanted to know—or didn't want to know—but another couple of hundred wasn't going to hurt my bank account any.

I called Hoffman's number, and when he answered I asked for Sarah, apologized for having the wrong number, and hung up. His car was in the garage when I got out to the Valley half an hour later.

At 6:10, he pulled out of the driveway and I followed him to a Vons market on Ventura where he came out with two bags full of groceries. He returned to his apartment directly, and I sat around outside yawning until 10:00, when he left again.

This time he went to the freeway. He drove at a steady fifty-five to the Hollywood Freeway, where he got off at the Highland exit. Hollywood was alive with lights and people on a Saturday night, and I thought for sure he was going to turn up the Boulevard and do a repeat of his trolling routine, but he kept going down Highland. When he got to Melrose, he signaled right and turned toward Beverly Hills. Just past the Pacific Design Center, he pulled over and parked and got out of the car. I stayed in my car and watched him as he crossed the street.

Above us, the massive bulk of the glass-sheeted Pacific Design Center seemed to pulsate with its eerie, purple-blue light, as if it were some huge, odd-shaped spaceship ready to scoop up the tiny art and antique stores on the street it hovered over and fly home. Halfway down the block, Hoffman stopped and went up the stairs that led to the front door of a converted two-story house. It looked like some kind of nightclub. There was music playing inside and a bouncer by the front door. I locked up my own car and crossed the street.

The place was squeezed snugly between a small antique store and a mystical bookstore that smelled of incense. It had a triple-peaked tile roof and curtain-covered windows all over its front. It was painted maroon and the ornamental Swiss chalet trim over the windows and doors was white, giving the place the impression of a gigantic cuckoo clock. A small sign over the doors said: MARIO'S AFTER HOURS.

The bulging, bearded bouncer at the front door looked like the giant in George Pal's *Atlantis, the Lost Continent*. He gave me the eye as I came up the stairs, as if he might do a few repetitions with me, but the older man standing with him looked me over as if interested in performing more visceral activities with my body. I could feel his eyes on me as I went inside.

The fact that the place had once been a house was even more apparent once you were in it. The front doors opened into an entrance hall and a staircase leading up. Small bunches of men clustered in the hallway, talking and smoking, some with drinks in their hands. The young ones looked too young to be drinking, and they were all in the company of older men who were busy fondling them. As I passed one group, I overheard one of the older men say: "Take my word for it, Phil, the kid's good. I did some footage on him last month. There isn't a better ass in the business. . . ."

I drifted past them into what had been a living room but was now a bar. The place was packed with people and smoke and noise. The walls were mirrored in diagonal strips, breaking up the colored lights that flashed in the ceiling in synchronization to the disco music. A small dance floor had been cleared in the middle of the congestion of tables, and cushioned benches lined the walls.

There were a few frantic-looking drag queens in the crowd and a smattering of lesbians, but the clientele was overwhelmingly male, and a good percentage of those were young hustlers like the ones Hoffman had picked up. The main concentration of hustlers seemed to be at the bench tables on the wall by the bar. They sat and stood, chatting and drinking and eyeing the older hawks who circled around, waiting for a score. I figured Hoffman would be over in that direction, so I headed that way.

Several sweaty shirtless male couples in skintight jeans were rocking on the dance floor. One of them as I passed held a small bottle of clear liquid up to his nose and inhaled, then threw back his head and laughed raucously. Amyl, probably.

31

"WHOOOOOEEEE!" he screamed, then smiled like a Cheshire cat and held out the bottle to me.

"No, thanks," I said, tapping my chest. "Pacemaker."

"It'll charge your batteries, man," he said, then offered some to his dance partner. He took a hit, and the two of them laughed and then started working out on each other's mouths.

Trying to get through the tangle of bodies, I was bumped into a squat, broad-shouldered bulldyke in a zippered jacket and jeans who looked as if she had just stopped in for a Miller after a hard day on the bulldozer. "Watch it," she growled.

"Sorry."

My attention was immediately diverted by the girl dancing with her, an absolutely breathtaking, raven-haired beauty in a strapless, low-cut evening gown. The girl's eyes grabbed mine and she smiled tantalizingly. I shook off the look and went to the bar where they were standing three deep.

After a minute or two, I spotted Hoffman, standing at the end of the bar talking to a slim, sandy-haired kid who looked no more than fifteen. I elbowed my way through the bodies and ordered a bourbon-water from the bartender, a mustachioed young man dressed in a summer undershirt and a construction worker's hardhat.

While I was watching Hoffman, a tanned, muscular young man moved in my line of sight and smiled. He was wearing a black cowboy hat and studded black leather pants and vest with no shirt. I shifted my gaze away, but he sauntered over like John Wayne and said: "I've never seen you around here before."

"No."

"Where are you from?"

I looked at him. He needed a shave. His eyes glittered brightly with reflections of snow. I was surprised he'd remembered to take the dollar bill out of his nose. "San Francisco."

He nodded and took a sip of his drink. His eyes roamed around my body for a while, then he said: "What's your line?"

"Producer."

A dark eyebrow raised under his hat. "What kind of stuff?"

"Chickenflicks. Maybe you saw my last picture—*Take Her, She's Nine.*"

He shook his head seriously. "No, I didn't. But if you're here to recruit talent, you came to the right place. A lot of producers come here, and a lot of the kids come here to display their wares, y'know, figuring to get a part."

I shook my head and stared over his shoulder at Hoffman, who now had his arm around the slim boy's shoulders. "I'm not here on business. Just pleasure."

A dark-haired adolescent walked into my view and gave me a big smile, thinking I was staring at him. I looked away quickly. I had the distinct feeling I was going to get into trouble before the night was over. I downed my bourbon and signaled the bartender for another.

"I was in a couple of chickenflicks myself," Midnight Cowboy said proudly.

"Really?"

He nodded. "Then I got too old."

He looked about twenty. So he knew what Shirley Temple felt like. "It's a hard business," I commiserated.

The dance number ended, and the girl in the low-cut evening dress and her bulldyke companion came back to their table, which happened to be directly in front of me. The girl was still staring. She looked at my crotch and ran a tongue around her lips slowly. Her eyes were at half mast, dulled by a Quaalude glaze. I could not help but stare at her—she really was beautiful—but I also couldn't help wondering what her game was. Maybe she was just tired of India-rubber dildos. The bulldyke was aware of the visual exchange and pursed her lips angrily. That made her look ugly, and she

33

didn't need a lot of help in that direction. She had a face like a brakeshoe on a 747. I looked away.

"You want to dance?" Midnight Cowboy asked me.

"No, thanks. Trick knee."

He smiled and reached over to put a hand on my ass. I grabbed his wrist and pulled it away. "I'm old-fashioned. I'm not used to these whirlwind courtships."

He had distracted my attention enough that I had missed Hoffman getting up. I scanned the room rapidly and finally saw him and the boy, moving through the crowd toward the front door. I pushed away from the bar without saying anything to Midnight Cowboy, and at that moment I happened to glance down at the black-haired girl. We locked stares again for an instant. That was all it took.

The bulldyke shot up from the table and charged me, snarling like a water buffalo. Light glinted off the heavy beer mug in her hand, and I threw my hand up instinctively to protect my face, at the same time putting my weight into the right hook I brought up into her chest. She screamed in pain as my fist sunk into her heavy breasts. She staggered backward, but she still held on to the mug. One thing I'd say for her: she had heart. She bellowed and started at me again, and I jabbed her with a left, then followed with a straight right and a left hook. Her eyes rolled up into her head, and she took a step backward and fell.

Someone grabbed me from behind and wrenched my right arm back into a hammerlock. A meaty arm wrapped around my neck. I looked up over my shoulder and saw the bearded giant from out front and said in a half-strangled voice, "Not my fault."

The black-haired girl who had been making gaga eyes at me all night was on the floor beside the unconscious bull-dyke, blubbering tearfully. "Tara! Tara!" She shot me a smoldering glance and said through twisted lips: "You've killed her!"

34

She stood up and started after me, but one of the circle of people who had gathered around the scene grabbed her. She fought against the arms that were restraining her, trying to get at me with outstretched bloodred claws.

"I saw it all," Midnight Cowboy chimed in. "She went after him for no reason."

A few people in the crowd nodded their assent, but Gargantua was apparently not in the mood to hold court. Still holding me in a hammerlock, he moved me speedily toward the front door, using me as a wedge to part the crowd. When we got outside, he let me go, then stared at me while I flexed my arm, trying to get the circulation back. There didn't seem to be any permanent damage, as far as I could tell; it would probably be good as new in a day or two.

"I wouldn't come back," the giant said. "Tara isn't about to forget you, and she can get a lot nastier than that. You caught her on an off night."

In the confusion, I had forgotten about Hoffman. I hurried down the street to where he had parked, but his car was gone. That left nobody here but us chickens.

Five

At 8:30 on Monday morning, Sylvia Calabrese returned the three messages I had left with her answering service. I was only half lucid, but I managed to tell her that I had something to report, and we arranged to meet at 2:00 that afternoon at the same restaurant as before. I figured that would give me enough time to get the film developed and tie up loose ends.

I was anchoring down one end of the bar with a vodka-tonic when she came in, twenty minutes late. She looked different. She had turned in her gray suit and joined the Saks Fifth Avenue brigade. Her mustard-colored linen skirt and jacket and yellow-and-olive striped blouse were expensive and smartly tailored, and her pale straw hat was adjusted at a stylishly jaunty angle. Her eyes were covered by a pair of large, round-lensed dark glasses, the kind that are darker at the tops than the bottoms. At least I wouldn't have to watch her eyes wander all over the room.

I expected her to come pouring out apologies again for being late, but she simply walked over briskly, eyed the manila folder on the bar in front of me, and said: "Is that your report?"

"Yes."

"What have you found out?"

"You're not going to like it."

"I hired you to find out the truth, not to be entertained." Her tone was assertive—the nervous diffidence she had displayed at our last meeting was completely gone. Perhaps it was just a defensive attempt to prepare herself for the bad news.

"Would you like a drink?"

"No, thank you."

I picked up my drink and the envelope and waved a hand at the empty lounge. We took a table in the corner, and I handed her the envelope and sat back, sipping my drink. She opened the clasp and removed the 5-×-7s. She looked through them slowly, then looked up at me. "Who are these people?"

"The man with the silver hair is Kenneth Dunland. He owns an Art Deco store on Beverly Boulevard. That's his house. The blond kid goes by the name Tony. His name may or may not be Bellonte. His address is in the report. I don't know the name of the other kid. I could probably find out if you really want to know, but I wasn't sure you'd want to go to the expense. It probably wouldn't be worth it. They're street hustlers."

Her shoulders squirmed. "What do you mean, 'street hustlers'?"

"Prostitutes. Your fiancé and Dunland picked them up in Hollywood. They all spent the night at Dunland's house."

"But . . . they're boys." She stared at me, open-mouthed, as if she still did not quite comprehend it. "You mean, Merle is . . . homosexual?"

"I'm afraid so."

Her face screwed up in revulsion and she began rubbing her arms. She shivered. "To think . . . that I let him . . . my God, it's disgusting."

"I know what a shock it must be. Would you like a drink now?"

She nodded weakly. "Thank you. I think I can use one. Scotch on the rocks, please."

I went to the bar and fetched the drink, and when I came back she was still staring at the photographs. She was taking it much better than I had anticipated. After her outburst the other day, I thought she might go hysterical on me, but there was no sign of that. She received the drink gratefully and took a large swallow. "You're sure about this? There couldn't be a mistake?"

"No. The night after these were taken, I followed him to a bar on Melrose called Mario's After Hours. It's a gay hang-out. A lot of chickenhawks hang out there, apparently—"

"Chickenhawks?"

"Older men who like young boys," I explained. "Hoffman picked up a kid there and they left together. I started to follow them, but I got waylaid by a jealous dyke who thought I was trying to cut into her action. By the time I got my act together, they were gone."

"What was that?" she asked, blinking up at me absently.

"It's not important," I said, seeing no need to go into it.

She nodded and put the pictures down on the table and looked away. "What makes it all the more horrible is that they're just boys. My God, how could he? How could I not know? How could he keep it hidden from me? He must be like a Dr. Jekyll and Mr. Hyde, some kind of monster. . . ."

Anything I could have said would have meant nothing, so I didn't try.

"What else did you find out?"

I took a breath. "I don't know what it means, but the same day Hoffman met Dunland—that afternoon, in fact—he met someone else. A state assemblyman named Ronald Eastland."

Her body tensed perceptibly. She leaned forward and repeated the name eagerly: "Eastland?"

"You know him?"

38

The question seemed to deflate her. She leaned back and her shoulders consciously relaxed. "No. Of course not. Why should I?" Her question seemed out of place, especially backed by the defensive tone in her voice. "What were they doing?"

"I'm not sure. It didn't seem to be any kind of sexual liaison, if that's what you mean. It might have had something to do with his work. There were county trucks and bulldozers working at the second location where they went, and it's in Eastland's district."

"Where was it?"

"In the Santa Monica Mountains above Pacific Palisades." I consulted my notes. "Bentomar Street, off Timoteo Canyon."

She took a greedy gulp from her drink. "You said they met somewhere else?"

"Right before that they were at a condo project up Mulholland called Skycrest Estates. Eastland followed Hoffman from there to the Bentomar Street location."

"What were they doing there?"

"As I said, I'm not sure. Hoffman seemed to be pointing out something to Eastland. I couldn't get close enough to tell what."

She looked away, lost in thought, then set her drink on the table and said in a suddenly very businesslike tone: "I don't see any purpose in going any further with this, Mr. Asch. I found out what I wanted to know. Or rather, what I didn't want to know."

"I'm sorry."

"Don't be. You saved me a lot of money, not to mention embarrassment. If I had married him and found out later what he was, I don't think I would have been able to bear it. If you'll just tell me what I owe you—"

"I haven't really figured it up yet. I didn't know if you wanted more work done. Six days work will come to twelve

39

hundred dollars. I haven't added up my expenses yet."

She opened her purse and took eight hundreds from her wallet. "That should cover it?"

"More than enough," I said, pocketing the bills. "I'll write you out a receipt—"

"That's not necessary," she said. "I trust you." She picked up the manila envelope from the table and stood up quickly. "The negatives are in here?"

"Yes. And the picture of Hoffman you gave me."

"That's it, I guess, then." She smiled and tried to hold it, but couldn't. She held out her hand. I took it. "I'll walk you out," I said.

At the door she paused and said: "I have to call a cab."

"You don't have a car?"

"It's being repaired," she said quickly.

"I'll drop you where you want to go—"

"Oh, no, I wouldn't think of it." She fidgeted. She seemed anxious to get away.

"It's no bother. Really."

She relented with an awkward smile frescoed on her face. "All right, then. Thank you."

We went outside to the parking lot. I pointed to the Plymouth and she got in. "Where to?"

"Down Wilshire. Toward Westwood."

She said nothing on the drive, but just sat there with the envelope in her lap, tightly clutched in her hands. About a mile from the restaurant, she told me to pull over anywhere. I found a space and parked, and she opened the door and stepped out. "Good-bye," she said through the window and walked away.

She walked to the entrance of a tall office building, and at the door she stopped and looked back to see if I was still there, before going inside.

Her behavior was strange, no doubt about that. The emotional transitions she made—from defensiveness to shock to eager alertness to almost casual stoicism—were a little bewildering in their rapidity. But then maybe that was just because she did not know exactly *how* to react; after all, she had just had the rug that she'd been about to stand on for the rest of her life violently yanked from under her. Still, there was something I couldn't put my finger on, something about her that was not quite kosher.

I sat there for a few seconds more, thinking about it, then shrugged it off and pulled into traffic.

Don't worry about it, Asch. So she's a little odd. Just think of her as your little Munchkin Queen bringing you gifts of green and let it go at that.

Six

I didn't think about her as my Munchkin Queen or anything else until the phone call a week later.

At the time, I was hallucinating on visions of Big Macs and
combing through the refrigerator, looking for something edi-
ble. A few days before, Mary Kay had decided that I needed
to be purged of my toxins and had cleaned out the icebox,
restocking it with assorted nutritional goodies from the
health food store. I had tried to explain to her that my toxins
had tenanted my body for a long time now and that to evict
them just like that, without notice, seemed unfair, if not
downright immoral. I argued that my system was not ready
for the unmitigated shock of goat-cheese burgers and jock-
strap molasses, and that withdrawal should be gradual. All to
no avail. She just told me that God did not eat meat and.
carted the load down to the trash, leaving me with two bags
of alfalfa sprouts, assorted fodder, and a bill for $33.50. And
now I was starving.

I had just picked up a loaf of 147-grain bread and was
staring at it, trying to figure out what I could put between
two slices of it, when the phone rang.

"Mr. Asch?" a female voice asked urgently.

"Yes?"

"This is Sylvia Calabrese."

"Oh, hi, Miss Calabrese. What—"

"I have to talk to you. Can you meet me?"

I looked down at the bread and squeezed it. It was working on stale. "When?"

"Now. As soon as possible." Her voice was as taut as a violin string.

"Is something the matter?"

"Yes. I need your advice. I'm in very serious trouble. I didn't know things would go this far. It's gotten out of hand."

She was way out in front of me, and I had a feeling that the longer we talked, the more distance she was going to put between us. "What's gotten out of hand? What kind of trouble? Is it about your fiancé?"

Her voice lowered suddenly and grew muffled, as if someone had just come into the room and she was cupping her hand over the receiver to keep from being overheard. "Yes. Listen, I can't talk about it over the phone. Where can we meet?"

"Where are you now?"

"Santa Monica."

I tried to think of a place not too far away where I could procure some sustenance. "You know where the Brown Bagger is in Venice? It's on Washington Street, just a couple of blocks from Pacific."

"I'll find it."

"I'll be outside on the patio in an hour."

"I'll see you then," she said gratefully, and hung up.

It was a typical Southern California, eat-your-heart-out-Chicago, February day—bright, sunny, and about sixty-eight—and the open air of the patio of the Brown Bagger was full. I was sitting at a table by the wooden wall, looking over the menu and listening to my stomach growl, when I saw a gray Firebird slow on the other side of the boulevard and recognized the bump of a head showing just above the window line. She should have tried sitting on phone books. She found a parking space directly across the street, took two attempts to parallel park, then opened the door and stepped out.

She stood by the car, glanced both ways at the traffic, which was light, then started across the street. Her eyes were on the traffic and mine were on her, but then I heard a car punch into passing gear and they snapped toward the sound.

She heard it, too, and her eyes widened as she saw the white Olds Cutlass bearing down on her. She broke into a trot, but she knew she was not going to make it and her mouth opened, probably to scream, but the scream never got out.

There was a loud sickening bang as flesh-sheathed bone met metal and she was tossed in the air like a ragdoll, her arms and legs flopping spastically as she sailed over the top of the car and smashed face-down into the street.

A woman behind me screamed, and then a collective gasp rose from the patio as the car behind the Olds slammed on its brakes and swerved to miss the body, sideswiping another car in the slow lane and sending it rebounding off the side of a car parked by the curb.

I ran into the street to where Sylvia Calabrese lay. She was not moving. Her clothes were in tatters and blood was spreading in a widening pool around her head. One of her arms was tucked awkwardly underneath her, obviously broken, the other was flung outward from her body as if still trying to ward off the car that was long gone. I picked up the wrist of that arm and felt for a pulse. There did not seem to be any.

Faces pressed around, looking down, and like a chorus from a Greek tragedy, voices asked: "Is she dead?"

I looked up. They seemed like the same faces I'd seen at every accident I had ever witnessed. "I don't know. Somebody call an ambulance. And some of you see if you can't slow down traffic. Otherwise, somebody else is going to get hurt."

Responding like automatons, a couple of men ran ahead and began waving their arms at the oncoming cars. Traffic was already beginning to jam up and the sidewalks were lined with open-mouthed gawkers, all angling for a view of the inanimate pulp that had been a human being a few seconds before.

I pushed through the crowd and went to the Vega that had run into the parked car. The woman driver was sitting behind the wheel, crying. I asked her if she was okay, and she said she thought so. The man who had sideswiped her stepped out of his car, which stood in a bed of broken glass in the middle of the street, and limped over. "Is she okay?"

"She's just shook up. How about you?"

"I banged up my knee a little. I'm all right. How about the woman who got hit?"

"I think she's dead."

"Jesus," he said. "That jerk didn't even slow down. He just kept going. I tried to miss her—"

"I saw," I told him, then walked to where Sylvia Calabrese's purse lay, its contents spilled all over the pavement. The wallet was still inside, and I pulled it out.

The driver's license in the wallet belonged to Nina Rivera, 421 Armacost Avenue, #5, Los Angeles. The picture on it was Sylvia Calabrese's.

There was a little over twenty-seven dollars in the money compartment, various credit cards and an Auto Club card, all made out to Nina Rivera, and some business cards. The business cards were all the same:

> Eldorado, Inc.
> 34410 Santa Monica Boulevard
> Santa Monica, CA
>   Nina Rivera, Office Manager

I could hear the sirens now, wailing plaintively in the distance. The man from the accident limped over and said: "The poor woman. Who was she?"

"I don't know," I said truthfully.

"Isn't her driver's license in there?"

"Yeah, it's here."

He looked at me strangely, and I walked away from him. I started back toward the restaurant, then stopped. The thought of hamburger right now nauseated me.

Seven

The air was filled with flashing red lights and the hard pink glare of road flares and waving arms and irritated cop voices shouting for people to keep moving and the sharp static of police radios.

The black-and-whites had arrived first, within a minute or two, followed almost immediately by the ambulance and more black-and-whites. I gave my statement to a patrolman while the photographer snapped pictures and the lab boys scoured the scene for bits of broken glass and paint flakes, and then gave it again to the white-hatted sergeant who was overseeing the investigation at this point. He seemed interested when I told him that the woman had been on her way to see me about something, just what I didn't know, but fortunately he was too busy to make much of it. He did say that he would be turning the case over to the detectives and they would want to talk to me about it.

When I left, half an hour later, the crowd was still hanging around, new ones replacing old ones at their watching posts, in spite of the fact that the only traces of Nina Rivera left were some bloodstains and an outline on the pavement.

Armacost was a narrow street of solid apartment buildings off Santa Monica Boulevard, most of them having been built in the days when the scale of architecture and property taxes were a lot smaller than they are today.

Number 421 was a two-story white stucco building divided down the center by a concrete walkway. A woman with her hair in curlers was coming down the walk as I was going up it and we said hello to each other as we passed. I loitered at the mailbox, waiting for her to turn down the sloping driveway into the underground garage, then went down the walkway, looking for apartment 5.

Each unit had a decorative cinder-block wall in front of it, enclosing a small, private patio. Nina Rivera's was a jungle of potted plants, and the jungle provided a convenient blind from nosy neighbors. I unlocked the apartment door with the key I'd taken from Nina Rivera's purse and closed the door behind me.

The curtains were all drawn and their heavy cloth blocked out the dimming daylight. The darkness was filled with an unnatural stillness, the air in the apartment was thick and tepid. My eyes began to adjust after a few seconds and picked out a lamp on a table. I went to it and turned it on. The living room, like the patio, was filled with plants. They stood in vases and overflowed pots on tables and hung from the ceiling in cradles of colored macrame, giving the tiny room the hot, crowded effect of a greenhouse.

In the middle of the room, two small, rolled-arm velour couches faced each other across a teak coffee table. A woman's corduroy jacket, brown, lay on the arm of one of them. The rest of the furniture—two chairs and an end table—were inexpensive wicker, Pier 9 Imports stuff. There was a small Sony color television on a stand, and a stereo console. An old rough pine hutch stood against one wall, its shelves filled by a couple of dozen paperback books and more pots filled with frothy green plants.

The kitchen-dinette was one step up to the left, and in it was a cheap formica dining table, surrounded by four Naugahyde chairs. For an heiress, the woman had not let her new wealth go to her head.

A hallway with a bathroom ran from the living room, and

the door at the end of it was closed. I went to it on tiptoe, for no reason I could think of.

The curtains were not drawn in the bedroom and light streamed in through the window above the bed. The bed was covered with a pink quilted spread, and a stuffed koala bear was propped up against the pillows. It watched me as I picked up one of the framed color photographs that sat on top of the mirrored bureau.

The photo was of an older couple—a short, red-haired woman and a taller, dark-complected man—standing with a collie dog in front of a white clapboard house, smiling into the sun. The other photo was of the same two people standing in front of the same house, but in this one the collie had been replaced by Nina Rivera/Sylvia Calabrese, wearing a red graduation robe and mortarboard. From the proud looks on their faces, they could only have been her parents, and although standing next to Nina Rivera made the man look like a giant, her father somehow lacked the stature of a cattle baron.

I left the pictures and opened the drawers. There were clothes there, a leather jewelry box containing a watch and some cheap items of jewelry, but little else. In the middle drawer, there was a white plastic scrapbook, and I pulled it out and sat on the bed while I looked at it.

The pictures in the book dated back to childhood, and the same couple as in the photographs on the bureau was always in attendance. The photographic record went through college, but there was little after that. I didn't know if that meant little had happened to the woman since then or she had just stopped carrying around her camera.

In most of the pictures, I noticed that Nina seemed to be standing alone or with other girls. When a man's picture did appear in the pages, he was usually alone, and it was usually the type of portrait picture shot for the school yearbook. In many of the later pictures, she appeared in stage costume—Shakespearean leotards, mostly—and in a few of those she was lighted by the glare of the footlights, bowing with the cast. There were several reviews clipped from the Cal. State-Long Beach paper to go with the pictures, and sections that mentioned Nina Rivera were underlined. Her notices were all favorable—particularly one for her portrayal of Ariel in the drama department's production of *The Tempest.*

The collection of clothes in the closet was sparse and it didn't take me long to go through it. Aside from a handful of lint and Wrigley's Spearmint wrappers, the search turned up a banking deposit slip dated two weeks before for Nina Rivera's checking account. The amount deposited was five hundred dollars, and it had been made by check. I put it in my pocket and went to the nightstand by the bed.

Her interest in drama seemed to have continued after she had left college. Tennessee Williams's autobiography was on the table—hardcover—and a bookmark stuck out from the middle of it.

There were some paid receipts in the drawer, and I went through them. One of them was last month's phone bill. I ran down the toll calls, looking for Merle Hoffman's number, but it was not there. One number in Glendale did crop up with noticeable regularity, however. She had made calls to it at least three times a week in the month, some of the conversations lasting as long as forty minutes. I took down the number and put the bill back and left the room.

The bathroom had a sunken shower with a tasseled canopy over its top, and there was a safety razor on the shelf inside. Aside from the usual fare in the medicine cabinet, there were several bottles of different prescription tranquilizers, all issued by a Dr. Finstin. It looked as if Nina Rivera was a little high-strung.

I went out to the kitchen. There was a cork bulletin board at the end of the kitchen cabinets by the wall phone, with a yellow Happy Face and an assortment of notes tacked to it. Market today. Call Rita. Cleaners. There was a note pad on top of a stack of papers at the end of the counter beneath the board. The name Clyde had been written in ink over and over on the top piece of paper, surrounded by delicate curlicues, as if she had been doodling while talking to Clyde, or at least thinking about him. The rest of the pad was blank.

I started sorting through the papers. Her checkbook was there. She had a balance of $934.07 in her account as of two days before, and five hundred of that had been the deposit slip I had in my pocket. There were no other deposits or withdrawals to the tune of hundreds of dollars in the past two months. Her balance had fluctuated between five hundred and one thousand dollars, which meant that wherever she had gotten the thirteen hundred dollars she had paid me, it had not gone through her account. She could always have gotten it out of a savings account, of course, but there did not seem to be any passbook around. The only other unusual thing I noticed about her check record was that every week for the past four weeks, she had made out a check for fifty dollars to a Carl Rivera. Ex-husband? Current husband? She had lied about everything else, there was no reason why she should not have been lying about that, too.

A paycheck stub was inserted in the plastic cover of the checkbook and I pulled it out. It was made to Nina Rivera, for the net amount of $162.81, from Eldorado, Inc. I took the deposit slip out of my pocket and checked the code number of the bank on the slip. The numbers matched.

I spent another twenty minutes going through the place, but there was no sign of the photographs or the negatives I had given her. Maybe they were in her car. Maybe they were in a safe deposit box. Maybe she had thrown them away. Maybe they never existed and I was imagining the whole thing. Things were not always what they seemed in Munchkinland.

I left the apartment key on the kitchen table and locked the door from the inside before I slipped out.

Eight

The office of Eldorado, Inc., was a dozen or so blocks from the beach, on a stretch of Santa Monica Boulevard lined with commercial buildings and shaggy palms. It had a subdued, ribbed-wood front, and large steel letters above the door spelled out Eldorado, Inc.

Inside, two rows of desks ran the rectangular length of the room. Three of the desks were occupied, all by women. The walls were filled with architectural renderings and blown-up photographs of model homes and condos from subdivisions developed or in the process of being developed by Eldorado, Inc.

The woman at the front desk was talking on the phone. She signaled me that she would be right off, and I nodded. She was in her mid-twenties, more cute than pretty, but not really a whole lot of either. Her hair was a dark explosion around her face and her skin was probably her best feature, smooth and deeply coppered by the sun.

The nameplate in front of her on the desk said:

Rita Jennings
Sales

Rita. Call Rita.
One of the other girls asked if she could help me, and I

said no, thanks, I would wait for Miss Jennings, and began casually strolling around the place, looking at the pictures on the wall. They were all out of my tax bracket, but it was something to do. As I browsed, I debated whether or not to use the direct approach with the woman, tell her who I was and why I was here. That idea died when I saw the two large pictures that occupied a shrinelike central place on the wall.

One was a blown-up photograph of the scrub-covered canyon, its sides deeply scarred by erosion. The other was an artist's rendering of a condominium project along the edge of a lush golf course and tennis courts. The pictures were supposed to be a before and after, but I had seen the project in between. The photograph was missing only some county bulldozers and a black Buick with a big red *A* on its license plate. The caption underneath said:

> **Seaview Country Club Estates**
> **—The Future of America**
> **A Development by Eldorado, Inc.**

I was still staring at it when Rita Jennings hung up the phone and said: "Yes, sir, may I help you?"

I approached her desk and smiled. "I'm looking for Nina Rivera."

"She isn't here right now. She stepped out for a little while."

She didn't know yet, then. "Do you expect her back soon?"

"I expected her back long before now," she said in a slightly irritated tone. "She went out for lunch over two hours ago."

I pursed my lips in disappointment and consulted my watch. "That's too bad. I have a plane to catch and I can't wait much longer."

"Is there something I can help you with?"

I thought about it and said: "My name is Anderson. Larry Anderson. I met Miss Ca—Miss Rivera last night. She knew the man I was with. He's also in the real estate business. Anyway, we got to talking and I told her I was considering investing some money in real estate out West, and she suggested I stop by her office here before leaving town to take a look at some of the things you people have going."

"I see," she said, her smile widening.

I waved a hand at the wall. "She mentioned that Seaview project."

"Seaview is our principal project right now," she said proudly.

I nodded and walked back to the rendering. She followed me. "It looks impressive enough. Where is it going to be?"

"Do you know Los Angeles?"

I smiled sheepishly. "Not very well."

"It will be in Timoteo Canyon, which is above Pacific Palisades, one of Los Angeles's more exclusive communities. The view will be magnificent and it will be about five minutes from the ocean. Did Nina tell you much about it?"

"No, not really."

"It's a monumental project," she said enthusiastically. "When it's completed, there will be six hundred homes, an eighteen-hole golf course, tennis courts, clubhouse, even a complete gymnasium, all built on wasteland being made usable through rubbish fill."

"Rubbish fill?"

She nodded, seemingly pleased by my feigned surprise. "Through an agreement with the county of Los Angeles, the sanitation districts have been contracted to fill in the ravines below Seaview with rubbish, which will then be covered by a thick layer of dirt. There are quite a few other rubbish-fill developments in Southern California, but this is to be the biggest ever undertaken. Not only that. Seaview will be the nation's first housing project to be totally solar powered, from heating to cooling. That's why we say that Seaview is the future of America."

"Guess the environmentalists can't kick up a fuss about that," I said, trying to invest my voice with a slight Midwestern twang.

"Governor Madden has already endorsed Seaview as being an inspiration. He's called it a 'shining example that technology and the environment do not have to be at odds,' and has already called for more projects of its kind." Her voice deepened and became intense as she quoted the governor.

"What'll the homes be like?"

"Here," she said, and went charging back to her desk. She pulled open the top drawer and brought back two pale blue sheets of paper. They were floor plans of different houses. One was a two-bedroom model labeled *Plan A*, encompassing 1,460 square feet; the second was a three-bedroom model called *Plan B*, which enclosed 1,927 square feet.

I looked them over and said: "How much will these be going for?"

"Oh, we aren't allowed to advertise a price until construction begins," she said, shaking her head.

"You must have some idea."

"I have a very good idea. But according to law, we aren't allowed to say."

"Upper hundreds?" I asked, winking.

She smiled slyly. "I would say that is a pretty good guess."

"When will construction begin?"

"At the end of 1981, when the landfill operation is complete."

"That's quite a ways off."

"We've already got over five hundred names of people waiting for the homes to go up. If you want to put yours on the list, now would be the time to do it."

"I can tell you're an honest woman," I said. "And a

shrewd businesswoman on top of it. What if I wanted two? Do you think they would be a good investment?"

Her eyebrows arched. "What business are you in, Mr. Anderson?"

"Tools," I said. "The Anderson Tool Company. It's a small company—only about seven hundred employees—but we're growing every year."

She nodded, totally engrossed now. "And where is that?"

"Hoosierville, Indiana."

"A beautiful city," she said. I could have said Calcutta and she still would have said "a beautiful city." She had a live one.

"Not so beautiful in the winter," I said. "That's why I'm looking for a home out here. The wife is tired of the snow. But while I'm living here, there's no reason I can't make a little money at the same time. And if these houses are going to be selling like you say they are, I might as well get in on the ground floor, right?"

"Right," she agreed. "And if you want my opinion, I would say that these homes will probably double in value in the next three years."

"Hmmm," I said, looking over the floor plans again. "It's mighty interesting, it surely is. But tell me something, being on top of garbage, doesn't it stink?"

"Oh, *no*," she said emphatically. "Have you ever been to a landfill project, Mr. Anderson?"

"No, I can't rightly say that I have."

"There is a twenty-foot layer of dirt between your house and the rubbish. You'd have to see the site to appreciate it."

She looked around the office and bit her lip. "I'm sure Lonnie can take care of things around here if I just slip out for a while. Things have been a little slow today anyway. Just a minute, I'll get my purse."

She went over to her desk and got her purse out of one of the desk drawers, then said something to one of the other girls and came back over. "Okay, Mr. Anderson. Let's go."

We went to a brown Celica and got in. As she headed down Santa Monica, I said: "That was real fortunate running into Miss Rivera like that. She struck me as a real nice person. I feel kind of guilty about cutting her out of her commission."

"You're not," she said, signaling for a turn at Twenty-sixth. "Nina doesn't have a sales license. She just runs the office, overseeing the secretaries and taking care of contracts and things. Did she tell you she sold?"

"Not really. I just assumed that she did. How long has she worked for the company?"

"Over a year," she said. "I've been working for Eldorado for six months and she was Mr. Laughlin's secretary—that's Clyde Laughlin, the head of our office—for at least that long before I came."

Clyde. The name struck me. She had been talking to or thinking about her boss while she drew curlicues around his name. Nothing particularly strange about that. Clyde was out as a mystery man—at least for the time being.

"Are you married, Miss Jennings?"

"Divorced," she said.

"Any children?"

"One. A little girl."

"I have two myself," I said, trying to sound proud. "Miss Rivera was telling me about her fiancé. I was trying to give her some tips on how to handle him."

"Fiancé?" she asked, surprised. "I didn't know she had one. I didn't even know she dated anyone."

"He works for the county. Name's Hoffman, I believe."

The name drew no reaction from her. She just shook her head and looked blankly out the window. We crossed San Vicente. Joggers were out en masse in the fading sunlight, trotting down the grassy divider that cut the street in half. I watched the chest of one magnificently lunged girl bouncing under her T-shirt in rhythm with her stride and said a little dry-mouthed: "We got into a long conversation about the man. He seemed like a real nice fella from what she said. You and Miss Rivera close?"

"Not really. Nina is kind of a private person. We talk, but mostly about business. She's a loner and keeps pretty much to herself. Where did you say you met her?"

"At a bar of a restaurant. I don't remember the name."

"Yesterday?" she asked, with a puzzled look on her face.

"Yeah. Why?"

"What time?"

"Oh, I'd say around sixish."

"Was she with a tall man with salt-and-pepper hair?"

"She didn't seem to be with anybody when I met her. I was sitting with a friend of mine—Bill Jackson—when we ran into her. She was sitting by herself. Why? Who's got salt-and-pepper hair?"

"Mr. Laughlin," she said. "He's vice-president of the company and the head of the office. They were the only ones left in the office last night when I went home. I was just wondering."

"No," I said. "I don't remember meeting anyone by that name. I'm sure she would have introduced him if he'd been around."

She turned on Sunset and headed toward the beach. I went on: "I told Miss Rivera after the sales pitch she gave me that with all her money she should be the one investing in her own project."

Her eyes flickered over me, then back at the road. "All what money?"

"She said her father died recently and left her a bundle."

She shook her head. "That's news to me. You sure we're talking about the same person?"

"I think so," I said, scratching my head. "Real tiny gal? About big enough to fit in a teacup? Black hair, wears it in bangs? Comes from North Dakota?"

"That sounds like Nina, all right, except for the fiancé and the money. And she comes from Glendale, not North Dakota. She's lived there her whole life."

"Her parents still live there?"

"I think so. I know she visits them all the time."

"Well, maybe I got it all mixed up. Maybe it was some distant relative in North Dakota who died and left her the money."

She gave me a funny look. "I don't know. All I know is that for the past six weeks she's been complaining that her father's out of work with a bad back and she's had to help support the family. Just last week, in fact, she went to Mr. Laughlin and asked for a raise because of it. She said she'd have to quit if she didn't get it."

"Did he give it to her?"

She nodded and said in a voice that had a catty undercurrent: "Lately, it seems Nina can do no wrong in this office. Mr. Laughlin really likes her."

"You don't sound as if you do."

Her cheeks flushed with embarrassment. "I didn't mean to give you that impression. I have nothing against Nina. I think she's a sweet person." The smile on her face looked a trifle fake, but I didn't want to press her on it just yet.

We turned at Timoteo Canyon Road and then forked off onto the same street up which I'd tailed Hoffman. She stopped the car at almost the exact same point Hoffman had, and we got out.

"Step over here," she said, waving me toward the edge of the embankment. She pointed down at the trucks that were dumping their loads of trash halfway up the ravine. As they moved out, bulldozers moved over the hills, like an ant colony, pushing and molding the garbage to make terraced plateaus.

"There, you can see the process. The elevations will keep building, step by step, until they are level with the top of the ridge. This landfill was originally slated to take four years, but things have been speeded up and we've cut the completion date down to three." She inhaled deeply and said: "Now, Mr. Anderson, take a whiff. Smell anything?"

I inhaled noisily through my nose. "No, ma'am, I surely don't. Tell me, doesn't that stuff settle, though?"

"The sections that will settle won't have homes on them. They'll be solid dirt fill. As will the roads, of course."

I nodded. "I'm real impressed that the governor has put his stamp of approval on it. I guess there couldn't be too much wrong with it. How about Assemblyman Eastland? What are his feelings about it?"

She looked at me strangely. "Assemblyman Eastland has endorsed the project, also. Why did you ask about Eastland? I thought you weren't familiar with Los Angeles?"

"Miss Rivera mentioned his name last night, I believe. This is his district, isn't it?"

"Yes, it is." She turned away, apparently mollified, and watched the bulldozers work. "That's where the golf course will be," she said, pointing. "And the clubhouse will be there. The houses will flank the edge of the fairways." She continued to point out what would be where, and her voice and hand motions became more and more animated as her sales pitch picked up in intensity.

"You seem to be real proud to be associated with this project," I said when she'd finished.

She nodded. "I am. It's not just a pioneering development. With all the energy problems we're facing, I believe Seaview will be an important prototype for many such communities to come."

"Well, I can't argue with you from what I've seen," I said. "And your enthusiasm is contagious. You've sold me, little lady. So let's just go back to the office and put my name on that wait list."

She beamed. "You won't regret it. Should I put you down for two?"

"Hell," I said. "Put me down for three."

"*Three?*"

"Why not? If I'm going to double my money in three years, I might as well make it worth my while, right?"

We returned to the car and started back. All the way, she babbled about the merits of Seaview and I tried to pump her about Nina, playing on her suppressed dislike of the woman. I found out that Nina had taken the state real estate exam three times and failed every time, which was why Rita found it slightly laughable that Nina had given me the impression she could sell. It was also a source of resentment, because around the office Nina was in charge, and she was not at all averse to reminding Rita of the fact. I also gathered from remarks she made that Rita thought Nina used her background in drama (she had been a drama major at Long Beach State) to manipulate people by playing on their sympathy. Nina liked the Camille role best, Rita said—especially the walking around with back of hand on forehead, saying, "Don't worry about me, I'll be fine." But she had to admit that Nina was competent and ran the office efficiently.

We got back to the office, and as I stepped out of the car I looked at my watch and said: "Jesus, I didn't realize how late it is. Listen, I'll tell you what I'll do: I'll be back in town on Wednesday, and I'll come in and we can get everything straightened out then."

She looked confused. "But—"

"I'll call you from Indianapolis tomorrow to confirm everything we've talked about. Now, I want three of those houses—the 'B' models, all of them. So you get it all set up so that when I get here, everything will be ready."

I grabbed her hand and pumped it and was saying good-bye when a blue-and-silver Seville pulled into the lot and a distinguished-looking man with salt-and-pepper hair stepped out.

"Oh, Mr. Laughlin," Rita Jennings said, before I could get

away. "This is Mr. Anderson. I just took him over to the site. He's going on our wait list."

Laughlin smiled and offered a lean hand. "Good to meet you, Mr. Anderson. I don't think you'll regret the move."

"Nina sent him in," she said. "They met last night."

The smile faded, turning to puzzlement. "Last night? It must have been late. We worked here until eight-thirty."

"I don't remember the exact time," I said, smiling affably. "It may have even been the night before."

"What did you say your name was?" he asked, his eyes narrowing.

"Anderson, Larry Anderson." I grabbed his hand and shook it again. "Glad to have met you, Mr. Laughlin. Your project is very impressive. Yes, sir, *very* impressive." I backed away from them, grinning. "I've got to run now or I'll miss my flight. I'll see you Wednesday, Miss Jennings, and thanks for your trouble."

I went to my car and unlocked the door. Rita Jennings was staring strangely at the dents in the side of the door and the coat hanger that served as my radio antenna. "Isn't it disgusting what they give you for rentals nowadays?" I called out to them. "I couldn't believe it when I saw it. I said to the guy at the counter, I thought you tried harder, and he just shrugged. What are you going to do?"

They were still standing there watching me as I waved and drove off.

Nine

Circus acrobats in harlequin costumes performed for me all night, except they did their act in the middle of the street instead of under the big top. Cars would head straight at them and they would stand calmly and wait and then, at the last minute, like the bull-jumpers of Crete, would put both hands out, catch the grill, and do a handspring over the top of the car. Every one of them would make the jump cleanly, but would come down on his face, and then I would run to him and turn him over and Nina Rivera would be staring up at me with dead eyes and a mocking smile on her blood-smeared mouth.

I woke up around 5:30 and tried to go back to sleep but couldn't, so I got up and went jogging along the beach. I came back, then got dressed and walked back over to Corso's, a tiny hole in the wall on the beach that serves the world's best spinach omelettes. I had one and read the sports page over about four cups of coffee, then took a walk along Ocean Front Walk.

The joggers and dog walkers were out, but it was a little early for the carnival parade of short-shorted roller skaters and luscious-thighed bikinied lovelies and jugglers and surfers and minstrels and old strollers and just plain freaks that would crowd the walk when the sun warmed up the beach, so I strolled along listening to the peaceful lapping of the waves and the harsh cries of the gulls. It didn't do much to settle my thoughts, however.

It was almost 9:00 when I got back to the apartment. I got in my car and drove down to Venice Division.

When I told the desk sergeant there that I wanted to talk to the detective in charge of the Rivera homicide, he took my name and told me to wait. After a few minutes, a sawed-off, middle-aged man built like a string of knockwurst came out of the back and said: "You Asch?"

He wore no coat, and the sleeves of his white shirt were rolled up to his elbows, exposing two beefy, werewolf-hairy forearms. He had a holster on his hip, and the butt of a snub-nose .38 protruded from it.

"Yeah, I'm Asch."

"I'm Investigator Mellerek." We shook hands. What little hair he had left on his head was pale yellow, and the bags under his eyes looked as if he'd packed for a long trip. He signaled me to follow him without saying anything more, and I trailed him into a large, dismal pea-green room filled with desks. The desks floated at all angles like barges in Hong Kong harbor, and about half of them were manned by coatless cops, none of whom seemed to be doing a hell of a lot. But then it was still early and a lot of them probably had not even gotten their first cup of coffee at 7-Eleven yet.

Mellerek went to a desk by the wall, gestured me into a chair, and sat down. He was apparently a man who felt that one gesture was worth a thousand words. Or even two. He hooked his thumbs in his belt and tilted his chair backward, nearly touching the poster on the wall behind him. The poster had the LAPD insignia on it and the words: LAPD HOMI-CIDE—OUR DAY BEGINS WHEN YOUR DAY ENDS.

"What can I do for you?" he asked disinterestedly.

"I'm just here to do my civic duty. I thought you might want to ask me a few questions."

"About what?" A fly landed on his nose and he brushed it away. He grunted as if that had taken a lot of effort.

"The Rivera killing," I said. "You've got the case now. I thought you might want to question me about it."

"You gave your statement to the patrolman, right?"

"Right."

"If I have any questions, I'll get in touch. There was no need to come all the way down here."

"Oh, it was no trouble. I just live a few blocks away."

We sat there staring at each other. That didn't seem to bother him. The fly bothered him more. It landed on his forehead and he brushed it away again, and his eyes followed it hatefully as it circled the desk.

"She was coming to meet me when she got it," I said.

"Ummm," he said, watching the fly. If curiosity killed the cat, he was going to live a long time.

"I'm a private detective. I did some work for her a week or so ago."

That brought his attention momentarily in for a landing. "What kind of work?"

Before it could take off again, I said: "She wanted me to tail her fiancé around. She was afraid he was playing her for a sucker, that he was just after her money. That's what she said."

He regarded me sleepily. "You found something wrong with it?"

"Not at the time, but later. Everything she laid on me was straight out of *A Midsummer Night's Dream*. When she came to see me, she told me her name was Sylvia Calabrese and that she lived on Pickfair and that her father recently kicked the bucket in North Dakota, leaving her a lot of money."

"Her parents live in Glendale," he said, smiling strangely. "And if her old man's dead, I'd hate to see the station's long-distance bill, 'cause I talked to him on the phone yesterday."

"What's his name?"

"Carl. Why?"

I ignored the question. "Did he come down to identify the body?"

"No. The old lady. He's crippled-up or something." He picked a little piece of yellow out of his teeth with a finger-nail, gave it a cursory inspection, then shrugged and wiped it on his pants. "So why do you figure the broad lied to you?"

I couldn't believe it. Somewhere inside his head, a neuron had fired. "I don't know, except that obviously she didn't want to be traced. That's probably why she paid me in cash, too."

"Cash?"

"Thirteen hundred bucks."

"How long did the job take?"

"Six days."

That brought him out of his lethargy. He put both his hands flat on the desk and said: "Shit. That's almost what I make in a month."

I had a good answer ready for that, but said: "Next month, I may not work."

That seemed to mollify him a bit. "What was the story on the boyfriend?"

"He likes boys. Young ones."

He shifted in his chair a little and raised an interested eyebrow. "Is that why she was coming to see you yesterday?"

"I don't know why she was coming to see me. She didn't say on the phone. All she said was that she was in trouble and needed advice."

"She didn't indicate what kind of trouble?"

I shook my head. "All she said was, 'I didn't know things would go this far.' When I tried to ask her about it, she said she couldn't talk on the phone."

"Did she say where she called from?"

"Santa Monica somewhere."

He turned slowly sideways in his chair and began fiddling with a piece of paper on the desk. "You got a look at the driver of the car?"

"Not a good one."

"Could it have been this fiancé you tailed?"

I shrugged. "It could have been just about anybody. The man had a big face and he was wearing a stocking cap. That's about all I can say. It happened too fast."

"Think you could put together a composite?"

"Not a chance."

He sighed. "A man wearing a stocking cap got on RTD 104 at Centinela ten minutes after the hit-and-run. That's about a block from where we found the car, half a mile from the scene. It had been stolen from the back of a Jeans West store in Santa Monica sometime between the hours of ten A.M. and noon. It belongs to a kid who works there. He came out to go for lunch and discovered it gone and called it in."

"Any prints?"

He shook his head tiredly. "Just the owner's. The guy must have been wearing gloves."

"Sounds pretty professional."

He made a face. "Professional-shmofessional. Five will get you ten that it'll turn out to be some punk kid who stole the car and was gonna strip it down and panicked when he saw a black-and-white and wasn't watching where he was going."

"The car speeded up when she stepped into the street. I saw it."

He waved a hand at me. "Sure, sure, only you don't know *why* he was speeding up. It'll be awfully hard trying to prove that whoever it was was aiming at the broad. Wouldn't make any difference if we could. When we catch the asshole, the D.A. will plea-bargain the fucker down to involuntary manslaughter anyway. But for now, it's a one-eighty-seven—murder—and that's the way I'm going to be playing it for a while. Which means I'm going to want to talk to this boyfriend."

If Mellerek ever got around to talking to Hoffman, I

would be surprised, but I had to give him the benefit of the doubt. "His name is Merle Hoffman. He's a sanitation engineer at Landfill Number Eight." I gave him Hoffman's home address, then asked: "Have you searched Nina Rivera's apartment yet?"

"We were over there, yeah."

"Did you come across a passbook for a savings account anywhere? There or in her car?"

"Why?" he asked defensively.

"I told you, she paid me in cash. If the thirteen hundred bucks didn't come out of her checking account and it didn't come out of her savings account, it might be interesting to find out where it did come from."

He mumbled something inaudible, then said: "I'll check it out."

"Also, I'm assuming that your boys didn't turn up a copy of the report I gave her or the photographs I took. Otherwise, you would've wanted to talk to me before this."

He scowled. "What photographs?"

"I took some pictures of Hoffman and an Art Deco dealer named Kenneth Dunland in the company of a couple of street hustlers they picked up at the Gold Cup. One was named Tony. Blond, maybe five-nine, one-fifty. Lives at the Valentino Arms, Apartment Six. I don't know the other one's name."

He took down the information and looked up resentfully. If things kept going like this, he might have to do some police work on this case. "We didn't find any pictures," he said grudgingly. "Or any report."

"That's kind of odd, don't you think?"

The fly was back. He waved it away, then looked at me as if contemplating the same technique. "Maybe. Then again, maybe not. What's your thought, that maybe this Hoffman character knew about the pictures and didn't want them spread around?"

68

"It might be something to ask him when you see him."

"It might be at that." His eyes looked almost hurt, as if they thought it was unfair, the weight of the bags they were being asked to carry.

"Remember," I said with exaggerated cheerfulness, "the day is just beginning."

"Huh?"

I pointed at the poster behind him and left.

Ten

The house was in an older section of Glendale, on a street lined with diseased elms. It was a prairie-style house, small and dingy white, with horizontally slatted sides and a row of small windows running directly under the roof soffit. An open-air cement porch projected from the front of the house, and to get to it I had to go up a cracked walkway that ran through a lawn that looked as if it were thinking of becoming an alfalfa field. In another few weeks, they would not have to worry about mowing it—they'd have to reap it.

Two rusted metal chairs and a warped wooden table kept me company on the porch while I waited for someone to answer my ring. The person who did was the short, chunky woman from the photographs in Nina's apartment. She looked older than in the pictures and her stiff-looking hair was more coppery than red. Her face was paper white and she wore too much makeup, and that, combined with the almost complete absence of a chin, gave her head the strange appearance of a bloodless balloon on which the features had been painted. Some of the makeup had smudged beneath her eyes, which were red from crying.

"Mrs. Rivera?"

She wiped her hands on her loose-fitting shift. "What is it?"

"I'm sorry to intrude on you, I know what a difficult time it must be for you, but I was wondering if I might ask you a few questions. My name is Asch. I'm an investigator. Your daughter was on her way to see me when the accident occurred."

She blinked and her head wagged back and forth like a warning sign on a railroad crossing. "What do you want?"

A male voice behind her said: "Who is it, Marguerite?"

"An investigator," she called out. "He says it's about Nina."

"Let him in."

She stepped aside. The room was stuffy and had the closed-in, sour smell of sickness. The decor of the place matched its architecture—shabby and out of date—but they had done their best with what they had to make it homey. Throw rugs of various shapes and colors were scattered over the wood floors, and the more threadbare pieces of furniture were covered with colorful knitted afghans.

The source of the sick smell was stretched out on a brown davenport in front of a television console, staring at the dead screen. Lying down, he appeared to be about six feet, and thinner than his picture. His eyes were sunken and the flesh seemed to hang on his long, bony face. He had a fleshy nose and thick black brows that joined above them.

On the scruffy maple coffee table beside him were several prescription bottles, a half-full fifth of cheap bourbon, and an empty glass. And the same framed picture of Nina on the stage in leotards I'd seen in her scrapbook. The man shifted his gaze from the screen to me and stared for a short time without saying anything, and suddenly I became aware of something else that filled the room besides the shut-in smell—a heavy, suffocating, almost palpable sadness. I found myself wishing he would turn on the TV, just to break up its oppressiveness.

"Well? Did you get the sonofabitch yet?" he asked belligerently.

His speech was slightly slurred and his eyes were glassy. He was not drunk, but he had been drinking. He had a right, I guessed. "I'm not with the police, Mr. Rivera. I'm a private investigator."

"Private? What do you want with us?"

"I was working for your daughter when she was killed. I'd like to ask you a few questions. I'll try to make it as brief as possible. I know what a bad time this must be for you."

"What would Nina be using a private detective for?" he asked suspiciously.

"That's what I'd like to talk to you about."

He winced painfully as he shifted his weight around on the couch, and his wife rushed over to adjust the pillow behind him. "My husband has a bad disk," she explained.

I shook my head sympathetically. "I had one rupture on me once. I know how bad that is. People don't realize it, but the back goes and everything goes."

His expression softened a little. I'd never really had a disk go, but I'd known people who had. You experience such intense pain you automatically join a club that separates you from the rest of the human race. It's like being a Mason or something—when you meet a fellow member, you are immediately taken by a feeling of fraternity. Here, at last, is someone who knows how you feel. "When did it happen?"

"Five weeks ago," he said.

"At work?"

"Naw," he said, waving a hand in disgust. "Right here. Stupid. I was in the garage, moving some stuff, and whammo, the next thing I know I'm on all fours and can't get up. The doctor says I should have surgery, but nobody's gonna cut my back."

"What's your normal line of work, Mr. Rivera?"

"Air conditioning. I'm a sheet-metal man." He looked at me self-consciously, as if realizing he was talking about his back to get his mind off other things, and indicated a frayed chair. "Siddown. What'd you say your name was?"

"Asch. Jacob Asch."

Mrs. Rivera perched herself on the arm of the couch next to her husband. Carl Rivera said: "Now, what's all this about Nina?"

"When was the last time you talked to your daughter?" I asked both of them.

Mrs. Rivera answered. "Saturday. She came by for dinner. I fixed lamb."

"Did you see her often?"

"At least once a week. And we talked almost every day on the phone."

"She confided in you about her private life?"

"Yes . . . she always told us what she was doing. She wasn't like a lot of children today, who run around and don't care about their parents. As a matter of fact, I don't know what we would've done around here without her the past month, with Carl out of work. She took money out of her paycheck every week and gave it to us, to help us out with the bills. I told her we'd get by, but she insisted—"

She was starting to run away with herself. She was rocking back and forth on the arm of the couch. Carl Rivera reached up and put a sympathetic hand on her knee, stopping her, and she looked down at him, surprised. Her eyes filled with tears and she said: "I'm sorry." She took a tattered tissue out of her shift and daubed her eyes with it, sniffling.

I waited for her to compose herself, then asked: "Did Nina ever mention a man named Merle Hoffman to you?"

"Hoffman?" Carl Rivera repeated the name. "I don't think so. You remember anyone by that name, honey?"

She shook her head, bleary-eyed. "No."

He looked at me. "Why? Who is he?"

"I don't know who he is, but according to her, he was supposed to be her fiancé."

Mrs. Rivera stopped sniffling and her eyes widened in bewilderment. "Fiancé?"

I nodded. "About a week ago, your daughter hired me to

73

do a background check on Hoffman. She said they were going to be married, but she had reason to believe he was trying to take her for a ride. She said she'd come into an inheritance from a relative who had died and was afraid Hoffman was just after her money." I did not tell them that Carl Rivera was supposed to be the dead relative or that she had given me a phony name and address. They might have been a little sensitive right now to having their daughter called a liar.

Carl Rivera tried to sit up and sucked in a pained breath. His wife put her hand on his shoulder and said gently: "Sit still, dear—"

He was not listening to her. He glared at me and said: "I don't know what you're trying to prove here, buddy—"

"I'm not trying to prove anything, Mr. Rivera. I'm just as baffled about the whole thing as you are. But I'm not making it up. Your daughter did come to me. She paid me. Thirteen hundred dollars—in cash."

The two of them looked at each other. Mrs. Rivera's mouth opened a little. "Where would Nina get that kind of money?"

"I take it there was no inheritance, then?" I asked.

"I don't know what you're talking about," Carl Rivera said.

"And she never mentioned Hoffman, or any plans she had to get married?"

They exchanged puzzled looks, and Mrs. Rivera said quietly: "She would have told us. . . ."

"Did she ever talk to you about any of the men she dated?"

She shook her coppery head and blew her nose. "The only man I heard her talk about recently was her boss—"

"Clyde Laughlin?"

She nodded. "I guess they'd gone out for cocktails after work quite a few times in the past month or so. He took her out to dinner a few times, too. She was floating around on cloud nine because of it. She'd had a crush on him ever since she started working for him a year ago. I told her not to get all excited about it. I knew how she was. She'd always wind up hurting herself in the end."

"How was that?"

She looked down at the tissue in her hand and twisted it around her fingers. "Nina was a real, well, shy girl, and she sort of used to like to dream about things. Y'know what I mean? She never had much of a social life. She had a tumor on her pituitary when she was just a little girl and it retarded her growth. The doctors cured it, but she was always smaller than the rest of the kids her age, and they used to make fun of her because of it. She was always real self-conscious about her height and didn't date because of it. Then, when she went to college and really started dating, she would get these crushes on certain boys. She would kind of, I don't know, fantasize that she was in love with them and they were in love with her and wind up getting hurt when she realized they weren't, that she'd made it all up. But it was only because she wanted to be loved so bad."

Nina had not lied about everything, just about Hoffman. It was Curlicue Clyde she'd had her sights on. "You think she was making up the whole romantic scenario with Laughlin?"

"I don't know," she said through the tissue. "He seems to have cared for Nina a great deal. He sent those flowers." She pointed to a huge arrangement of red and yellow flowers in the corner. "And he called to tell us how sad he was about it and how he was going to miss her."

I nodded. "When she came over here on Saturday, did she seem upset?"

Carl Rivera's eyebrow cinched in the middle. "Like how?"

"I told you she was coming to meet me when the accident occurred. She'd called me about an hour before and said that she was in trouble and wanted to talk to me about it. Her exact words were, 'I didn't know things would go this far.' You have any idea what she could have meant by that?"

They exchanged puzzled looks, then shook their heads.

"Could it have something to do with her job at Eldorado?"

"Nina loved her job," Mrs. Rivera said. "Mr. Laughlin just gave her a raise, in fact. She was already in charge of the office, but he told her he was going to delegate even more responsibility to her in the future. She was real happy about that. He'd already put her in charge of a special project they were working on. She said for the first time, she was getting to use her real talent on the job."

"Her real talent?"

She nodded. "Acting. Nina was a good little actress." She picked up the photograph on the table and handed it to me. "That was her playing Ariel in *The Tempest*. That was when she was going to Long Beach State. That was Nina's big passion—acting. She tried to pursue it as a career for a while, but the competition was too fierce. And then there was her size. It limited what kind of parts she could play."

The woman was still in shock and she was doing reruns of her daughter's life in her head. I understood and I felt sorry for her, but I tried to steer her back to the episode that dealt with Laughlin and Eldorado. "Did she say what the special project was that she was assigned to?"

Mrs. Rivera put a hand thoughtfully to her brow. "No. I think it had something to do with that Seaview development they're building, though. She said she couldn't talk about it."

Carl Rivera had not said anything for some time. He just sat with his arms crossed, fixing me with a brooding stare. Finally, he said: "You said Nina was on her way to meet you—"

"Yes."

"Were you there when it happened?"

I hesitated. I had been hoping he would not ask that. After a few seconds, I said: "Yes."

"How did it happen?"

"She got out of her car and was walking across the street when the car hit her."

His body tensed. "I don't know, but I get the feeling—all these questions you're asking, you saying she called you up saying she was in trouble—that you don't think it was an accident?"

I stared at him. "That's for the police to decide."

His face grew hard and he stuck his chin out. "I'm asking for your opinion. You were there. You saw it happen. You think it was an accident?"

"I don't know—"

"What do you mean, you don't know?" he said, his voice rising belligerently.

"All I know is that the car speeded up when your daughter stepped into the street."

Mrs. Rivera's right hand clutched her throat. "You mean the man *tried* to hit her?"

"That's what it looked like."

Carl Rivera regarded me craftily. "You told that to the cops?"

"I gave them a statement, yes."

"What'd they say?"

"The car was stolen. They're working on the theory that the thief panicked and ran down your daughter by accident."

He nodded slowly. "You know what I think?"

"What?"

His eyes grew hard and hateful. "I think you're nothing but a fucking ambulance chaser. I been sitting here since you started talking, trying to figure out what your angle is in this thing, and I've finally nailed it down. You want to convince us that our daughter was murdered and the cops aren't gonna do jack shit about it so that we'll pay you to look into it. I don't even believe my daughter hired you. You're just making up all that crap to play on our grief, just to suck some blood money out of it—"

"I have a copy of the report I gave her in my files, if you'd like to see it—"

"I don't want to see anything you've got, mister. I just want to see your ass out of this house." He started to sit up, and his wife reacted immediately, putting her hand on his shoulder. "Don't do that, dear," she said. "You'll hurt yourself."

His mouth was twisted by hate, not pain. "You're just goddamn lucky, mister, that I can't get up, because if I could, I'd kick your ass clear into the street."

Mrs. Rivera huddled over him protectively, as if trying to shield him from his own fury. "You'd better leave."

I nodded and stood up. "I'm sorry to have bothered you both." I left them huddled together there on the couch, trying to work out their grief in different ways, and feeling glad, like he said, that he couldn't get up.

Eleven

The proceedings of the County Board of Supervisors were kept on the third floor of the County Hall of Administration, in the executive office of the board. The agreement between Eldorado and the county was filed there.

The agreement had been signed on December 14, 1977, by Supervisor Burt Casey, and what it basically said was that the county was to pay Eldorado, Inc., $1.4 million over the next five years for the privilege of using the canyons below the Seaview site as a garbage dump and landfill. But there were some other clauses buried in the garbage of legal language that were not so basic.

Land, as well as money, had changed hands. In exchange for some low land the county needed for its landfill operation, Eldorado had received some county land on the tops of the canyons. But because there was a difference in acreage between the two parcels, the county was to pay Eldorado another $1.2 million in "compensation." No consideration apparently had been given to the fact that the low land was absolutely useless to Eldorado as development property or the fact that the higher land had to be worth considerably more per acre.

The county agreed to build an access road to the site—on

solid earth, because garbage has a tendency to settle. It also agreed that the dirt used to cover the garbage would be taken from the tops of the canyon ridges, which would coincidentally provide nice, terraced slopes for Seaview, free of charge. And the sanitation district was to pay all the property taxes on the land while all this was being done, of course.

All in all, it was a charming contract—for Eldorado, Inc.

While I was there, I had the clerk check his indexes and see if he had anything on Mirabelle Canyon or Skycrest Estates, Hoffman's first stop.

The file on Mirabelle Canyon went back to 1966. In that year, the City of Los Angeles issued a conditional use permit to the county and sanitation districts, which owned a good chunk of Mirabelle Canyon, so that the canyon might be used as a landfill. The canyon was zoned for residential and the city had to give its permission before it could be used for anything else. The permit was to last for fifteen years, but in granting it the city had stipulated that "the filling operations be completed at the earliest possible date in order to permit progressive development of recreational areas." The "recreational areas" to be developed were a public park and a golf course that was to be built and administered by the county.

Considering the condition of Mirabelle Canyon, it did not seem that the county was going to make the 1981 deadline, but that really did not make a hell of a lot of difference because in the file there was a memo dated 1979 from the County Department of Parks stating that the plans for a park in Mirabelle Canyon were being aborted as there was no public money available for the project. That memo had apparently made quite a few people mad, for there was also a sheaf of letters in the file from irate homeowners in the area expressing bitterness over the scrapping of the park project and demanding to know why the landfill operation had been stopped.

One particularly vituperative letter writer, a Dr. Aaron

Goldman, wrote that he had bought his house in Skycrest Estates only because of the promised park. Now, he contended, the landfill had been stopped and the area below his house was "an eyesore." He went on to say that he intended to sue the city and the county for breach of promise. I took down the good doctor's address and gave the clerk back the file.

Facts can be like junk. You take that first hit and it's kicky enough to make you want to try some more and you do, telling yourself all the while that you're cool, that you're just chipping, you can quit anytime you want. Then you wake up one morning to find you're hooked. A fact junkie can get high just digging them up and putting them together. I was starting to feel a little high by the time I walked over to the State Corporations Commission and started going through the file on Eldorado.

Eldorado, Inc., had been formed in 1974 and was described as a land-development company. From the look of the yearly audits in the file, the company appeared to be in good financial shape. Seaview was listed as its only current project, but it had built three other housing tracts in the past four years—in Torrance, West Covina, and Pasadena. At the time of incorporation, the principal officers had been Joseph Pallisgaard, president; Clyde Laughlin, vice-president; and Emma Dysinger, secretary-treasurer; and from what I could determine that lineup had not changed. The company's officers were also its stockholders. Pallisgaard owned fifty-five percent of the stock, Laughlin twenty-five, and Dysinger twenty.

Just for the hell of it, while I was there, I ran the three names through the commission indexes. In a little under an hour and a half, I had a list of four corporations in which the three were also officers, together and apart. All of the companies were involved in finance, real estate, or land development. In all of them in which his name cropped up,

Pallisgaard controlled a majority of the stock. Whoever he was, Pallisgaard seemed to be the heavyweight of the trio.

There was nothing I could possibly pull out of it but trouble. Nobody was paying me and I had no prospects. My client was dead and she had never really been my client anyway. I didn't owe anybody a damn thing. What did it matter that somebody had used me, played me for a sucker? A lot of people had done that in my life. Take the thirteen hundred and walk away, Asch. Who cared what kind of a dirty mess the woman had gotten herself into, and then gotten wiped out for her trouble? What did it matter that she was coming to you for help when she'd gotten killed? Nobody could help her now.

All that was on one side. On the other was just curiosity. That was all. And I was too smart to let that get the better of me.

I always cursed those stupid broads in the horror movies who heard the noise upstairs in the haunted house and went up to see what it was with a candle in their hands that you knew goddamn well was going to blow out. I could never work up any sympathy for them when they bought it. The dumb bitches deserved what they got. A person with any smarts would head for the front door, not the stairs. Being the smart person that I was, I went downstairs and started out the front door. I almost made it, too. But the pay phone there stopped me. I used it to call Landfill Number Eight.

A man with a gruff voice answered the phone.

"Merle Hoffman, please."

"Not here."

"When will he be in?"

"Good question," the man said testily. "He didn't show up today."

"He didn't call in?"

"No, he didn't call in."

"Did you try him at home?"

"You try him at home, mister," he said. "I'm god-damn busy."

"Sorry to have bothered you," I said, and hung up. Actually, he was the one who had bothered me.

I got Hoffman's home number from the phone book and dialed it. I let it ring eight times before giving up. Then I picked up my candle and went out to the car.

Twelve

I ran my finger down the panel of buttons by the gate in front of the Oak Knoll until I found 345. When nothing happened, I pushed it again, then began stabbing buttons at random. On the fifth try, a man's voice asked who it was and I told him it was Parcel Post and I had a package for him. He buzzed the gate open and I went inside.

My elevator companions to the third floor were an auburn-haired beauty dressed in a skimpy bikini and terry-cloth cover-up and a tan little blonde in white shorts. The blonde's tan little ass was being squeezed halfway out of her shorts and I couldn't help but stare lasciviously. I thought that this was a strange place for Hoffman to choose to live. All the heterosexuality must have disgusted him. But then, you could never tell; maybe he had an attack of it every once in a while.

The two girls got off at the third floor and went down the hall, chatting amiably, and I waited until they had turned a corner before I started looking for 345.

I found it without much trouble, at the end of a corridor cul-de-sac. I stood pressing the buzzer for a couple of minutes, scanned the hallway and, when I was sure nobody was coming, went to work on the lock with my set of picks. It took five minutes, but then the tumblers clicked and I turned the handle and slipped inside.

The place was one big room with a twenty-foot ceiling and an open sleeping loft upstairs. A wrought-iron banister ran across the front of the loft to keep anyone up there from dropping into the room unannounced. Nobody dropped on me. Nobody screamed at me to get out or demanded to know what I was doing there. Nobody did anything.

I closed the door behind me and stood listening to the silence that filled the place, and an uncomfortable feeling of déjà vu began to creep over me. I instinctively smelled the air for death, but could not even pick up the smells of life. Just the characterless, impersonal, paint-and-fabric smell all new apartments seem to have.

The shag carpeting was dark brown, the walls beige. There was a cream-colored sectional sofa arranged in an L around a glass coffee table, some fat stuffed chairs, and a glass-and-chrome stand of shelves on which were arranged at various levels a row of books, a television set, and an AM-FM stereo tuner. There was a French Provincial dining set with cane-back chairs, and in the corner a small, pale writing desk. The walls were covered with prints by Reynaud and Mondrian, and an assortment of magazines lay over the top of the corner table.

I went to the desk and opened the drawers. There was nothing in them but some unused stationery with Hoffman's name on it, some pens, and a pencil sharpener. Not a letter, not a receipt, not an unpaid bill, not a canceled check. Nothing.

The drawers in the kitchen were well stocked with kitchen utensils, but that was all. Some dishes sat in a wire drying rack by the sink. There was very little food in the icebox—butter, some moldy cheese, a loaf of bread. I took out a carton of milk and sniffed it. Sour. I went up the carpeted stairs to the loft.

The loft was small, and the king-sized bed, end table, and mirrored chest of drawers were cramped together to utilize the space.

The bed was made, but one edge of the brown-and-white grid-patterned spread was rumpled, as if somebody had sat down on it and not smoothed it out again.

There were more magazines in the drawers of the end table, a shade more hard-core than the assortment downstairs. They were the ten-dollar variety, and the photographs in them varied between flat-stomached, well-hung young men wearing leather jackets and nothing else—with a little mild bondage thrown in for good measure—and contortionist ménage-à-one-to-cinco acts among older men and varying combinations of teenage boys. Hoffman's tastes seemed to flip-flop between stroking leather and plucking chickens.

A search of the chest of drawers did not turn up much. One of the drawers was half empty, and what was there was disheveled, as if someone had grabbed something out of it in a hurry. There was also a large gap in the clothes hanging in the closet, which lent a possible significance to the suitcase-sized gap between the two pieces of Tourister luggage on the shelf above.

There were some things missing from the bathroom—toothbrush, razor, shaving cream—but then there were also some things there that probably shouldn't have been, like toothpaste and deodorant.

I suddenly became conscious of myself in the mirror above the sink. The week had taken its toll, the crow's-feet seemed to have cut more deeply at the corners of my eyes. Some women say that lines add character to a man's face. If it was true I was rapidly developing a lot of character. Little wonder. Picking up other people's dirty leavings, following pedophiles around until all hours of the morning fried out of my skull on speed, snooping around in other people's apartments sorting through their underwear—I was in a character-building profession, all right.

The person in the mirror seemed to be leering at me. I said good-bye to him and left the apartment and took the elevator down to the garage. Hoffman's parking slot was empty. I hadn't expected it to be anything else.

On the way into Beverly Hills, I stopped off at the public library and did a little reading in the research room, then drove over to Dunland's store. A big white Rolls was parked in the lot next to Dunland's Jag, and I parked next to it. A bell bonged somewhere in the back of the store when I opened the front door and stepped in.

The place was much deeper than it was wide, and every square inch was filled with something, giving it the look of a pack rat's cave. It was dimly lit and had a rich, musty smell, a combination of old furniture polish and dust that had settled in and stayed.

Dunland was halfway back inside the cave with an elegantly dressed and coiffed woman, discussing the merits of a large ebony desk. He called out that he would be with me in a moment, and I said, "Sure," and began browsing.

The place had everything from large pieces of furniture to cut crystal to painted lacquer panels to old movie posters to framed reproductions to old *Vogue* covers. There were lampshades and cigarette lighters, bureau mirrors, paintings, and pieces of stained glass. But for all its variety, the stuff had one thing in common: It was all Art Deco from the twenties and thirties and embodied a time when the word *style* had a somehow more permanent meaning than it does today. The crystal was all elegant, the cigarette cases were inlaid with mother-of-pearl, the furniture was ornately carved and made of only the most exotic fabrics and woods—macassar ebony and amaranth and shagreen and ivory. At least that was what the book in the library had said. Myself, I wouldn't know macassar ebony from plain old ebony, and I hadn't even known what shagreen was until I'd looked it up in the dictionary.

My browsing was stopped by a bronze and alabaster cobra

floor lamp. The tail of the snake was coiled around the base and the reptilian body rose up to a hood that supported an opaque glass bowl. The cobra bared its fangs at me and its beady eyes dared me to pick up the price tag around its neck. Not one to be easily intimidated, I did. Five hundred bucks. I dropped it just in time to avoid being struck.

"I'll have the desk delivered tomorrow, Mrs. Ackerman—" Dunland was saying as he walked the woman up front past me. "And don't worry, I know he's going to love it."

"Just make sure it's before three," the woman said. "I want Charles to be surprised."

Charles would be, I thought. When he got the bill. Then I thought about the Rolls outside and changed my mind.

Dunland fawned over her all the way to the door, then came back to me. "May I help you?"

He wore a V-necked brown velour shirt and faded French jeans and white canvas loafers with no socks. Through the crook of the V, a mat of dark hair and some strands of gold chain showed. The hair on his head was prematurely gray, and up close I could see that he was probably less than forty. He had a jutting chin and a prominent forehead that protruded from his face like the overhang of a cliff, shielding its features from the elements. Under the overhang, his eyes were dark, cavelike hollows, and his nose was sharp and pointed.

"I'm just browsing," I said. "A friend of mine suggested I come here to look around. He said you have the greatest collection of Art Deco in L.A."

"Kenneth Dunland," he said, offering his hand. "I'm the owner."

"Jacob Asch."

The hand was warm and unpleasantly damp. The little fingernail was much longer than the rest—almost like a woman's false fingernail—and I wondered if he used it just to snort cocaine or employed it for more exotic purposes. There was a cat's-eye ring on that finger and two gaudy diamond rings on the second and third fingers of his left hand. The man did like his jewelry.

"A pleasure, Mr. Asch. Are you a collector?"

"To me, Art Deco was the last real attempt to achieve a coherent, internally consistent decorative style."

I hoped he had not read the same book, or at least not recently. Apparently he hadn't, because his eyes lit up and he reached out and touched my arm affectionately. "I can see you are a man of taste. That's so rare today. So many people have none, or what they do have reflects their personalities—boring, boring, boring."

"Sometimes I think I was born in the wrong time," I went on. "The twenties and thirties were a time when people weren't embarrassed by luxury. They pursued it as a life-style. People today are so *uptight*."

He beamed. "You are so right. What line of work are you in, Mr. Asch?"

"I have an agency," I said vaguely.

"Theatrical?"

"Partly." To get him off that track, I stepped over to the cobra lamp and touched the glass bowl. "I just *love* this."

"A unique piece. I got it in only last week. It was from Norma Tarya's estate."

"The silent movie star?"

"Yes." He smiled coquettishly. "You couldn't possibly remember her. You're much too young."

"I told you I was born in the wrong time."

He laughed a phony laugh and said: "If you remember Norma, you must not be kidding." He waved his fingernail at the store. "Is there anything in particular you were looking for?"

I strolled slowly, looking at everything. "Not really. My friend just knew about my passion for Deco and told me I had to come in and see you." I picked up a cigarette case and turned it over in my hand. "I believe you know him. Merle Hoffman."

"Merle is a good friend of mine," he said in a voice that was suddenly tense. I looked at him. His eyes were looking at me in a new way now. They were adding and subtracting, making small, rapid calculations as they studied my face. "How do you know Merle?"

I went back to studying the cigarette case, then put it back on the shelf. "We met at a club on Melrose. Mario's."

"Yes, I know the place," he said. Some of the tenseness seemed to drain from his voice, but there was still a residue left behind. He smiled warily. "Is that where you live, in the Valley?"

"No. The Marina. But I go out to the Valley a lot. I have a lot of friends out there." I went over the brightly colored vase covered with geometric designs and said: "Ah, a Fauré, isn't it?"

"Torgini," he corrected me.

"Hmm." I held it up. "The style is similar."

"Yes. Torgini was a disciple of Fauré's."

I breathed a little easier; the slip had not been too bad. He seemed to breathe easier, too. Only a true collector would know a Fauré.

I put the vase down and asked: "When was the last time you talked to Merle?"

"Monday."

"I tried calling him at home this morning, but he didn't answer. He isn't at work, either. I called there and they told me he hadn't been in in a couple of days. You wouldn't happen to know where he is, would you?"

"I'm afraid not."

I nodded. "We were supposed to get together for a drink today. Funny. Did he mention to you about going away anywhere?"

He shook his head. The suspicion was back in his eyes. "No, nothing."

"Think he could be with Nina?"

The suspicion was now clouded by confusion. "Nina?"

"Nina Rivera."

"I don't know any Nina Rivera."

"Very short woman, black hair?"

He shook his head.

"She works for Eldorado, the development firm that's putting in that big development over by the Palisades. Seaview Country Club Estates."

His expression turned hard and his chin jutted out even further. "Who are you?"

"I told you, I'm a friend of Merle's—"

"You're no friend of Merle's," he snapped. "What do you want?"

"I just want to talk to Merle—"

He put his hands on his hips and leaned toward me from the waist up. "Who sent you here?"

"Nobody."

"Well, as you can see, Merle's not here. So unless you want to buy something, I wish you would leave."

His face was flushed and the air made a whistling sound as he breathed angrily through his nose. I was not ready for the aggressive reaction I'd triggered, and there was not much I could do now to try to salvage the situation except come clean. "I'm a private detective, Mr. Dunland. I'm working on a case and I think Merle might be able to help me—"

"Just get out of my store," he said. "Go tell your bosses at Seaview or whoever you work for to shove it."

"I'm not working for Seaview," I said, taking a card out of my wallet and handing it to him. "I'm working for myself. It's a personal matter. Truthfully."

"Truthfully?" he said shrilly. "You come in here lying about being a collector and some great friend of Merle's and then you have the nerve to stand there and try to use the word *truthfully* on me?"

He made no move to take the card, and I pushed it at him.

91

"Look, if you see or hear from Merle, Mr. Dunland, just give him this and ask him to call me. It could be important."

He glared at me and made a broomlike sweep of the air with his hand. "Get out, get out, get out."

Since I couldn't afford his prices anyway, I put the card down on the shelf by the Torgini and got out.

Thirteen

A kiosk and an electronic gate guarded the entrance to Skycrest, but the kiosk was empty and the gate was up, so I drove right in. Shadow Mountain, the street Dr. Goldman, the disgruntled homeowner, lived on was the first one on the left as you entered the gate, and it curved to follow the edge of the mountain.

Construction was incomplete on at least half of the condos on the right side of the street, and nobody seemed to be in a particular hurry to finish them. Cement mixers, wheelbarrows, and piles of lumber sat silently on unlandscaped dirt lots alongside the unpainted, unplastered structures, but there were no workmen around. The condos on the left side of the street—the ones visible from below—were mostly all finished and were built to look like French villas, with truncated blue tile roofs and lots of white-trimmed oval windows and ornamental iron balustrades striping their upper stories. I parked outside the one that should have been Goldman's and got out of the car.

A white-haired man dressed in work overalls was kneeling in the flower bed at the edge of the brick walkway that led to the front door, digging the dark soil with a spade. When he saw me approaching, he stood up and wiped his hands on his overalls and said: "Yes?"

"I'm looking for Dr. Goldman."

"I'm Dr. Goldman." He was short and wiry with a seamed, weather-beaten face and quick, beady, bird eyes.

"My name is Asch, doctor. I'm a private investigator." I held out my license and said: "I have a client who's interested in what's been going on here at Skycrest. I ran across your letter in the Board of Supervisors' file."

The bird eyes regarded me as if I might be poison seed. "Who'd you say you were working for?"

"He's an author. He's writing a book on corruption in local government. I found your name in the file and I thought it might be a good one to put in the book."

The dark eyes twinkled. "You want a case of corruption in government, son, I'll give you a dilly. Come on in."

He led me into a sun-washed living room and told me to sit down. I picked out a soft-looking, cream-colored sofa in front of the white marble fireplace and lowered myself into it.

The room was large, tastefully decorated in ochers and creams, and from the paintings on the walls it looked as if Goldman was a fan of Japanese art. A beamed ceiling rose above the room to form a trapezoidal ocher canopy, and the sliding glass doors that opened onto the backyard gave the place a spacious feeling.

A handsome, gray-haired lady who looked a good ten years younger than Goldman's sixty-odd came into the room, and I stood up.

"Mr. Asch," Goldman said, "this is my wife, Dora. Mr. Asch is an investigator, Dora. He's working for a man who's writing a book about corruption in government and he's thinking of putting us into it."

She smiled pleasantly and gave me her hand. "So very nice to meet you, Mr. Asch. It's about time somebody took notice of what's been going on." She turned to her husband. "Would you men care for some coffee? I just made some."

"That would be lovely," I said.

Goldman said he would have some, too, and she left humming.

"I like your home," I said. "It has a nice feel to it. Classy, yet homey."

He smiled. "Thank you. We like it. That's what makes it that much harder to take what's going on."

"How long have you lived here?"

"Six years in March," he said. "We bought the place two years after I retired."

"What kind of medicine did you practice, doctor?"

"I was a thoracic surgeon. I was the head of surgery at Valley Hospital for seventeen years." He said that like a medal winner reciting his battle exploits at a Veterans of Foreign Wars convention.

I nodded. He didn't say anything else, so to get him started I said: "Where did you live before you moved here?"

"Van Nuys. We lived there for twenty years. But when we heard about this place, we decided to make the move. It seemed like a great place to retire. We liked the floor plans the developer showed us; it was above the smog, and at the same time still close enough to everything not to be inconvenient; and with the golf course and park going in, it would have been perfect. Dora plays tennis, you see, and I play golf. Only now, instead of spending our time playing golf and tennis, we spend it sweeping dust out of the house that blows up from that mess the county left. And what really makes me mad is that we can't even sell the place now without losing a lot of money."

"Why?"

"Let me show you something," he said, and stood up. He opened the sliding glass door and led me outside to the small grassy backyard. A high iron fence ran along the back side of the yard, and he went to it and pointed through the bars. A few inches on the other side of the fence, the side of the canyon dropped away steeply until stopped by the dry dirt plateaus. A dust devil moved across the top of one of them like a miniature tornado. "How would you like to wake up every morning and look down at that?"

"It isn't very attractive," I admitted.

"*Attractive?* It's an abomination. And because of it, a lot of us here who would like to sell out and move can't. I bought this place for one hundred and three thousand dollars. Its value has gone up since then, but only a fraction of what houses elsewhere have gone up. It's all supply and demand. Because of that eyesore down there and the fact that there isn't any prospect of it being cleaned up, nobody wants to buy. If I sold out and bought somewhere else, I'd be taking a bath, especially the way interest rates are today."

"And you blame the county for that?"

"Certainly I blame the county," he snapped. "Who else?"

"How about the developers?"

He shook his head. "They got hoodwinked just like we did. They can't even afford to finish half the condos they'd originally planned to build. You saw those across the street. They've been sitting like that for the past two months. They'd planned to sell them before they were completed, but they didn't have a chance, not after the county pulled its men off the job."

"When was that?"

"Last August. One day the trucks were working, the next they were gone." He snapped his fingers. "Just like that. No notice, nothing. We all thought they'd be back, but they just left everything looking like that, just big ugly mounds of garbage with dirt on top. It wasn't bad enough that they had to scrap the park, but they had to stop the landfill, too. The developers or even we homeowners might have been able to do something with it if they'd finished. But what can you do with it like that? We don't have earthmovers. I'll probably be dead before there's even any grass growing down there."

"Aren't they supposed to come back and finish it?"

He threw up his hands. "Who knows? I can't get any straight answers out of those damn bureaucrats, and I'm sick of trying. We've given up trying to talk to Supervisor Casey. I went to three different board meetings and he refused to even give me the floor. Once I tried to grab the microphone and he had me barred physically from the hearing room."

"Have you talked to anyone else about it?"

"I talked to one of Maher's deputies, I can't remember his name."

"Jerry Maher?"

He nodded. "I always thought he was the only honest one on the Board of Supervisors. I thought for sure he'd do something."

"What did his deputy say?"

"He sympathized with our plight but said there wasn't much he could do, that it wasn't in Maher's district. He suggested I talk to Burt Casey's people. That was before I knew the extent to which Casey was mixed up in this thing."

"Did you go back to talk to him after you found out?"

"What would be the point?" he said, his face reddening. "They're all in cahoots with each other. They've all got their hands in the till, I don't care how honest they say they are. Not Maher or anybody else on that board is about to turn on one of his own. They'd be too afraid of retaliation." He wheezed and something rattled in his chest and he coughed. He brought up some phlegm and spat it through the fence. "The only person who expressed any real interest was the engineer for the sanitation districts who was supervising the rubbish fill. He was the one who first came to me to apologize for what was going on. He was very upset about the whole thing. He said the sanitation districts were being manipulated by Burt Casey and a bunch of his crooked buddies."

I knew what he was going to say before I asked it, but I asked it anyway. "What's the engineer's name?"

"Hoffman. Merle Hoffman."

97

Mrs. Goldman stuck her head out of the door and said in a singsongy voice: "The coffee is ready. Come and drink it before it gets cold."

We went inside. A tray with a coffeepot and three cups and a plate of chocolate chip cookies were on the glass table. Mrs. Goldman sat down and asked me if I wanted cream and sugar and I said, "Please," and she poured it.

Her husband was about to sit on the couch, and she looked at him petulantly and said: "Don't sit on the furniture with those dirty overalls."

His eyebrows squirmed. "Where do you want me to sit, woman? On the floor?" But he scooted to the edge of the sofa and perched there, scowling like Snoopy's vulture.

"Have a cookie," she said, holding out the plate. "I baked them yesterday."

I thanked her and took one, and after complimenting her profusely on her culinary wizardry, I asked the doctor: "When did Hoffman come to see you?"

Goldman slurped some coffee and took a cookie. "When the county people were first pulled off the job. But we've kept in contact since then. He's going to help us fight this thing." The motion of the cookie stopped on the way to his mouth. "You won't say anything about that to anybody, will you?"

"About what?"

"About him helping us. He's a nice young man and I wouldn't want him to lose his job."

"I doubt he'd lose his job, even if somebody found out what he was doing. Once somebody has a civil service rating in this county, it's easier to get him indicted than fired."

He cackled and took a bite of cookie. "I know what you mean there, son. Still, I guess if somebody didn't like a fella, especially somebody like Burt Casey, he could make trouble for him. Have him transferred out to Castaic or something. You know what I mean."

I nodded. "I won't say anything about it. But how's Hoffman going to help you fight it?"

"By giving us information, for one thing. He was the one who told us why the county trucks were pulled off the job."

"Why were they?"

He leaned forward and scratched the air with a bent finger. "To use on another development being put up by a friend of Casey's, that's why. Seaview Estates. They wanted to complete that job quicker, so they pulled all the trucks they had on this one and killed the park. That's going to be the basis of our suit, that there was collusion between Casey and the Seaview people."

"Wait a minute, doctor," I said, holding up my hands. "You just left me in the dust. What suit are you talking about?"

"We got sick and tired of trying to get action from the bureaucrats, so some of us decided to form a homeowners' group. We think we've got the basis for a damned good civil suit. The developers think so, too. They're thinking of joining us."

"Do you have an attorney?"

"We're in the process of getting one right now. You ever hear of Louis Metzger?"

I said I hadn't.

"Well, he's supposed to be the best at these things. He's expensive, but what the hell. If I lose the money selling the house or I give it to a lawyer, it's gone all the same. And this way, I'll get some satisfaction out of it, sticking it to Casey and his cronies." His face brightened with an idea. "Say, maybe the suit would make a good part in your client's book. You know, how to fight back against the system. You *can* beat city hall."

"I'm sure he'll want to put it in if he can. Publication deadlines are a problem, though."

"When do you think the book will be out?"

"Oh, next year sometime."

I finished my coffee and thanked Mrs. Goldman again for her hospitality. Goldman shook my hand at the door and said: "I never did ask, son, what's your author's name? I got to know if I'm going to buy the book."

"Lee Desmond," I said. Lee Desmond was a talent agent I knew who handled freaks as clients—dwarfs, acromegalic giants, and recording stars who claimed to be the reincarnation of Rudolph Valentino. I had no idea why his name popped into my head, but Goldman didn't seem to find anything wrong with it. He smiled impishly and held up a blue-veined hand. "You know, these bureaucrats downtown are making a big mistake. They think just because these old hands shake a little bit, they still can't cut out a heart. They're going to be surprised when I cut out a few of theirs."

"I'm sure they will," I said. "I'm sure they will."

Fourteen

It had been almost two years since I had last seen Marty Savich. Years before that, we had both worked at the *Chronicle*, Marty for the political desk and I on the crime beat. But after my newspaper career came to an abrupt and bitter end when Marcus Simon, the owner of the *Chronicle*, had refused to back me up and I'd wound up spending six lovely months as a guest of the county for refusing to reveal my news source for a story I'd done, my contact with Marty had become sporadic, and finally nonexistent.

As a reporter he had been tough, relentless, and totally incorruptible, and like most investigative journalists who spent a lot of time sniffing around the political arena, he had come to look upon all professional politicians as inveterate thieves and liars. That was why I had been surprised six months ago when I heard he had quit the paper to go work for Jerry Maher. But not *that* surprised. If he had gone to work for any politician, Maher would have had to be the one.

Like Savich, Maher had started his career as a muckraking newsman. As anchorman on the Channel 6 "Evening News," he would nightly name names, blasting giant corporations and local politicians to the cheers of his TV audiences. When some of the program's sponsors complained to the station management about being among the blasted and Maher refused to tone down his approach, he wound up being replaced by a less controversial and more controllable anchorman, one of those perfect-toothed, brush-cut boys who deviates from his copy only when making an occasional cute aside to the perky weather girl to his left.

Maher dropped into a hole after that, but reemerged a few years later when he announced his candidacy for the Board of Supervisors. The experts had given him little chance to defeat his opponent, a veteran politico who had occupied the same seat on the board for the previous twenty-five years, but that old political warhorse soon turned into an old gray mare when Maher appeared on television with documents spelling out some pretty shady land deals in which the man had been involved, along with an arrest report dating back to 1939 showing that he had been caught that year at L.A. International Airport trying to steal one of those mini-tractors the airlines use to tow around their planes. When a reporter had asked Maher what he thought his opponent could have possibly wanted with a tractor, Maher had merely shrugged and said: "I have no idea. Maybe he wanted to steal an airplane."

The electorate got the message and Maher had wound up with 55 percent of the vote.

Since taking office, Maher had received a lot of criticism about the way he used his position, and most of it was from the boys sitting alongside him in those high-backed chairs. Most of those boys had been able to stay in office simply because they were masters at prestidigitation, adept at directing their audience's attention to their right hands with a line of patter while the left ones were pulling doves out of their coat pockets.

Sure we've got smog, they would say, but what the heck can we do about it when those fat cats in Washington won't crack down on Detroit? Every night you could hear one of those board members on the evening news, whining bitterly about being hamstrung by the federal government or the administration in Sacramento.

That was where Maher would step up and point out that the local Air Pollution Control District—which just happened to be represented by the five members of the Board of Supervisors—had recently granted a variance to Standard Oil to allow its El Segundo plant to keep operating even though it was in flagrant violation of county clean-air standards. Then, with a magical flair all his own, he would pull out of his pocket a couple of 5 by 7 file cards, his face showing a slightly bewildered expression, as if to say, Gee, how the hell did those things get in there? And read off some very generous campaign contributions Standard Oil happened to have made to the reelection committees of several members of the board.

Watching Maher's magic lessons, the public was starting to become educated, and the other four members of the board were starting to smile and sweat a lot, like Daffy Duck staring down the bore of Elmer Fudd's shotgun. And they were becoming reluctant to try the big tricks. No more rabbits or doves. Handkerchiefs were easier, but even those could be risky when your audience had your repertoire down in advance. Everyone was just a little on edge, the old backslapping confidence was gone, which probably had something to do with why Maher's colleagues did not stand up and sing "For He's a Jolly Good Fellow" every time he walked into the hearing room.

Maher's offices were on the eighth floor. The reception room was walnut paneled, carpeted in thick green pile, and filled with pale brown, plump leather chairs and rented plants. A waist-high partition cut the room in half, and behind it half a dozen secretaries fulfilled Parkinson's Law by grinding out their daily quota of paper on their typewriters. An attractive brunette at the desk in front took my name and asked me to be seated, and a few minutes later Marty came out of the back, his hand thrust out and a broad smile on his handsome face.

"Jake!" he said, pumping my hand with genuine warmth. "Christ, how long has it been? Three years?"

"Longer, I think."

"Must be, must be."

Although it was painful to be objective about it, he held his thirty-six years better than I held mine. He was still built like a middle linebacker, and even though his sandy hair had thinned a bit in front, his smooth-jawed, athletic good looks were still intact.

He wore no coat, but the Ivy League necktie, the neatly buttoned candy-striped shirt, and the black patent-leather loafers were all touches I'd never seen before.

"Well, I'm glad I came in. Now I've seen everything—the Savage Savich wearing a tie."

He looked down at himself. "Jerry likes his deputies to look neat. You know how it is. Public image and all that."

He whisked me back into a small office, cluttered by an oversized desk and a congregation of filing cabinets, and set me into a leather chair. A poster on one wall showed a little fish swallowed by a bigger fish. The message did not really have to be spelled out, but it was: THERE IS NO SUCH THING AS A FREE LUNCH. He settled behind the desk and asked: "So how's the P.I. business?"

"Not bad. It has its days—both kinds. How's politics?"

He looked up at the ceiling and exhaled a gust of air. "Hectic. But interesting."

"I have to admit, when I first heard I couldn't believe it. Marty "If His Lips Are Moving He's Lying" Savich going to work for a politician."

He grinned. "I couldn't believe it myself, if you want to know the truth. When Jerry offered me the job, I was really reluctant. If he'd been just another politician, I would've turned him down flat. But I liked what he had to say and what he was trying to do, so I said, what the hell, I'd give it a whirl. So far, it's working out."

"No regrets, then?"

"Like you say, it has its days—both kinds. But it's a good feeling being able to shape things, having an effect and seeing it. That's something I never felt at the paper, even when I broke a big one. There are other benefits too. Job security, for one thing. And I don't have to add that the pay is a hell of a lot better than writing a political column for the *Chronicle*."

"Sounds like you've found your niche in life."

He shrugged. "Not politics, if that's what you mean. I don't think I could ever work for anyone else in this business but Jerry. That's the one big drawback about the job—dealing with obtuse bureaucrats and crooked old ward heelers and coping with their torrent of bullshit. The job can be frustrating. We're trying to accomplish certain things around here, but it's hard to clean up the swamp when you're up to your ass in alligators."

We both laughed, and he said: "Why do I have the sneaking suspicion that you didn't come over to see how I was enjoying working for Jerry Maher?"

"Because you know me," I said. "You ever hear of a condominium development called Skycrest? It's up Mulholland."

He turned it over in his mind. "Skycrest, Skycrest . . ."

"The county was doing a landfill project there. They abandoned it in midstream, which made the homeowners there very unhappy. They're getting ready to launch a suit against the county over it. I talked to one of them. A Dr. Aaron Goldman. He says he talked to someone in this office about it."

"He might have."

"You don't remember?"

His chest heaved with a tired sigh, and he stabbed a finger

105

at the door. "See that door? It's a revolving door for the walking wounded. Everybody has got problems, and because of Jerry's reputation as champion of the downtrodden they all seem to come here. Just yesterday, for instance, I got one of the ray people in."

"If I may be so bold, what are ray people?"

He looked at me as if I were a little dense. "People who claim they're being bombarded by rays. You know, gamma rays, X rays, UV rays—"

"Oh. Sure. *Ray* people. For a minute, I didn't know what you were talking about."

He nodded. "Anyway, this guy comes into the office wearing a stocking cap and down vest. And under all that—he shows me—he's got on long underwear. It's ninety degrees outside and this fruitcake is dressed to go skiing. He sits down there, right where you are, and tells me it's to protect him from the rays that are coming down out of his attic and attacking him and his son. The rays are giving him sores, he says. Guess who's responsible for the rays?"

"The CIA."

"How'd you know?"

"Who else has access to such diabolical weapons? They've got the ray market cornered."

"Yeah," he said, shaking his head. "So I tell the guy someone will be out to investigate and call the Psychiatric Emergency Treatment Center and they go out to his house and find that his fourteen-year-old son hasn't been in school for two months. They ship the joker off to the Laughing Academy and get help for the kid."

"Goldman isn't a ray person. From what I can see, he's not suffering from paranoia of any kind. He's a retired surgeon and he's in control of all his faculties."

"I'm sure he is. My point is, we get inundated with calls and letters from people like this Goldman every day. It's impossible to keep them all sorted out. We'd have to have a

106

staff of three hundred if we were going to investigate all of them. What did he say we told him?"

"That it wasn't in Maher's district."

"Whose district is it in?"

"Burt Casey's."

"Ah." He picked up a pencil from the desk and put the eraser end in his mouth.

"So is the Seaview development," I added.

He put the pencil back down on the desk next to two others and looked up at me. His eyes flickered with interest. "What does Seaview have to do with this other thing?"

"Apparently what happened was the county trucks being used for the landfill at Skycrest were pulled off the job and put on Seaview."

"I see," he said. "I wasn't aware of the tie-in. I might have paid more attention to this Goldman or whoever he was if I had."

"Casey was the big mover in the Seaview deal with the county?"

He nodded.

"I looked up the agreement. It smells."

He arranged the pencils in a neat row, side by side, then messed them up and began rearranging them again. "Sure it smells."

"You think Casey took a payoff?"

"Casey has had his hand under the table for the past twenty years. There's no reason to think he would start changing his habits with Seaview."

"Why hasn't your boss done something about it? I thought he's supposed to be the taxpayers' watchdog."

He looked up. "The agreement was signed before Jerry took office, for one thing. For another, Jerry is interested in seeing Seaview succeed. He thinks it is an important project, in spite of how it came about. He wants to see Southern California lead the nation in the development of solar. He's even proposed the use of county funding to do it. Trying to hang Burt Casey would be like spitting in the wind. We'd never be able to prove he took a bribe, and even if we could the county would never indict him."

"Why not?"

"It isn't public yet, but Casey has the Big CA. Terminal. The doctors have given him six months, if that. He's going to be stepping down next month. Governor Madden will appoint someone to take his place . . . with the approval of the rest of the board, of course."

"Any idea who the someone will be?"

He hesitated, then said: "Right now, the odds-on favorite is Ron Eastland. He's an assemblyman from the Thirty-eighth. He and Madden are very tight. They went to law school together at Loyola."

"Eastland," I repeated.

He caught my tone and asked: "Yeah, why?"

I debated whether to spill what I had, then decided to. I was tired of carrying it around by myself. Together, we might be able to make some sense of it. We'd done it before.

He waited until I'd finished, then said disbelievingly: "You're not suggesting that Eastland is involved in some way in Hoffman's disappearance? Or the death of that girl?"

"I'm not suggesting anything. I just don't like the connections, that's all."

He stared at me. "Eastland is a big supporter of Seaview, but I wouldn't call that much of a connection. It's in his district, there's no reason he wouldn't talk it up."

"It's nice that his district got picked for the site," I said. "Especially since he's probably going to sit in the seat of the man who set up the whole deal."

He glanced at me scoffingly. "You're pushing a bit there."

"Maybe. What's Eastland's story, anyway?"

He shrugged. "An up-and-comer, picked to go places. He's good-looking, young, bright, articulate—everything the aspiring politician should be."

"Sounds like a wet dream by the National Committee. What's his record like?"

"He's strong in his district. He has a reputation for getting things done. Of course, his friendship with the governor doesn't hurt him any there. He carries some weight of his own, though. Has a couple of important committee positions, on Ways and Means and the Subcommittee on Energy. He's chairman of that."

"Is he honest?"

"We haven't done enough work on him to know. He looks okay on the surface, but that doesn't mean much. And even if he's honest now, it doesn't mean he'll stay that way. Especially if he gets on the board."

"Power corrupts, and all that jazz?"

He nodded. "People don't realize just how much raw political power a board member wields. Probably more in this state than anyone outside the governor. L.A. County has a bigger population than forty-four states. Its annual budget is four billion, which is bigger than the budgets of thirty-six states. And it's all controlled by the five men who sit on the board, which makes your local supervisor a damned good man to know if you need a favor. Hell, I don't have to tell you how it works. You're a builder and you need a piece of property rezoned from residential to commercial so you can put up a shopping center. A little contribution to the old campaign fund and the Planning Commission—the members of which just happen to be appointed by the board—votes in your zone change. Or say you're a developer and you want to put in a huge housing development in Malibu, but Malibu is on cesspools and a project of the size you're contemplating needs sewers to take care of the waste. And the people who live in Malibu now are quite content with their cesspools and they don't want sewers. So you call your friendly supervisor and he proposes a sewer bond, and just to make sure it passes he arranges for the sanitation district to be gerrymandered to concentrate all the yes votes, which have already been polled. And for extra measure, a couple of weeks before the election, county health inspectors descend on Malibu issuing citations to septic tank owners for health violations. That last little number Casey pulled off a couple of years ago."

"Nice."

"Yeah. And those kinds of favors cost." He squinted at me and leaned forward. "You know what a deputy job like mine is supposed to be worth? A hundred grand a year, three-quarters of that tax-free, under the table. You can imagine what the market value of a supervisor's job is. Hell, sometimes I feel like a schmuck taking home my five hundred dollars a week and not reaching for the gravy."

"Knowing you," I said, "you'd probably just spill it on your tie."

He grinned sheepishly. "Probably. The point is, whoever steps into his shoes is going to be inheriting twenty-five years of connections, and you can be goddamn sure there will be a lot of pressure from those connections to keep up the relationship."

"What about your boss? Isn't he susceptible to the pressure? Or is he as honest as he comes off, all righteous indignation and moral integrity?"

I had meant it as a joke, but obviously he did not take it that way. He stiffened and said in a serious tone: "I'll tell you just how honest Jerry is. When he calls his wife to tell her he's going to be late for dinner because he has to work late, he makes a check out to the county for thirty-five cents. And that's the truth."

I waited for the Lily Tomlin raspberry, but none was forthcoming.

"Sounds a little gonzo to me."

"He does it for a reason," he said firmly. "Jerry is trying to make changes in county government. Real changes. The vested interests don't want change. They want things like they have been. They'd love to see him make one little fuck-up they could use to get him out. He's not about to give it to them." This was the church, this was the steeple. From the religious tone in Savich's voice, I would have been willing to bet that Maher's face adorned the altar.

The phone on the desk buzzed and he picked it up. "Yes? Yes. Right. Right away." He hung up and said: "Shit."

"Trouble?"

"What else? I've just been told we're having an emergency meeting to hammer out some problems with the rapid-transit proposal we're working on. I'm going to have to cut this short." He sat very still for a moment, thinking, then said: "From what you've said, I take it you've been looking into this on your own. I mean, you're not working for any-body, right?"

"Right."

He nodded and stood up and came around the desk. "I'd really like to discuss it some more with you. And I'd like you to meet Jerry. What are you doing tomorrow morning—say, around eleven-thirty?"

"Nothing that I know of."

"You know where the hearing room is downstairs? Why don't you meet me there around that time? We're holding some hearings into the County Hospital, but they should be breaking up then."

"Okay."

"Good." He stood up and came around the desk and slapped me on the shoulder as he walked me to the door. "I'm sure glad you stopped by. It's been too long."

We shook hands at the door, and then the phone rang again and he said he would see me tomorrow. He charged back to his desk, looking like a man about to be up to his ass in alligators.

Fifteen

Whatever was going on at the hospital when I came through the back door of the Hall of Administration the next morning was important enough to make the evening news, because the stage at the front of the auditorium was bright with television lights. I went down the aisle and took a seat with the forty or so other spectators who had come to see their government in action.

The room must have held close to a thousand people. It had a high ceiling and pink marble walls, and at the head of the room thick red velvet curtains rose to the ceiling, providing a regal backdrop for the five supervisors who sat on an elevated platform in high-backed leather chairs, like Supreme Court justices. Behind the bench where they sat, several burly uniformed marshals stood surveying the audience for any sign of insurrection.

Jerry Maher occupied the center seat. He signaled to a bailiff in front of the bench and handed the man a piece of paper. The bailiff took the paper to the witness table, where a man sat trying to smile for the cameras. The man had a soft, round face, which right now was shiny with sweat. He stared at the note while Maher asked: "Do you recognize that note, Mr. McCallum?"

"I'm not sure," the man said weakly.

"That is your handwriting?"

"Yes."

Maher leaned forward. "In the third paragraph of this note, the initials *N.D.* appear. Who would N.D. be?"

The man mopped his face with a handkerchief. "I don't know. I imagine it would be Nick Drake. I can't think of anybody else it would be."

"And you wrote this what date?"

"I believe it was sometime prior to my November memo to Dr. Harris. I don't know the exact date."

"There is no date that I can see."

"No, sir."

Savich slipped into the seat next to me. "Glad you could make it, Jake." He looked up at the stage. "This should break any minute now."

"What's going on?"

"A big capping ring has been operating out of County Hospital. Jerry is in charge of health services. We've been working on the investigation for almost a year."

"What was the purpose of making this note, Mr. Mc-Callum?" Maher asked.

"I guess—I take notes to refresh my memory when I'm preparing a report. I can go back that way and use the information pertinent for the report."

Maher seemed to be concentrating on some of his own notes. "But you don't remember writing this?"

"No, sir."

Maher looked at him contemptuously. "You make notes to remember, but you can't remember this note?"

The man's eyes darted around. He mopped his brow again. "Yes, sir. I mean, no, sir. I mean, I must have written it, but I just don't remember it or what it refers to."

Maher shook his head sadly. "You are excused, Mr. McCallum."

The man smiled gratefully and scurried away from the table like a trapped animal that had just been released, and Maher moved that the hearings be adjourned until the following morning.

"Come on," Savich said. We got up and went through the partition that separated the supervisors from the spectators. Maher was talking to the media people who crowded around him with microphones and poised pencils, hoping for a juicy quote. He glanced up at our approach.

"Jerry," Savich said, "this is Jake Asch."

Maher offered a subdued smile along with his hand. "This is a distinct pleasure, Mr. Asch. I've heard about you for some time."

I had seen his face enough on television to be familiar with the features—the thick black hair, dusted with gray, the broad nose, the dark, pouched eyes, the thin-lipped, turned-down mouth that always seemed to be frowning in faint disapproval—but seeing them transmogrified into living, three-dimensional flesh made them somehow unreal, like seeing a movie star off the screen for the first time.

He was shorter than I had imagined, no more than five-five or -six, but he radiated something that either added inches to his height or cut down my own, I wasn't sure which. It could have been an illusion, a combination of things coming together to play on my own susceptibilities—the stories I'd heard about him, the distance the TV screen puts between its celebrities and the mass of its lowly viewers—but I didn't think so. What he gave off was firm, almost tangible: an inner strength and self-assurance that was immediate and compelling. He said: "Let's go up to the office where we can talk."

The reporters continued to crowd around Maher, firing questions like arrows, but he warded them all off with a wave of his hands. "I have no comment right now, fellas, and I won't have until we've heard all the testimony. So if you'll excuse us."

We pushed our way through them and out a side door, down a maze of corridors to a private elevator. "You had that guy sweating on the stand," I observed as we stepped in.

"That sonofabitch deserves to sweat," he said contemptuously. "He's been letting a group of cappers illegally use the County Hospital for its base of operations for the past year. He's not the one I'm really after, though. He's just a pathetic little man who's trying to save his pension. The one I'm after is his administrative head, Nick Drake. He's got connections to half the shyster lawyers in this town, but I'm going to nail his ass on this one."

From the tone of his voice, I believed him. We left the elevator and went down the hall to his office. He said good morning to the battery of secretaries, then took me back into a paneled office not much bigger than Savich's. Savich trailed behind us. Framed plaques and awards from various civic organizations covered the walls, and through the large picture window the mountains of Pasadena hovered hazily in the smog.

"Marty told me about your conversation yesterday."

I nodded, but said nothing.

"I found it interesting, to say the least."

I still didn't say anything.

He watched me for a few seconds, then asked: "How would you like to go to work for me for a while?"

The man did not go in for long preambles. I was too stunned to say anything but: "Doing what?"

"Officially, your title would be deputy, but you would be working a special assignment."

"I don't mean to sound redundant, but doing what?"

He put the fist of his right hand into the palm of his left and leaned back. "Marty told you that there's a seventy-thirty chance Preston Madden will pick Eastland to fill the vacancy on the board left by Burt Casey's retirement. Before we rubber-stamp him into that seat, I want to find out exactly who he is and what he's connected to."

"You have any reason to believe he's connected to anything he shouldn't be connected to?"

"Not yet. But your questions about Seaview intrigue me."

He paused to glance at Savich, then went on: "Marty told you Eastland is the chairman of the Assembly Permanent Subcommittee on Energy. What he didn't tell you was that Eastland recently ramrodded through his committee a bill that he co-authored, Assembly Bill Twelve Eighty-three, which will provide low-interest loans to construction companies installing solar devices in their housing projects. Up to now, all low-interest loans have been handled through the Municipal Solar Utility Program and have been granted only to individual homeowners. Seaview will qualify for the loan once the actual construction begins. He's also made several speeches to the Assembly praising Seaview as a landmark project in the energy crisis."

"You think he's been gotten to?"

"I don't know. I do know that Joe Pallisgaard is very friendly with Preston Madden. He was a big contributor to his last campaign. Which means that if he also happens to be pushing Eastland, Madden will have a double reason to put his old school chum in." He hesitated thoughtfully, then said: "The thing that really bothers me about Eastland is not that he's politically ambitious—I haven't met a politician who wasn't, it's in the nature of the beast—but that he has the potential to go further than most. He has the looks, the charm, the personality, and he's aware of it. You can be damn sure other people are aware of it, too. Which means that in his case, his ambition will make him susceptible to offers to get him where he wants to go."

"Where does he want to go?"

"That's one thing I'd like to find out," he said. "What I've tried to do here since I got in office, Mr. Asch, is map out where the lines of power go in this state. As you know, the boroughs system and the party machine never got a foothold

116

in California. The real power here is concentrated in the hands of a few groups—lobbyists, organized business, organized labor—people who control enough money to buy the media. Those kinds of people don't care about political parties and party politics. They care about performance. And if they thought Eastland would be the one who would do a job for them, they would do anything they could to put him in."

I thought about the sign in Savich's office. "And there's no such thing as a free lunch," I said.

"That's right," he responded gravely. "There isn't. But before I sit next to Eastland at that hearing table, I want to know exactly what's on the menu and what the tariff is going to be."

"Fair enough," I said. "But why me?"

His dark eyes glanced past my shoulder to where Savich was leaning against the closed door with his arms folded. "Marty gives you a strong recommendation and I trust Marty's judgment. That's one. Also, I was anchorman at Channel Six when they jailed you for contempt. I don't know if you are aware of it, but I did some strong editorials calling for your release. It took a lot of guts to do what you did. You could have gotten out at any time by giving that judge the name of your source, but you didn't. I've admired you a long time for that."

I was aware of it. When I'd been thrown to the wolves for that story I'd done on the Lawson trial, Maher had openly blasted Marcus Simon, the owner of the *Chronicle*, for "abetting this insidious attempt to subvert the First Amendment." In fact, during the six months I'd spent in that little barred room, I probably would have broken down a dozen times if it had not been for Maher and a lot of other newsmen like him who'd kept reminding their audiences of the importance of what I was doing. Sometimes, when I thought about those six months and broke into a sweat, I wished they would have all kept their mouths shut. I could have squawked, walked, and all I would have had to deal with would've been my own conscience. Instead, the bastards had added peer group pressure to compound the issue.

I did not say that to Maher, though. I just said: "Okay, but I don't understand why you have to call in outside help at all. You've got a lot of people on your staff just as qualified as I am. Marty, for instance. Why not use one of them on it?"

He shook his head ruefully. "Normally, I'd do just that, but right now I can't spare anybody. We're trying to put a rapid-transit plan together, and these hospital hearings just got underway, and on top of that it's budget time. The CAO has turned in a four-billion-dollar budget, which means with Prop. Thirteen now we've got to trim it by over half a billion. I've got everybody on the staff working day and night trying to figure out what programs we can cut without turning the walking wounded loose in the streets."

"How would I fit into the new budget?"

"You mean how much would you be getting paid?"

"That's what I mean."

"You'd be getting a regular deputy's salary, which is about five hundred dollars a week. It's not your regular rate, I know, but there are a few extras, like the use of a county car and a gasoline credit card and a comprehensive health insurance plan in case you get sick or injured on the job. That brings the total up a little."

The irony of going to work for the same county that had locked me in a cell for six months appealed to me. Especially going to work for Crusader Rabbit. But Crusader Rabbit or no, I liked Maher. He might seem a bit of a nutter, but I was convinced of his sincerity, and I liked what he was trying to do. All that and five hundred a week to look into something that I would probably still be looking into for nothing.

"Okay." I said.

"Good." A pleased smile crinkled his eyes, and he said: "Marty, get—what do you like to be called? Jake?"

"That's fine."

"Get Jake set up, will you? W-Four, insurance forms, and all that? He can work out of Sam's old office."

Savich came off the wall. "Right, chief."

Maher rose to his full five-foot-six and proffered his hand. "I might as well tell you before you start, Jake, you're not going to be winning any popularity contests when you start asking questions out there. And you'll probably hear a lot of stories about how I'm a publicity freak who crucifies people for press coverage, that I'm just using the board as a political football to get into higher office. I don't mind the stories. In fact, I take a certain satisfaction in them. They're usually propagated by nasty small-minded little men who can't understand how anybody could be uninterested in power for its own sake or doesn't use his office to make a dirty buck. What I'm trying to say is don't expect any red carpets to roll out when you mention my name."

"I was never partial to red anyway," I said. "And I never adjusted well to popularity. In high school, I was voted 'the man most likely to be found dead in a motel room—alone.' "

He smiled sardonically. "Well, let's hope that the prophecy doesn't come true while you're working here. The publicity wouldn't do me any good at all."

Sixteen

I was issued my own office, complete with secretary, an ID card saying I was an official deputy for Jerry Maher, an ARCO credit card with the county's name embossed right on it, the keys to a new white Chevy Malibu parked in the Hall of Administration's underground parking lot, and the keys to the executive elevator that dropped into said garage. There was a certain feeling of importance that automatically came with all those cards and keys, but after four days of combing through campaign contributions and corporation records, those feelings of importance were starting to weaken, along with my eyes.

Campaign contributions are filed in the office of the Secretary of State, supposedly to provide John Q. Public with the opportunity of checking up on the honesty of his elected public officials. Only the reality was not quite that simple, and unless John Q. knew just what he was looking for in that morass of names and numbers, more likely than not he would never find it.

Say a businessman wanted to contribute to a politician's campaign but didn't want good old John Q. to know about it. He might funnel his donations through faceless organizations with names like Businessmen for Better Government or

Citizens for Honesty in Politics, organizations that might not even be in existence six months after the election. Or he might give through DBA businesses, and since donors are listed on the rolls by name and not by the nature of their business, links to the businessman might be difficult to recognize. Or he might donate through one or more of the law firms with which he dealt. Or, if he had a number of corporations, he might not make contributions at all, but then all of his individual corporate officers might—from the vice-prez all the way down to the treasurer. Even *buildings* can legally give to the candidates of their choice, even though it might be hard for a twelve-story office building to find a voting booth big enough to vote in. Eastland had his share of all such entries.

After four days of sifting through files and shuttling back and forth between the Corporation Commission and the City and County Licensing Bureau and the County Assessor's office, I'd managed to come up with $9,200 that had been donated to Eastland's last campaign by business concerns with which Joe Pallisgaard, Clyde Laughlin, and Emma Dysinger had some connection, either as corporate officers or owners, and another $7,500 that had been chipped in by three law firms with which the trio did business.

But it wasn't only Pallisgaard and his cronies who had donated to the cause. Several other big developers had made significant contributions, as had the California Real Estate Association and the California Mortgage Brokers. Ronald Eastland, it seemed, was the darling of the real estate set.

The next step would be to prove influence, which meant going through Eastland's voting record on those issues in which the real estate interests had a stake. That way I would find out if there was a positive correlation between the way he voted and the way they would have wanted him to vote. I was in the process of doing just that, plus going through Eastland's credit reports with a fine-tooth comb just to make sure some of those donations did not accidentally find their way into his private bank accounts, when I stole a little county time to drive out to Landfill Number Eight. I didn't really feel guilty about the theft. After all, I *was* investigating Eastland and Hoffman *did* look like he might be a hostile witness.

The weather had soured overnight, and a gray, misty drizzle speckled my windshield as I pulled up in front of the engineer's trailer. A mud-splattered red Ford pickup was parked outside, but nobody was around it.

The trash caravan was light today, and there were long gaps between trucks as they pulled up to the kiosk to be weighed. I knocked twice on the door of the trailer, then opened the door and went in to get out of the rain.

The room was empty and smelled of stale cigarette smoke and old coffee. The source of the coffee smell was in the back, a Mr. Coffee with an inch residue of tar-black brew. The paneled walls were covered with topographical relief maps of the landfill and surrounding area, with the contours and different elevations marked by different colors.

There were more maps on the two scarred desks, and on one of them was a mug half-filled with black coffee. The mug was still warm, but barely. I started to go through a sheaf of papers stacked on the edge of the desk. They were mostly memos from the Joint Administration Office, written in some undecipherable technical jargon about compactions per square foot and cutfills and vertical depths. There were also some pieces of paper with telephone messages for Hoffman. Most of the names I didn't recognize, but two of them I did: Detective Mellerek, Venice Detectives, and Kenneth Dunland. From the number of slips, it looked as if Dunland had called at least three times.

I had my hand on the desk drawer when the door of the trailer was opened by a husky man wearing a yellow rain slicker and a yellow hard hat. He had a pouchy-cheeked face and a dark mustache and sideburns. "What are you doing in here?" he asked harshly.

I showed him my ID. "I'm with Supervisor Maher's office."

His demeanor loosened up immediately. "Oh. Sorry if I snapped at you there. I'm not used to people walking in here. I'm the supervisor, Don Carruthers."

I wondered if he had been the one I'd talked to on the phone. Maybe they didn't roll out the red carpet at the mention of Maher's name, but they didn't tell you to get lost, either. Not if they worked for the county. I was getting to enjoy having the weight of the office behind me. "Jake Asch."

He held out a hard, rough hand permanently stained black by grease. "What can I do for you?"

"I'm looking for Merle Hoffman."

"Join the club," he said in an Oklahoma twang. "I think everybody wants to know where Merle is. You, the cops—"

"Nobody's heard from him since he didn't show up for work?"

He shook his head. "Not a word."

"When was that."

"A week ago last Monday."

"Why were the cops looking for him? Did they say?"

"They wanted to ask him some questions about a hit-and-run accident that happened the other day. At first, I thought that's maybe what happened, that Merle had run the woman down, then got scared and ran. But hell, Merle wasn't at work for a couple of days before that."

I nodded. "Have you got a couple of minutes, Mr. Carruthers? I'd like to ask you a few questions."

"If you don't mind going for a ride," he said, shrugging. "I've got to go up to the line to check out a piece of equipment."

"I don't mind at all."

We went outside, and he pointed at the pickup and we got in. The road wound sharply upward, zigzagging up the side of a smooth-faced dirt embankment. The tops of the mountains above us faded into a soft gray mist. Some of the mist fell onto the windshield, barely enough to keep the wipers working.

"You an engineer, too, Mr. Carruthers?"

"No. I just keep things coordinated around here. Merle is the engineer. He oversees both this and the School Canyon fill."

"Have any theories about what might have happened to him?"

He shook his head. "Not unless he had an accident or something. Or he really *is* in trouble with the cops. It has to be something like that. I can't figure it any other way."

"Why not?"

"Because Merle isn't some goddamn flake that would just take off and leave. Somebody else might do something like that, but not Merle. Merle's goddamn married to this job. I mean, most of us who work this fill are really proud of our work, we all take pride in our jobs, but Merle oversees this site like a mother hen." He paused. "In a way he is. I mean, he did design it."

The words "design" and "dump" struggled with each other in my mind. "What exactly does Hoffman do here? I'm not really sure what a sanitation engineer is."

"Don't feel bad. Not many people are. People think 'dump' and right away all they can think is 'trash.' I know I did when I first came out here ten years ago. I said, 'I know what a dump is,' but I sure didn't. It's a lot more complicated than people think. Everything is carefully planned out. The fill schemes and the contours of the plots are all meticulously designed. Merle is the best rubbish man in the business. He knows just where to lay it and how much to grade the contours so they'll get just the right amount of runoff and won't settle out too bad. Some people, like me, are good at cutting fills, but Merle—Merle's the greatest with rubbish."

It seemed like a dubious claim to fame, but I was not about to rain on his parade. He took his eyes off the road and said: "Why are you looking for Merle, anyway?"

"I want to talk to him about something," I said. "The Seaview project."

He nodded knowingly. "He call your office?"

"Not that I know of. Why?"

"Because he called everyone else he could think of about Seaview. I told him if anyone would be likely to do something, it would be Maher—"

"Do something about what?"

We reached the top of the grade and the road leveled off. "When the county signed the contract with Seaview, Merle was working on a project in Mirabelle Canyon. He'd been working on it for a couple of years. It was another one of his babies. He designed it and nurtured it and got it off the ground, and then the funding got yanked and the county pulled its equipment off. When Merle found out they'd reallocated the funds earmarked for Skycrest to Seaview, he got pissed off. He said Casey was behind it, that a deal had been made and he wasn't going to let him get away with it. He said even the Environmental Impact Report had been fixed. What made it such a personal thing with him was that part of the money was pulled out of here."

"How?"

"Our operation here is self-supporting. You come to dump, you pay. About forty percent of that revenue is paid to the city of L.A. for the use of their land, and the rest is used to take care of our operation costs. Whatever is left over after that goes into a trust fund the county uses to acquire and implement new sites. Actually, once the money goes into the trust fund, we have no control over it. The county can spend it wherever the hell it wants. But it was Merle's understanding that it would be earmarked for the Skycrest project. When he found out that Casey was behind the move, he hit the ceiling. Merle doesn't like Casey anyway. Casey has pulled some shit in the past with the sanitation districts. Merle always said he was a crook."

"Did he say how the Environmental Impact Report had been fixed?"

"No. He just said it was a whitewash."

"When did all this happen?"

He shrugged. "He's been bitching about it for the past six months, but he'd really been on a rampage the last couple of weeks before he disappeared. I don't know what the hell happened to him to get him so worked up; he wouldn't tell me exactly. All he said was that they'd try to put some pressure on him to get him to shut up."

"By 'they,' do you mean the Seaview people?"

"I guess so. Merle never really said. All I know is that it really sent a hot hair up his ass. He started calling everybody and his brother, to raise hell about it."

"Who did he call?"

"Quite a few members of the board of the sanitation district, Assemblyman Eastland—"

"Eastland?"

"Yeah. Seaview is in his district."

The road narrowed, and we drove along the edge of a precipice that dropped in a sheer, smooth incline to the base of the mountain. Looking over the edge was like looking down the face of Hoover Dam. Carruthers saw me staring out the window and said proudly: "That's where we started, eight years ago."

"That's garbage?" I said in disbelief.

"About five hundred feet of it. There's fifteen feet of dirt cover, but below that, it's paper."

"Mind-boggling," I said truthfully.

We passed between two rocky outcrops, and then the road

dipped and leveled off again and we were on a flat, gray plateau perhaps a quarter of a mile across. It was totally barren, a wasteland devoid of any life forms at all except the procession of trucks that moved across its surface. The sterility of the place was unearthly and had an unsettling effect on me. Even the surrounding mountains had been stripped of their vegetation and had the haunting look of scraped bone.

The trucks were grinding to a halt in front of a dirt bank at the end of the plain. Before we reached there, Carruthers peeled off the road and we bounced across the rutted surface to an access road that led up the side of the dirt embankment. From the top of the embankment we had a good view of what was going on below.

Two huge DK8 caterpillar tractors moved back and forth in perfect coordination, shoving the garbage that was being dumped by the trucks into one huge pile at the end of the embankment.

"Is that just one day's garbage?" I asked, pointing at the pile.

He nodded. "We figure each person has about seven pounds of garbage to get rid of at the end of every day. Nobody in the country knows how to handle trash like we do. The entire county sanitation district disposes of twenty-eight thousand tons of trash a day. We take care of about twenty-eight hundred tons at this site alone."

I looked back down at the cats. I could not see their drivers; against that gray, wasted surface they moved like robotized moon mobiles. Carruthers pointed a finger and said proudly: "Those drivers are highly skilled. Driving one of those things over paper is like driving on marshmallows. You wouldn't think it, but you could flip easy, you didn't know what you were doing."

I nodded, remembering. "I used to drive one of those babies a long time ago, when I worked construction one summer. They're hard enough to drive on hard pack, never mind the mush."

"The dozers will build that pile there to about twenty feet, and then at five, when we close, we'll cut it off and a scraper will take dirt from the side of the mountain and cover it over. By six, there won't be a piece of paper showing."

He looked up at the darkening sky. "Unless the goddamn rain erodes some of it away."

"Interesting," I said. There was certainly no problem getting him to open up. Just get him started and he'd talk trash all day. "You think Hoffman could have gone somewhere to get away from the pressure, whatever it was?"

He waved the thought away with his hand. "You want something from Merle, you don't ever try to force it out of him. I learned that a long time ago. Just makes him madder than hell. And one person you don't want to see mad is Merle. I've had to pull him off of more than one guy who made that mistake."

"You mean pull off as in fistfight?"

He nodded and smiled, as if enjoying the instant replay in his head. "Merle is a hell of a scrapper. Just last month, we were out having a beer in a little shitkicker's joint we go to sometimes after work, and some big dude started mouthing off. There were four or five of us, and trash guys are kind of cliquey. It's funny. We're kind of like lumberjacks or truck-drivers or something. I've seen a bunch of guys from a land-fill come into a bar and say, 'Okay, all you other fuckers leave.' That doesn't sit too well with some guys, y'know? Anyway, I guess whatever we were doing didn't sit too well with this one asshole, we were talking too loud or something, and pretty soon he gets lippy and then words start going back and forth between him and Merle and the next thing I know, the guy is laid out on the floor."

The tractors were directly below us, laboring like monstrous yellow beetles rolling their dung. Trucks continued to rumble down the road and dump their loads. "Slow day to-day," Carruthers said, watching them. "It's the rain."

I had no idea if Carruthers was aware of Hoffman's homosexuality, but he did not appear to be. "You and Hoffman go out socially much?"

He pushed out his lower lip and said: "Not really. I'm married and Merle isn't, so that'd be kinda tough, if you know what I mean."

"Hoffman ever talk about getting married?"

His eyebrows raised in surprise. "Merle? Merle's a confirmed bachelor."

"He ever mention a girl named Nina Rivera?"

"The cops asked me the same question. Who is she?"

"Possibly a friend of Merle's?"

He paused to reflect on that. "I never heard him mention the name."

"How about Sylvia Calabrese?"

He shook his head. "Merle never talked much about the chicks he went out with."

For good reason, I thought.

Carruthers stopped the truck in front of a huge scraper, the tires of which were as tall as the roof of the truck. He got out and bent down to inspect one of the scraper's front tires, which was flat. He looked like a pygmy squatting next to it.

"Shit," he said, standing up. "These fucking tires cost five thousand apiece."

The rain was starting to come down a little harder now. He came back to the truck and got in. He sat there, staring at the tire tight-lipped, then started the truck again.

"Did you ever hear Hoffman mention the name Joseph Pallisgaard, Mr. Carruthers?"

He ran the name through his mind, then shook his head. "Can't say that I have."

"How about Clyde Laughlin? Emma Dysinger?"

"No. Who are they?"

"The owners of Eldorado, the company that's building Seaview."

"I'm sure he knows who they are, then." The man's pouchy face grew thoughtful. "I sure wish I knew what the hell's happened to Merle. It's really got me worried. You think he really might be in trouble with the cops, that he might be hiding out somewhere?"

"I don't know."

He stared hypnotically at the wipers working on the windshield and said: "Shit, I just hope nothing's happened to him."

We drove down the embankment and across the dead plateau to the road. When we got back to the trailer, I wrote my office number on a page in my notebook and ripped it out. "If you hear from Hoffman, Mr. Carruthers, I'd appreciate your telling him to get in touch with me. Tell him we're on his side, okay?"

"Yeah, sure."

Another man wearing a rain slicker came out of the office and shouted to Carruthers: "Did you take a look at the scraper, Don?"

"Who the fuck was driving it last night?" Carruthers yelled back angrily. "Freddie?"

"Yeah."

"Well, get somebody over there to change that tire. We're going to need it tonight."

I stepped out of the truck and waved at Carruthers and went to my car, leaving the two men to talk their trash.

Seventeen

Dunland had a helper today. A slim young man with a neatly clipped mustache and brown hair cropped short in back was showing a couple around the store, with Dunland nowhere in sight. He gave me a coquettish smile as he floated by about six inches off the floor. Then Dunland came out of the back, responding to the bell sounded by the opening door. He was wearing white jeans with a rope belt; a khaki shirt and a navy blue shirt open enough to expose his impressive collection of gold chains. "You again," he said.

"Don't hurt my feelings. I'm a sensitive person."

He tried to shoo me away with his fingernail. "I told you the last time you were here I have nothing to say to you."

"Things have changed. The last time I was here, I wasn't on county business." I showed him my ID. "I'm with Jerry Maher's office."

"I don't care who you're with. You people can't come around here harassing me and upsetting my business. I have friends, too. Political friends. So just get out of here. I have nothing to say to you."

"Have the police been around to talk to you yet?"

He took a step toward me, his narrow shoulders hunched. "Don't you hear? I said get out."

131

His voice was rising in volume, and the couple being shown around the store looked at each other nervously. The assistant tactfully steered them farther away. I watched them, not moving, then looked back at Dunland. "Did you tell the cops about the blackmail attempt?"

It was a shot in the dark, the bullet melted down from what I had so far. It turned out to be a bull's-eye. He blanched and began blinking rapidly, then said very quietly: "I don't know what you're talking about."

I nodded my head toward his assistant and said: "You want your customers to hear all this or do you have someplace where we can talk privately."

He thought about it, then relented with a wave of his hand. By the time we'd gotten to the little office-storeroom full of cardboard boxes and packing paper, he had regained his composure. He closed the door behind us and folded his arms defiantly. "Well?"

"Pictures," I said.

"What?"

"About a week before Hoffman dropped out of sight, a woman named Nina Rivera hired a private detective to get something on Hoffman, on the pretense that she was Hoffman's fiancée and thought he was chipping on her. What the detective got were pictures—of you and Hoffman and two street hustlers you picked up outside the Gold Cup. The reason she did that is that she worked for an outfit named Eldorado, Inc., and Hoffman had been running around town bad-mouthing a big housing project Eldorado is working on. He was pointing fingers and using words like 'political corruption' and making a general nuisance out of himself. To get him to stop, they tried to use the pictures as leverage. You still want to tell me you don't know anything about this?"

He glared at me hatefully. "What is this, some sort of shakedown? In case you haven't heard, there's a consenting adults law in this state—"

"Adults, yes; kids, no."

"Both those kids were over eight—" He cut himself off, realizing he had stepped into it.

"Look, Mr. Dunland, I'm not trying to shake you down, and I could care less what you or Hoffman or anybody else does with his spare time. It's none of my business. I'm only interested in finding Hoffman."

"Why?"

"I know how Hoffman feels about what's been happening with the sanitation districts. I just got through having a long conversation with one of his co-workers about it. Supervisor Maher doesn't like it, either. If political corruption is involved, we want to expose it. Hoffman may be able to help us do that, and at the same time we may be able to help him. Right now, he may need some help."

"What's that supposed to mean?"

"The hit-and-run case the cops are trying to solve is Nina Rivera. If they knew that she'd tried to blackmail Hoffman, it would give him a motive for murder—"

"That's ridiculous," he said vehemently.

"Is it? Hoffman's co-workers apparently have no idea he's gay. He must not want it known. And although the county would have no grounds to fire him just because he's homosexual, it would have if it could be proved he's been playing around with children."

"I told you, those boys weren't children. They were both over eighteen."

"Uh-huh," I said. We locked stares, until I said: "What did he tell them when they contacted him, to go to hell?"

He looked away quickly. "I haven't the slightest idea what you're talking about." But he did. He was lying. There was no doubt in my mind anymore.

"Look, Mr. Dunland, your friend is in over his head. He's been trying to twist the arm of the Incredible Hulk. You don't do that without getting thrown across the room. Considering everything that's been happening, I realize it must be hard for you to believe that anyone in county government can be on the up-and-up, but we're prepared to give Hoffman some help if he needs it. You, too."

"Me?" He put a hand on his chest. "Why should I need help?"

"In case someone tries to approach you about the pictures."

"I came out of the closet a long time ago," he said disdainfully.

"But Hoffman hasn't."

He said nothing.

"You say Hoffman didn't kill Nina Rivera. Maybe not. But somebody did. The question is why. She was on her way to meet me when she was run down. She was pretty shook up about something. She told me she hadn't thought things would go this far and she needed advice. Now what do you think she meant by that?"

He rubbed his forearm with his long-nailed hand. "How would I know?"

"She was *killed*, Mr. Dunland. Maybe it was an accident, maybe no. Maybe she just knew too damn much. Maybe Hoffman knows too much, too. Maybe that's why he split, to keep from winding up like Nina Rivera."

I was trying to scare him enough to start him talking. He seemed to be teetering on the edge.

"What did he have on Seaview?" I asked.

Dunland's face was crowded with indecision.

"He told someone he wasn't going to let Casey get away with it," I persisted. "How did he intend to stop him?"

Dunland pulled back from the edge. The moment was gone now. He went to the door and opened it. "If that is the extent of your little speech, perhaps you'll leave and let me get back to work."

I took out a business card and wrote Maher's office number on it and put it down on the top of the wrapping counter. "That's in case you lost the other one. I know you wouldn't have thrown it away."

As I went by him, he said: "I was serious about having influential friends of my own."

"I'm sure you were."

"I suggest you don't come back here anymore."

Unless prepared to be attacked by angry chickenhawks, I thought of adding, but left without saying anything.

On my way home, I stopped off at the Blue Whale and had some swordfish, then went home and took down a couple of stiff Old Granddads, and relaxed on the couch with a collection of Algren to stop thinking about the case for a while. My mind was working on it overtime, but I wasn't getting paid for it.

I must have nodded out, because when the phone startled me awake I was still on the couch, with Algren open on my lap and my drink beside me, still upright. I fixed that by getting up and knocking it over, spilling watered-down bourbon and melted ice all over the cushions.

I staggered to the phone and picked it up and a voice like a cheese grater said: "Asch?"

"That would depend."

"On what?"

"On who this is."

"This is Merle Hoffman. I understand you want to talk to me."

I looked at my watch. Eleven-forty. "I wouldn't mind it, but couldn't you have picked a better hour?"

"It's now or never. I can't take the risk of being seen. They were following me."

"Who?"

"I'll tell you when I see you. I'll be at 77312 Sunset Terrace. Meet me there."

"Dunland's house?"

"Yeah, half an hour."

I must have held the receiver for five seconds before I realized I was talking to a dial tone. I hung up and tried to gather my thoughts, but they had scattered in the hills and were refusing to gather. I went upstairs and got a jacket anyway and went out to the car.

Rain still dribbled down out of the skies, good rear-end weather, and I drove carefully along Sunset. In spite of the rain and appropriate to the witching hour, half the people on the Strip looked as if they had just flown in from a Sabbat. The disco freaks and groupies and rock 'n' rollers were out in force in their glitter makeup and silver space jackets.

The lights were ablaze in Dunland's house as I pulled up, five minutes early. The Jag was in the driveway, but Hoffman's Merc was not out front. He probably hadn't gotten there yet. I pulled in behind the Jag and parked. As I stepped out of the car, I could hear the hard-rock music blaring inside the house. That was not right somehow. Rudy Vallee should have been coming out of that house.

I sat there for a minute, just listening to the rain patter on the roof of the car, then pulled up my collar and made a dash for the front door. A small metal plaque there said:

If you don't swing
Don't ring

I rang anyway.

After a couple of minutes of standing there with nothing happening, I put my ear to the door and pressed the button again. Over the sound of the music I could hear chimes from deep inside the house, like echoes in a cave. Maybe he couldn't hear the bell over the music. I tried the handle. Locked.

I went around to the living room window and peeked through the sliver of light between the drawn curtains, but there was nothing there worth seeing, and after getting wet tapping on the window with my car key, I trotted back to the driveway.

A door in front of Dunland's car led into the house. As I reached the door, the music inside stopped, and a deep male voice began giving a recital of the song titles that had just been played. Dim honkings drifted up the hill from the boulevard. I stood there, debating what to do.

The door handle turned when I touched it. I pushed it open and felt around inside for a light switch. I was in a tiled kitchen. Sets of copper pans hung neatly above the stove, spice containers sat in even rows along the drainboard, faucets gleamed. Either Dunland had a maid or he was an immaculate housekeeper. I wondered if his icebox was also filled with acidophilus and goat cheese.

"Dunland!" I called out. The only voice that came back was that of the disc jockey on the radio. I went through the kitchen into the living room.

The room was a monument to Art Deco. The walls were high-sheen white except the one on which a Rousseauesque jungle mural had been painted. The floor was silvered mat glass illuminated from below with soft lights. A zebra skin that looked real flowed from the floor up onto a low stuffed couch with white plastic arms that took up one end of the room. It appeared Dunland had a thing for animal skins. In front of the couch was a coffee table with a goatskin top, and flanking it were two sheepskin chairs with ebony arms that curled up from the floor like elephant tusks. The skins had a disconcerting effect on me. So did the lions and leopards that peered from the mural on the wall. But then, anything would have had a disconcerting effect on me at that time, even the woman's voice coming from upstairs, talking about how soft her hair was when she used Organo Shampoo. I went toward the voice, feeling like a rat following the Pied Piper.

In the entryway by the front door was a chrome and Plexiglas staircase guarded by a chrome statue of an ibis-headed Egyptian god. I went up the stairs slowly.

There were three doors along the hallway that ran from the top of the stairs, but only two of them were open. Light spilled out of the first one. So did the woman's voice talking about Organo Shampoo. The voice was making me jumpy. I didn't give a rat's ass about Organo Shampoo, but I went there anyway.

"Dunland?" I called out as I stepped inside. No answer.

It was a large, open bedroom, with high-sheen white walls like the living room and a large-square tile floor. There was not much furniture in the room, but what there was was tastefully arranged and suggested opulence. There was a gondola-shaped love seat covered with white fur and a backless bucket-seated chair made of leather. Two brass stand-up lamps anchored both sides of the bed, and a series of staggered Caucasian-walnut shelves ran almost to the ceiling, forming the headboard. The stereo tuner was on one of the shelves in reach of the bed, and I located the source of the sound—two speaker cabinets in the corners, partially concealed by being recessed into the walls.

The bed was about the size of a polo field, and from the way it looked a game might recently have been played in it. The covers were thrown back and the chartreuse satin sheets were rumpled. On the shelf above the pillows was a fifth of Southern Comfort. Beside them were two amyl poppers, unused, and a mirror on which lay a razor blade and some white powder that had been chopped into neat lines. I wet a finger and dipped it in the powder and tasted it. Coke.

There was a phone beside the bed. It had been ripped out of the wall.

Opposite the head of the bed was a walk-in closet with sectional folding doors and another door that presumably led into the bathroom. The bathroom door was partially open and the sound of running water came from behind it. I went to the door and pushed it open all the way.

He was sitting on the tile floor, wedged between the bathtub and the toilet. He was nude. His head hung over his chest, but I didn't have to check to see if he was still alive. The average human male body holds only about twelve and three-quarters pints of blood, and seven of Dunland's had to be on the floor and walls. His face was gone. Standing in for it was a bloody, gray, sticky pulp.

The long, graceful neck of a heron protruded over the porcelain edge of the sink and peered at me with one bird eye. It was an Art Deco piece made of brass and it looked heavy. The blood was starting to cake on it. Two blood-soaked towels hung over the edge of the sink, and one lay on the floor. It looked as if the guy had been doing some cleaning up when I interrupted him. I backed away from the door on sick legs.

He must have been in the closet, because when I heard the scraping of a door I started to turn in that direction. I caught a flash of yellow and that was all before something that could have been a fist or a sap or a sackful of horseshoes smashed into my left temple. Disco lights exploded in my head, and since I'd never taken disco lessons I did the only thing I could do. I fell down.

I tried to roll over and get up, but the horseshoes came down on my head again and the disco lights and the music died, and I was sucked down into a silent, still vortex of black.

Eighteen

The engineer working the mixing board was very good. He faded the music back in very slowly and gradually, and then someone was talking to me. It was the engineer.

He was telling me how swell he thought it was that I was awake and all about what he'd been playing while I was asleep.

My cheeks felt cool. I groaned and opened my eyes. Both of those actions seemed appropriate. The reason my cheek was cool was that it was resting on the floor. I pushed myself up onto all fours and looked to make sure all my limbs were still there. That was when I realized I was not dressed in what I had arrived in.

I was wearing a shorty black silk bathrobe with red and yellow Chinese dragons all over it, and it smelled as if it had been laundered in Scotch.

I tried to think of a good reason why I would have gotten undressed and slipped into a Scotch-laundered bathrobe decorated with Chinese dragons, but could not come up with one. I didn't even like Chinese dragons. Then I saw the heron by my right hand. It was following me. Pretty birdie. The birdie was covered with blood. Somebody had shot the pretty birdie. Poor birdie. I looked at my hand. It was sticky with blood, too. Then it started to come to me. In pieces. I felt like throwing up.

The robe fell open and I looked down at my chest. There was blood smeared on it. That made me take a closer look at the robe. Whoever had bought it had bought it with just the yellow dragons. The red ones had been dyed recently.

My skull felt like somebody had been working on it with a power drill. Just to make sure they hadn't, I ran my fingers over it. I sucked in some air, but managed not to scream when I touched the egg behind my ear. The roaring in my ears pounded in time to the wailing of rock guitars. I stayed on all fours for a while, trying to think, but nobody came to give me a doggie-biscuit reward, so I struggled to my feet and looked around for my clothes. That was when the music stopped and I heard the voices.

They were muffled, indistinct whisperings beyond the door, and when they stopped for a moment I thought I'd imagined them. My mind playing tricks on me. Then I heard them again. Downstairs, but louder now. Coming up the stairs.

My body tingled with a sudden rush of adrenalin, and my eyes scanned the room in panic. If those voices belonged to the cops, I'd have a nice time trying to explain being here in a Chinese bathrobe smelling like a Shriners' convention with a dead body in the other room. Then again, if they belonged to the goons who had done the job on Dunland and who were now coming back to finish the job on me, I probably wouldn't have to explain anything to anybody.

My eyes lighted on the heron. The blood on my hand probably meant that my prints were all over the damned thing. I felt the slip-knot tighten around my neck. I bent down to pick it up. That made me dizzy, and I had to steady myself on the bed to keep from falling.

I went into the bathroom and wiped off the bird with one of the bloodied towels and put the statue back in the sink. I could always pick it back up if I needed to use it on some-body. I pulled the door shut until it was just a crack and peeked out.

The seconds dragged their mummy feet. I tried not to look at Dunland, tried not to think about him being there. I felt nauseous enough already. My palms were soapy with sweat. I prayed for cops.

Led Zeppelin shouted from the radio. I could not hear the voices anymore.

I held my breath as I saw the bedroom door being prod-ded open. A hand and the brown sleeve of a sheriff's uniform came through the door, holding a .357, and I let the breath go in a sigh of relief. I pulled open the door and stepped out. "Don't shoot—"

The deputy dropped into his firing stance, both hands firmly on the grip of his pistol, which was leveled at my chest. "Freeze!"

I froze. The gun was steady in his hand. "Charlie!" he called, never taking his eyes off me. "In here!" Then to me: "All right, you, hands on head. Now!"

I put my hands on my head. "This isn't what it looks like," I said lamely. "Really it's not."

He came toward me slowly, still holding the gun in both hands. "Just shut up and keep your fucking hands on your head."

I shut up and kept my fucking hands on my head.

The scene was held for a detective-sergeant from Sheriff's Homicide downtown named Baatz—as in belfry—and I would not have been surprised if he might have kept a few of the furry little critters as pets. He looked more like a high priest of the Church of Satan than a cop. His head was shaved smooth as an egg, and a pitch-black mustache drooped evilly over the corners of his mouth and ran down to his chin. His deep-set, dark eyes gave the impression that he was looking at you from the bottom of a well.

I wondered if the image was a true reflection of his personality, or if it had been purposely cultivated for the effect. He probably got great results from his interrogations, especially in alleys after midnight. His suspects probably peed all over themselves, certain that they had fallen into the clutches of the Fiend. It was well after midnight, we were not in any alley, and the Fiend had long ago given up hope, if he had ever had any, that I was going to pee on myself.

He did not seem terribly thrilled when he learned who I was working for, but maybe for that reason he didn't read me my rights immediately. After running me through my story a couple of times at the house, he drove to County General where I had five stitches sewn into my scalp, then over to Sheriff's Central where we started going over it again.

I didn't lie to him, not really, but I did leave a few things out. I told him about Hoffman's midnight phone call, but maintained I'd been looking for the man for personal reasons, namely the Rivera homicide. I filled him in on the background—the photographs, Nina Rivera's phony front, my discussion with Dunland that afternoon about what Hoffman had been into with Seaview, the threats he had made, and my suspicions about a blackmail attempt. I left out Eastland's name, though, and denied that my visit to Dunland's house had anything to do with what I was working on for Maher (which was partially true).

I knew this was no time to be holding back—I knew I was in deep shit—but I wanted to talk things over with Maher before I spilled everything. I didn't owe him my neck, but I did owe him my cover.

Baatz kept hammering at my story, especially at my contention that I'd been hit over the head and undressed to make me look good for the murder, and after a while I felt like Foghorn Leghorn trying to convince Henry Hawks I was not a chicken. Evidently he had never seen those pictures where the cop looks at the suspect and says, "Your story is so screwy it *has* to be true," because after I told him I would be happy as a clam to try it out on the lie box, he read me my rights and had me booked without bail. Murder One. He did allow me my one phone call, and before I went into lockup I woke up my attorney, Paul Ellman, with the news. He was overjoyed to hear the sound of my voice and bitched that if I *had* to kill somebody, couldn't I at least do it at a civilized hour? But he did say he would be down later. He also promised to get word to Maher.

I was put into a cell with two other men, neither of whom quit snoring when the door clanged shut. They were sound sleepers. Sometimes at home I woke up drenched with sweat hearing that sound in my nightmares. They didn't even wake up when it was real.

Fortunately for me, I was so tired I fell asleep before I had time to think about my situation or where I was. I slept through the breakfast call, too, but got up when they told me it was time to take the polygraph.

I was taken to a soundproofed interrogation room on the second floor where a young uniformed Chicano wired me up and took me over the salient points of my story. His face remained perfectly impassive while he asked the questions, and after running four tests he told the deputy who had brought me down that he was through, and I was taken back upstairs to lockup. I was not told if I'd passed, but then I hadn't expected to be. That was the way things were in jail.

Paul Ellman came to see me that afternoon. He said he had talked to the D.A. and been told that whether or not I was to be arraigned would depend on what Baatz came up with in the next seventy-two hours. If they didn't arraign me by then, he would have me sprung on a habeas writ. He had talked to Maher, who said he would do everything he could, but was not tickled pink about it. The publicity had apparently already started. My arrest had been blasted over several afternoon television news shows, and the papers would be jumping on it tomorrow. He said no matter what evidence they turned up pointing to my innocence, they would probably hold me for three days, and I shouldn't count on being let out before then.

It was after Paul left that the uncertainties of my situation really began to get to me. What if this frame was set up well enough to bind me over for trial? There was no bail on murder. I could be here for months. The thought of it made me break into the shivering sweats. I was not one who handled jail well. Spending six months in County had left emotional scars on me that split open every time I got near a cell, never mind in one. I'd never been claustrophobic before then, but that six months had left me that way. And now the minutes dragged, and with every one the walls moved in, inch by inch, like an episode from a very bad Fu Manchu serial.

By the morning of the third day, the ceiling was about down to my bunk when the turnkey unlocked the cell door and told me to shake my ass.

I was taken downstairs to a soundproofed room like the other one with a two-way mirror on one wall and a long pale wooden table and some hardwood chairs. Paul Ellman was sitting in one of the chairs, pulling some papers out of his briefcase, which was open on the table. He put the papers back as I came in, then stood up and pushed out his hand. "How are you, kid?"

He had that same rumpled yet indefatigable look he always had, as if he had just made a quick trip to the bathroom to freshen up after an all-night poker session and was now back, ready for another game. His gray hair was sticking out on all sides, and he kept brushing it back with a hand, even though he knew it was a losing battle.

"I'm okay. How does it look?"

"Looks good," he said, then pouched his cheeks out by

filling them with air. They usually looked as if they were stuffed with nuts anyway, but the pouching completed the transformation into a big, friendly squirrel. I wondered if Baatz would fall for the illusion. I knew some D.A.'s who must have thought that Dracula might as easily be a flying squirrel as a bat after Paul had gotten through with them. In court, he had an uncanny instinct for the jugular.

The door opened and Baatz came in, trailed by a thickly built black man with a close-cropped natural. The black man had on a jacket and tie, Baatz had on neither. "This is my partner, Sergeant Walker."

Walker might have nodded, I was not sure. He folded his arms and stood back against the wall. Baatz waved offhandedly at a chair. "Sit down, Asch." When I did, he said: "I took the liberty of phoning Mr. Ellman here, since you expressed the wish to have counsel present when answering questions."

They looked at each other and sparks came out of their eyes. I found myself looking forward to the confrontation. The High Priest of Satan meets Dracula the Flying Squirrel.

Baatz came around and sat down in front of me on the edge of the table, letting one leg dangle over. He watched the dangling foot swing loosely for a few seconds, then asked: "You like dead bodies or something?"

I was not sure what I was supposed to say to that, so I just answered: "Not particularly. To tell you the truth, I find their company pretty dull."

"Really," he said, still looking at the foot. "Well, for somebody who finds them dull, you sure like to hang around them a lot. Herrera and your friend Gordon in the D.A.'s office tell me you're good for a couple a year."

Al Herrera, besides being an old personal friend, also happened to be a sergeant with Sheriff's Homicide, which was why I'd dropped his name to Baatz as a character reference. "Where is Al? I thought he'd at least drop by to say hello."

"Arrowhead. He's on vacation."

"Look, Sergeant," Paul broke in, "let's get down to it. My client's story has checked out right down the line. He passed your lie detector test. Either have him arraigned or cut him loose."

Baatz turned his head slowly and looked at Paul. His face was an expressionless mask. "His story does not check out down the line, *counselor*. There are quite a few things about it I don't like."

"Such as?"

"Such as him being found at the scene in a bathrobe—"

Paul smoothed down an unruly strand of gray hair with a manicured hand and said: "Come on. He explained that—"

"Yeah? Well I don't happen to like his explanation."

"Do you think I do?" I asked. "I don't like being undressed by strangers."

Baatz didn't look at me. "I also don't like his prints being found on one of the glasses by the bed."

"The plot sickens," I said.

Paul held up a hand and said with a little impatience: "It's obvious, isn't it? Whoever undressed him was trying to make him look good for the murder. So he put the glass in his hand. That would make it look like he was there drinking with Dunland, they got into an argument, and he killed him."

Baatz nodded as if he understood. "Then why didn't he also put Asch's prints on the bird? That would have made him look even better for it." Score one for the Scourge of Satan.

"Maybe there wasn't time," Paul said.

"Maybe. And maybe your client wiped his prints off the bird. Maybe that was what he was doing when the deputy arrived on the scene. There were no prints at all on the bird. None." He looked down at me. "How about it, Asch? I might like your story a little better if you copped out to that. I can understand it. You panicked when you heard the deputies, you took the bird—"

"Don't lead the witness," Paul said angrily.

"We're not in court now, *counselor*," Baatz snapped back.

Paul looked at me. "Don't answer the question." He shook his head sorrowfully and leaned back in his chair. "Just what are you contending was Mr. Asch's motive for murdering Dunland?"

Baatz shrugged. "They didn't like each other. They argued that afternoon."

Paul made a belittling gesture. "A slight disagreement. Hardly a motive for such a passionate slaying. In fact, that argument corroborates my client's story of what he was doing at Dunland's house—looking for Hoffman."

"Maybe he wanted to see how the other half lives and couldn't handle it," Walker chimed in.

"Ah. You're back to the sex-orgy theory. Of course. He went up to Dunland's and wound up being seduced, then killed Dunland out of guilt, shame, or whatever."

"It's been known to happen," Walker said dryly.

"Except there are a couple of things wrong with it. Number one, the autopsy showed that Dunland had not ejaculated recently before death and there was no semen in any of his bodily orifices, which means that it was a pretty dry encounter. Two, my client has no record of homosexuality—"

"Ever hear of a place called Mario's After Hours, Asch?" Baatz cut in.

Paul looked at me. I didn't say anything.

"It's a gay bar over on Melrose, in case you've never heard of it, *counselor*. Specializes in young, tight stuff. Dunland used to hang out there a lot. Ever been there, Asch?"

"Don't answer," Paul instructed me.

Baatz turned on him angrily. "It doesn't matter whether he answers or not. We've got him positively identified as having been there. It seems he got into a slight altercation with a bulldyke and punched her out. People around there remember his face quite well."

"It's all right, Paul," I said. "They can check that out in my files. I have copies of the report. I was working for Nina Rivera. I tailed Hoffman there."

"Face it," Paul broke in. "You don't have a case. Nothing fits according to your scenario. For instance, what time did the call come into the West Hollywood substation that there was a disturbance at Dunland's?"

Baatz looked the question at Walker, who said: "Twelve-forty-two."

"The anonymous call," Paul said contemptuously, "from a concerned citizen doing his civic duty, but who didn't want to leave his name. Right." He turned to me. "What time did you leave your house, Jake?"

"Eleven-forty-five."

Paul stood up. "That means my client would have had to drive all the way from the beach to Dunland's house, have a glass of Scotch with him and maybe a friendly blow job that was never consummated, then freak out and bludgeon him to death, all in a little under an hour. Tell me another one."

"Only we don't know your client left his house at eleven-forty-five or even if he left from there at all. He has no witnesses. And no toll calls were made from Dunland's house after nine-thirty, which means that if your client did get a call from Hoffman like he says, it was from somewhere else. So the way it looks, I can tell you anything I want. I've got him at the scene, dressed in Dunland's robe, I've got his prints all over everything, I've got a witness who will testify that he visited the victim the afternoon of the murder and had an argument with him, and I've got him positively identified as a frequenter of a gay bar where Dunland used to hang out. So no matter which way you slice it, *counselor*, I've got motive, means, and opportunity."

My heart sank in my chest.

Baatz stabbed a finger at Paul. "So just make sure he stays available—*real* available—in case I want to ask him some more questions."

I blinked at him, confused. "I don't understand. You're cutting me loose?"

"For now," he said, as if he hated the words. "It doesn't mean you're out of it. Not by a long shot."

"Come on," Paul said, closing up his briefcase and standing up. "Let's get you checked out."

We started for the door and I stopped, remembering suddenly something I'd wanted to tell him. "Oh, Sergeant, there is one thing. You know I told you that before I got hit, I saw a flash of yellow?"

"Yeah?"

"I've been thinking about it, and I know what it was. It was a raincoat. You know, one of those yellow slickers. They wear slickers like that out at Landfill Number Eight. I saw men working in them when I went out there."

Baatz and Walker exchanged significant looks: "You're just coming up with this now?"

"I've had a lot of time to think about it," I said, grinning.

He didn't grin back.

We went downstairs and got my stuff back from the property clerk, then went outside. The sun was shining and the rain had cleansed the air, giving a bright, hard look to the street. I took a big, gulping breath and said: "The way Baatz was talking, I thought they were going to arraign me for sure."

He shook his head. "There was no sweat. I knew they were going to cut you."

"Sure you did."

"I did. Really."

I gave him a doubting look. "How?"

"You passed your polygraph, for one thing. Those cops will scream bloody murder in court about the things being inadmissible, but they really put a lot of stock in them." He paused knowingly. "And then there was the palm print."

"What palm print?"

"The one they found under the sink in the bathroom. They don't know I know about it. It was a bloody print and it was smooth, so they figure the guy was wearing gloves, but it was a big hand—bigger than yours or Dunland's. The guy must have missed the spot when he was wiping everything down."

"Then why the hell did they hold me all this time?" I said hotly.

He shrugged. "They're cops. If I was a cop, I would've held you, too."

We started down the street. "How did you find out about the print?"

He smiled slyly. It made him look more like a fox than a squirrel. "I still have friends in the D.A's office." As we walked on, he said: "Oh, and don't let them bullshit you about your friends Herrera and Gordon. They went to bat for you pretty good. I know."

I nodded. "Thanks for being there, Paul. I appreciate it."

"Don't worry. You'll get a bill in the mail. Your car here?"

"They must have impounded it. But I'm going to walk over to the office right now and talk to Maher. He'll want to know what's happened."

He stopped and shifted his briefcase to his other hand. "You want a lift?"

"No, that's all right. It's just a couple of blocks."

He nodded and offered his hand. We shook firmly and he said: "Try to stay out of trouble, will you? And that means out of this case. I know you're going to be tempted to poke around in it yourself, but fight the urge. These guys aren't going to take it as a joke if they find you messing in their business."

"Yes, sir."

He frowned. "I'm serious."

"Yes, sir."

He stared at me dubiously. "Just remember what I'm telling you. Baatz was not bullshitting when he said you weren't out of the woods yet. They could come and pick you up anytime. Print or no print, you're still their number one suspect."

"I'll lock myself in my room and watch reruns of Mary Tyler Moore."

He waved and went to the parking lot, and I walked up Temple, my face tilted up to catch the sunshine.

Nineteen

The secretaries looked at me kind of funny when I came into the office. I asked Jenny if Marty was in his office and she said yes, and I went back there. He looked up, startled, when I opened the door.

"Jake! Jesus. When did you get out?"

"Just now. I have to see Jerry."

He stood up uncertainly. "Yeah. Sure. But how . . ."

"You might as well sit in, that way I'll only have to tell it once."

We went down the hall to Maher's office. The door was open. Maher was at his desk, poring over some papers with a harried look on his face. When he looked up, the expression changed to surprise, then to a scowl, the meaning of which I was not ready to interpret. "It's good to see you out and about," he said, standing up and offering his hand.

I took it. "Yeah. It's good to be out."

"They let you go or your lawyer spring you?"

"They didn't charge me. Yet."

He nodded. "How did they treat you?"

"Like I was a prisoner or something."

"Bad?"

"They didn't break out the rubber hoses, if that's what you

mean. But then they didn't have to. It's bad enough without anybody going out of his way to make it bad."

"I did all I could to get you out. There wasn't a hell of a lot I could do."

"Yeah, I know. Thanks for trying, anyway."

He acknowledged that with a nod. "What the hell happened, anyway?"

"The day of the killing, I went out to Landfill Number Eight to talk to some of Hoffman's co-workers. One of them told me some things that interested me enough to make me want to talk to Dunland. Dunland was the one I took pictures of with Hoffman when I was working for Nina Rivera. Dunland didn't have much to say, but that night, around midnight, I got a call from Hoffman—or somebody claiming to be Hoffman. He sounded a little paranoid, said some people were after him, and asked me to meet him at Dunland's house. I asked him who was after him, but he wouldn't say. He just said he would explain it all when I got to Dunland's. When I got there, I found Dunland in the bathroom. Whoever killed him—at least that's the way it looks—was still there, hiding in the closet, and he sapped me. When I woke up, I found myself dressed in Dunland's bathrobe and the cops downstairs."

He sighed and asked in a tone that was almost a rebuke: "Have you seen the papers?"

"No."

He reached under the desk and came up with a folded *Chronicle*, which he tossed to me. The story was splattered all over page one:

MAHER DEPUTY HELD
IN SLAYING OF HOMOSEXUAL

The story described the murder scene and how I had been booked after being found there in a "seminude condition" by officers from the West Hollywood Sheriff's station re-

154

sponding to an anonymous phone call about a disturbance at the house. Dunland, a "known homosexual and owner of a prestigious Beverly Hills Art Deco store," had been beaten to death with a heavy instrument, according to the article, and there was a statement by Sheriff Clement Rayburn that the killing had possibly been "sexually motivated." There was also a little background sketch on me—my previous association with the *Chronicle*, my stint in County for contempt—along with the fact that I'd been working as a P.I. and had recently joined Maher's staff as a deputy.

Now I knew what the scowl meant. "Nice," I said.

"Isn't it?" Maher said gruffly. "The phone has been ringing off the hook ever since you were arrested. Citizens' groups, concerned parents' groups, antisodomy groups, gay rights activists, Christian antipornography groups, all demanding an explanation."

"Shades of Anita Bryant."

"This isn't funny. The media has been on it like a pack of sharks in a feeding frenzy. The blood in the water is being purposely leaked, of course. Sheriff Rayburn has just been waiting for something like this to happen so he could embarrass me publicly."

"What's Rayburn got against you?"

"He was using the sheriff's helicopter for personal purposes, to survey some real estate he was buying. I called him on it in the papers. He's just been waiting for a chance to get even."

I was getting winded trying to stay ahead of his political enemies. "My head doesn't make a good football. Wrong shape. It's not pointed enough at the ends."

He ignored that and said: "How much do the police know about what we're doing?"

"Some, not all. I told them I went up to Dunland's looking for Hoffman, which is true, but I told them it was for personal reasons, because of Nina Rivera. I never mentioned Eastland's name or the fact that we're investigating him."

He nodded, satisfied. "If that got out, Eastland and his people would be all over us, screaming 'smear campaign.' The situation is bad enough the way it is."

"It may get worse."

He leaned forward tensely. "What do you mean?"

"They let me get by with my story so far, but that situation may not be permanent. I have a strong feeling that the heat is going to be turned up. The cops don't know what we're doing, but somebody sure as hell does. Like whoever had Dunland hit."

"Hit?" Savich cut in.

"I was set up, either by Hoffman or by somebody who knew I was looking for Hoffman."

"But why?" Maher asked.

"To stop me and to stop you. I think Dunland was killed because he knew something—something Hoffman told him. I was still poking around in it, so I was a threat, too. What better way to get rid of me than by framing me for Dunland's murder? Dunland would be dead, I'd be in jail, and you'd be so embarrassed politically that you couldn't do anything with your hands but use them to cover your ass."

They both stared at me. "Look, let's take what we know," I said. "One, Hoffman was pissed at Casey for meddling in the sanitation districts. I got that from a friend of Hoffman's out at Landfill Number Eight. He was especially pissed when the Skycrest fill was scuttled. It was his pet project, and he had been calling everyone in town—Eastland included—to try to stop the county contract. Why he never called here, I don't know—"

"He did," Savich interrupted.

I shot him a glance. "What? When?"

"About a month ago. He called and demanded to be put through to Jerry, but Jenny wouldn't do that, of course. She says he sounded a little nuts, he was so insistent about it, but she wound up shunting the call to Barry Gresham. Barry thought he sounded a little wacko, too, but he told Hoffman to come into the office at two the next afternoon. Unfortunately, some emergency came up the next morning and Barry couldn't make the appointment, and he couldn't get in touch with Hoffman to tell him not to come. When Hoffman came in and Jenny told him, he got pissed and left. He never called back. I guess he thought he was getting the old bureaucratic fast-shuffle."

"Why didn't you tell me this before?" I asked, a little pissed myself.

"I only heard about it a couple of days ago, while you were in the bucket. Hoffman's name came up in a conversation and Barry told me about it. Hey, you've been around the office, you know how many crank calls like that we get every day. Remember the ray people? Hoffman never really told Barry specifically what he wanted, and when he didn't call back again Barry just forgot about it."

"Shit."

"That's ancient history," Maher said, waving a hand. "Go on with what you were saying, Jake."

"This guy I talked to, Carruthers—he's a supervisor out at the landfill—told me that Hoffman had made some remarks to him shortly before he dropped out of sight, remarks about someone trying to pressure him into cooling his vendetta against Seaview and Mr. Casey. But the pressure only made him madder. I think it was in the form of certain photographs that I was hired to take." I took a breath and went on. "Just before she came to me, Nina Rivera deposited a five-hundred-dollar check in her checking account. The bank code number of the check was the same as Eldorado's bank. I think she was paid the five hundred to pose as Hoffman's fiancée so I'd work for her. There are a few good reasons they used her for the job. One, she had acting experience. Two, she was hung up on her boss, Clyde Laughlin. She probably would have done anything he asked her to. Three, her father's laid up with a bum back and she's been helping her parents out. The money would have come in handy."

"You could never prove that was what the money was for," Savich said.

"No. But that was why I went to see Dunland, to get him to confirm that a blackmail attempt had been made. Dunland was in those pictures, too, and I figured since he was involved, Hoffman might have told him about them."

"Did he?"

"Dunland wouldn't admit it, but he did make a slip about the boys in the pictures being over age, which means he knew there were pictures."

Maher watched me darkly and asked: "Where are you going with all this?"

"Let's just assume that Hoffman told whoever contacted him to shove the pictures up his ass. Let's also assume that somebody at Seaview really wanted to shut him up. What could he do? One, he could just let things alone and hope Hoffman kept running into stone walls like he's been doing. Two, he could try to scare him so bad he'd either shut up or rabbit. Or three, he could get him out of the way altogether by having him taken off.

"Now let's say that Nina Rivera found out about it, got nervous, and wanted out. When she called me to set up a meet, her exact words were, 'I didn't know things would go this far.' Let's also say that whoever it was who paid her to play Sylvia Calabrese found out that she was going to spill the setup to me, and sent someone to stop her."

"All this over the county contract with Seaview," Maher said skeptically.

"It does fit the facts."

"All except one—motive."

"The county contract is worth ten billion dollars to Eldorado. I call that a hell of a motive."

He put his palms out. "You don't seem to understand. There would have been no way Hoffman could have gotten the county to rescind the Eldorado contract. Even if Hoffman could have proved Casey had taken a bribe, nobody would have done anything about it. Pallisgaard and his people know that. Then there's your Dr. Goldman and his lawsuit against the county, or are you forgetting about him? The county contract with Eldorado is bound to come up in that suit. Or do you think that Pallisgaard and his partners are going to have all the homeowners of Skycrest bumped off, just to keep things quiet?"

"Maybe it isn't the county contract," I offered. "Maybe Hoffman found out something about Seaview that isn't likely to come out in Goldman's suit. Something nobody knows about."

"You could make just as strong a case for Hoffman as the killer," Savich said. "He's the one who called you. If Nina Rivera needed money, like you say, she might have been trying to work a number on Hoffman herself. Say she approached him and he got violent. She got scared for her own safety. She sure as hell wouldn't go to the cops after she tried to blackmail the guy, so who does she call? You. If Dunland knew about the blackmail attempt, as you say he did, he could also have guessed who ran her down. Hoffman would've had to get rid of him. Or maybe it was a crime of passion. You say Hoffman came off like a Macho Man at the dump. Maybe he has ambivalent feelings about his homosexuality and took them out on Dunland."

"But why would he invite *me* up to the house?"

Savich shrugged. "Maybe he really wanted to talk to you. Maybe he wanted to turn himself in. Maybe he wanted to bitch about Seaview. Maybe he never intended to kill Dunland. Maybe they got into an argument while they were waiting for you to show up and he killed him. When you walked in, he panicked and tried to pin it on you. He knew you were looking for him, maybe he wanted you to stop. I don't know the answers, Jake. I'm just trying to point up that there is as good a case for Hoffman as anyone at Seaview."

"Maybe. But you don't think it's worth looking into?"

"No," Maher cut in. "I don't. This office does not investigate homicides. That's a police job. If they caught me trying to do it, they'd run me out of town on a rail. They're trying to do that now." His eyes dropped to the desk and his voice dropped with them. "That's why I'm going to have to suspend you, Jake, until this situation is cleared up."

That possibility had crossed my mind, but now I found that I had not really expected it. He looked up and said: "You're still a police suspect. I'm sorry. I really am. But until the cloud of guilt is blown away, that's the way things are going to have to be. I'm having a hard enough time holding off my attackers as it is without adding another front to the battle. You understand, don't you?"

"Sure." I wanted to get mad about it, but somehow I couldn't. I could see the position he was in. "What about Eastland?"

"We'll just have to proceed very cautiously. There are a lot of people looking over my shoulder right now. I may put Marty on it or I may put it on the back burner until things cool down. By then, who knows? The cops might come up with Dunland's killer and you could get back to work. I'm sure this is just a temporary situation."

"Does this mean I lose my pension?"

Dark lines appeared at the corners of his mouth. "Pension?"

"Never mind. It was a joke."

He looked at me sadly. "I hate to do this, Jake. I really do. You were doing a hell of a job. Only I have no choice. I hope you can see that. Murder just isn't political business."

"Yeah?" I asked. "Since when?"

I left them and went down to my office to clean out my desk. While I was doing that, Jenny buzzed me from up front. I picked up the phone.

"There's a man out here from the Bureau of Consumer Affairs to see you, Mr. Asch."

"What does he want?"

"He wouldn't tell me."

160

"Send him back."

A thin man wearing horn-rimmed glasses stepped through the door. Everything about him was neatly pressed, from his brown suit to his slicked-down hair. "Mr. Jacob Asch?"

I went on clearing out my desk. "What can I do for you?"

"My name is Patterson. I'm an investigator with Consumer Affairs."

He was slick, all right. The piece of paper was in my hand before I knew it was there. I looked down at it. "What's this?"

"A summons," he said. "An administrative hearing will be held next Wednesday in the State Building, Room One-oh-seven, at nine-thirty A.M. You may bring counsel."

I stared at him blankly. "Administrative hearing for what?"

"For the revocation of your private investigator's license," he said tonelessly.

"But . . . why?"

"Certain charges of misconduct have been brought against you—"

"What charges?" I shouted at him.

He adjusted his glasses nervously. "I have no idea. I'm just a process server."

"Yeah? Well, you're lucky you caught me in," I said sarcastically. "I had only a few minutes between getting out of the slammer and getting fired."

"It wasn't luck. I followed you over from the Sheriff's Department."

"You . . ." I rolled up the summons into a tube and held it in front of his face. "I think you'd better get the fuck out of here before I shove this thing up your ass."

His eyes grew wide behind the glasses and he scurried out of the door. I sat down heavily at my desk and stared at the tube of paper. "And they thought Chicken Little was a nut case," I said to nobody.

161

Twenty

The case against my license, Paul found out, was being pressed by the attorney general's office. Apparently they had a stockpile of complaints against me dating back three years, the latest being from the Riveras, who were claiming that I had unethically tried to solicit business from them. I wanted to go over and talk to them about it, find out what their motivation was, but Paul told me to stay away, that it would just look like I was trying to intimidate the witnesses and go worse for me. He seemed pretty confident that no administrative judge would yank my license on what the A.G. had, and if they did we could always appeal, he said. Already my attorney was talking appeal. That did wonders for my confidence.

I went home and locked my apartment door and tried not to think about it. To hell with them. If they wanted me, they were going to have to come and take me. I spent a lot of the next two days in a half-stuporous state, immersed in my bathtub in steamy hot water, drinking beer or bourbon (whichever was handier at the time), and listening to Billy Cobham cranked up on the living room stereo. As a matter of fact, Billy just happened to be on the stereo on the morning of the third day, when knuckles sounded on my front door. I turned down the volume and went shirtless to the door.

"I kind of thought you might be home," Baatz said. "I could hear that thing down the block."

He wore a gray turtleneck and blue slacks and his shoes were shined. Walker was with him. He might have had on the same suit and tie he'd worn three days ago, or maybe he had a closet full of them. His shoes were dusty.

"Is this something official, or are you just checking up to see how well I'm adjusting to life on the outside?"

"Let's say it's semiofficial," Baatz said. "Can we come in?"

I shrugged and stood back, and they walked in and looked as if they expected to find something incriminating behind the door. Walker gave a disgusted look at the room. Articles of clothing were flung over the backs of chairs, empty beer cans littered the tables, and on the coffee table in some waxed paper was the day-old remains of a Sloppy Joe I'd apparently been working over. The memory of it was kind of vague.

"Looks like it was a hell of a party," Baatz said, looking around.

"It was, it was. I've been celebrating."

"I hear Maher suspended you."

"Yeah."

"That's too bad."

"Well, that's the way it goes: first your money, then your clothes." I brushed a couple of newspapers off the seat of the couch. "Here. Sit down, sergeant and sergeant. My home is your home."

Walker looked at me strangely. "You been drinking, Asch?"

"Not in the past six hours, but thanks for reminding me. I told you guys I was celebrating." I started for the kitchen where the bourbon was. "You guys want a little bracer to fire up the old boiler?"

"No, thanks."

"Come on. I can't celebrate alone. The big one is on Wednesday, though. I *know* you guys are coming to that one. Room One-oh-seven in the State Building."

Baatz's expression grew vexed. "What the hell are you talking about?"

"Wednesday. The administrative hearing to pull my license. Come on, sergeant, don't tell me you didn't know about it. I thought for sure you guys would be testifying for the prosecution."

They looked at each other. "I never heard a thing about it," Baatz said.

"Sure. The A.G. loves me. They've gone to a lot of trouble to dig up people from my past. It's going to be sort of a 'This Is Your Life'—"

"The A.G.?"

The hardness in his voice made me stop. I came back without a drink. "Yeah, why?"

"Because that's why we're here," Baatz said. "Ever since I cut you loose, Asch, my phone hasn't stopped ringing. It's either the D.A. wanting to know why I let you go or the sheriff wanting to know how the investigation on the Dunland homicide is progressing or the A.G.'s office wanting to know if I have any other suspects in the case." He frowned and stuck out his lower lip. "Now, hell, I'm just a working cop, y'know? I've been with the S.O. ten years now and worked homicide five, and in all that time, you know how many times I've talked with the sheriff? Four times. Now, suddenly, we're on a first-name basis. It's all buddy-buddy."

He leaned forward and put an elbow on one knee. "What I'd like to know, Asch, is why is everybody so interested in a fag killing? And in you in particular?"

"I'd like to know the answer to that one myself," I said.

He nodded. "I called a friend of mine on C.I.I. to see if I could find out. He did some checking and it looks like the interest is being generated in Sacramento. Somebody with enough juice to move people in the A.G.'s office. But he couldn't pinpoint the source. But somebody wants your ass. I thought maybe you might have some ideas who."

"Not who. Maybe why."

"Okay. Why?"

"There are a couple of possibilities. Somebody might be trying to get at Jerry through me. There are a lot of people in positions of power in this state who would like nothing better than to see Maher off the board."

"And two?" Walker asked.

"Maybe I've been nosing around in something somebody doesn't want me to nose around in."

Baatz stroked his mustache. "Such as?"

"The Rivera killing."

He threw up his hands. "You're not going to get off on the Rivera broad again? I don't want to hear about that shit. I've got enough problems of my own to worry about without doing the LAPD's job, too. Let's get back to the political angle. What were you working on for Maher before he suspended you?"

I shook my head. "Sorry."

"I want to know," he said in a voice that was supposed to be tough.

"That's nice."

"Why won't you tell us?"

"Because to tell you the truth, I'm a little paranoid right now and I don't know who sent you or who you report back to. What I was working on for Jerry was—and still is—a politically sensitive matter. To spill it to you might jeopardize the investigation, not to mention some political reputations. Look what's happened to mine. My arrest makes page one and my release gets honorable mention in the back of section two. If I gave you something, Rayburn or whoever you hand it to could use it however he wanted, whether it had

165

anything to do with your investigation of Dunland's murder or not."

Baatz sucked on the insides of his cheeks until they formed skull-like hollows. "I didn't really think you were going to go tough guy on me. From what Herrera said, I thought we might get some cooperation from you on this. I guess I was wrong."

"Hey, I'm not trying to go tough guy on you, sergeant. You two are the ones who came in here with the hard act. If you want, you guys can come to the hearing on Wednesday and testify that I obstructed justice, but you may have to line up. I think somebody is already coming with that routine."

"It seems to me that you've got enough enemies around without making two more," Baatz said.

"You have a point there," I admitted.

"Then—"

"Don't you think you guys better get back downtown? Maybe a senator or somebody has been trying to get in touch with you. You wouldn't want to miss the call."

Baatz's face reddened. He exhaled loudly and stood up. "All right, Asch. We'll play it your way. For now. But watch your step. That's just friendly advice. You don't have Maher behind you now. You're out in the open. Fair game."

I turned my palms up. "Without Maher, who'd want me? I'm too skinny. There wouldn't be enough to feed the wolves."

He grinned. "You know what they say: The closer to the bone, the sweeter the meat."

Just as they reached the door, it opened and Mary Kay stepped in, roller skates in hand. She had on a gray sweatshirt and blue UCLA track shorts. She started a little, surprised by the presence of strangers, and looked questioningly at me.

"Mary Kay Blane, Sergeants Baatz and Walker, Los Angeles Sheriff's Department."

They looked at her legs appraisingly and smiled. She scowled back, then grunted rudely and brushed past them.

"Don't take it personally," I told them. "She thinks all cops are the spawn of the Devil. Your appearance probably just confirmed it for her. She thinks you all get secret communiqués from Wall Street and the FDA."

"What is she, some kind of a fruitcake?" Walker asked.

"I don't know. I'd have to check your communiqués before I answered that."

"Come on," Baatz said disgustedly. "Let's get out of here. I think he's as loony tunes as she is."

I closed the door and turned around. Mary Kay was standing by the sink, still holding her skates. "What did the pigs want?"

"They were digging for truffles, but the ground was too hard."

She gave me a look that doubted my sanity and said: "You didn't leave me any money last week."

"I asked them to let me out so I could pay you, but they wouldn't."

"You were in jail?"

"Yeah."

She put down the skates. "What for?"

"Murder."

That did not seem to surprise her. "When did you get out?"

"Three days ago."

She waved a hand at the room. "You did all this in three days? This place is a shithouse."

"I've been busy."

She made a disparaging sound, then started moving around the room, picking up crumpled pieces of waxed paper and beer cans, testing their weight for empties. She made a face when she got to the Sloppy Joe. "You should have been in jail for murdering your body. This stuff is poison."

"I had to find something to take the taste of chipped beef out of my mouth. Alfalfa sprouts just didn't make it."

She grunted and took the load into the kitchen and dumped it in the wastebasket. "Who did you kill, anyway?" she asked casually.

"A man named Dunland. A nobody. I was a political prisoner."

She came back into the living room. "*All* prisoners are political prisoners."

"One of my cellmates was in for hitting a home run off his wife's head with a baseball bat. The other one tried to rob a Seven-Eleven with a bag over his head. Only he forgot to punch the eyeholes in it and stumbled into some cops on the way out. I don't call that very political. Or even very bright."

She folded her arms and shook her head obstinately. "You miss the whole point. The prison system in this country is purposely counterproductive, and those men are victims of it just as much as you. It has been carefully designed to perpetuate antisocial tendencies in order to provide the ruling class with an excuse to maintain an oppressive police state. Do you really think that by sticking a man in a cell you can reshape his thinking and make him into a productive human being?"

I was not really listening to her. I'd heard the speech before, anyway. I was listening to Baatz's voice echo in my head about Sacramento, about people there who would have enough weight to move wheels in the A.G.'s office. A state assemblyman might have that much weight. "Maybe you're right," I said absently. "Maybe we should revamp the whole system. More capital punishment, that's the only way to solve the problem. Get these swine thinking right. Capital punishment for *all* crimes. That way, there would also be lots of organs left over we could use for transplants. Solve two social problems with one daring stroke."

She put her hands on her hips and struck a belligerent

pose. "You have to be kidding. Studies have proven that capital punishment is no deterrent to crime."

"I don't know how they figure that," I said, scratching my head. "You gas a guy for shoplifting and he's sure as hell going to be deterred from shoplifting again—"

"You're a fascist," she said, trying to keep her voice under control. "I won't work for a fascist."

I saw immediately I had gone too far. I had visions of all my crockery and jelly glasses flying out of the window and shattering on the courtyard below. "Aw, come on, Mary Kay. I was just kidding."

She stared at me tight-lipped, not saying anything.

"Really." I went up to her and put my arm around her shoulders. "You know my sense of humor. Sick."

She shook off my arm and went into the kitchen and began slamming dishes around in the sink. I didn't say anything, figuring better to lose a couple than lose them all. I went into the bathroom and shaved, then took a shower and got dressed. When I came out, she was vacuuming the living room. The place no longer looked like the inside of a burned-out beaver dam.

She hit the button on the vacuum cleaner and the motor whined and died. She really did have great legs. I found myself wondering, as I did every once in a while, what she would be like in the sack. Probably took her sex instruction from some Maoist manual on guerrilla warfare. Attrition was the key—wear your enemy down. Besides, our relationship was delicate and somewhat tenuous, and I would do nothing to alter it. A good lay you could find anytime, but a good maid?

"Where are you going?"

"Out to dig some truffles before they take my truffle-digging license away."

"Well, before you dig anything, how about my fifty bucks?"

"Fifty?"

169

"As of last week, my rates went up five. Cost of living increase."

"Have pity on us poor political prisoners."

"Don't blame me," she said. "Blame the system."

I took two twenties and a ten from my wallet and handed them to her. "I think that's just about what I'm getting ready to do."

Twenty-one

The walls of the suite's front office were covered with posters telling people to ride the RTD and to turn down their thermostats to conserve energy. The room was quite warm.

The receptionist holding down the desk was a young, auburn-haired girl with pale, freckled skin. She told me that Mr. Eastland was not in and asked if I had an appointment. When I told her no, she smiled sympathetically and said it would be impossible to see Mr. Eastland today, that he was flying up to Sacramento that afternoon, and what was it I wished to see him about. I smiled back and asked if Mr. Eastland would be coming in at all today, and she smiled, "Yes, but—" and I said that was all right, that I would wait, and took a chair. That was when she stopped smiling.

After about half an hour of her staring at me, the front door opened and a tall, dark young man in a chocolate-colored corduroy coat came in looking as if he were in a hurry. He stopped at the receptionist's desk long enough to say: "Have you booked my flight yet?"

"Two-thirty," she said, then her eyes flickered over to me.

He didn't catch it and started into his office, and I stood up. "Mr. Eastland—"

He turned, the smile on automatically. "Yes?"

The smile alone would probably take him a long way. He had great teeth. The rest of him was heartthrob, too. He had a nose that might have been called patrician, if you were inclined to use words like that, and his ruggedly squared jaw offset the femininity of his long-lashed, liquid-brown eyes. His brown hair was boyishly disheveled. I had the feeling it would always be boyishly disheveled. It was a message to male voters that he was much too busy with important matters to bother with little things like hair care, and it would make female voters want to mother him. I didn't object to that. After all, if you want to win the Series, you have to cover all the bases. What bothered me was that it had not been disheveled when I had seen him at Skycrest, but neatly combed, and about half a shade lighter.

"My name is Asch," I said. "I'd like to talk to you, if you've got a moment."

"I'm sorry, but really, I'm very busy—"

"It'll just take a moment."

"What's it about?"

"I have a problem you might be able to help me with."

"Are you one of my constituents?"

"No, but this really is important."

"Look, maybe my secretary can help you—"

"I doubt it." I leaned toward him and lowered my voice. "Not unless she knows who paid off the mortgage on your house."

The smile froze and he glanced quickly down at the woman to see if she had heard. "Peggy, I'll be with this gentleman in the office. No calls."

We went back into a yellow-walled office cheaply furnished in orange and yellow. The wall behind the desk was covered with framed black-and-white glossies of Eastland in the company of various beaming political figures. Governor Madden was in at least half of them, and I also recognized two U.S. senators, one of them current, and an ex–vice-president.

He peeled off his coat and hung it over the back of the swivel chair behind the desk and sat down. He had a pale yellow, short-sleeved, button-down shirt, pleated tan slacks, and dark brown Gucci loafers. I sat on the orange couch, and he crossed his legs and swiveled sideways to face me. His easy-smiling composure was back. "Now, what's all this about my mortgage?"

"Three years ago September, the balance of the mortgage on your house at Seven-seven-one-six Capri Drive, Pacific Palisades—a total of nineteen thousand five hundred dollars—was paid to First Mortgage Deed and Trust. The money was acquired through an unsecured loan you received from First City National Bank in Beverly Hills. The interest on the loan was paid for one year, after which time you defaulted on the loan. But your credit rating seems to have gotten through all that unscathed, because six months later you were granted a car loan from B of A for seventy-six hundred dollars. A station wagon for your wife, I believe."

I had gotten all that from Leon Rosen after I had picked up certain discrepancies in Eastland's credit report. Leon was a retired bank examiner who made a nice, tax-free living selling confidential bank information to various lowlifes like myself who were willing to pay the fare. Because he had to spread the wealth with his ex-colleagues, the fare usually came high. In this case, it had set me back two hundred dollars.

Eastland's smile ran like watercolors into a frown. "Just what are you trying to say?"

"First City National is not your bank, Mr. Eastland. You bank at B of A. That brings up certain obvious questions. Such as who arranged for the unsecured loan and why your credit rating was not affected. But hell, maybe it'd be better to save those for the TV cameras." I touched my thumbs together and framed his face in my hands. "That'd be great dramatic stuff—a close-up of your face while Jerry Maher fires off those questions at you."

His eyes widened in recognition and he shook a finger at me. "Now I know where I've heard that name before. You're

Maher's deputy. The one who was arrested for murder."

"It's tough being a celebrity—people stopping you on the street all the time, begging for autographs. . . ."

"Is that who sent you over here, Maher?"

"I don't work for Maher anymore. He let me go. No, I dug all this up by my little old self. Jerry doesn't know anything about it. Yet."

"Well, I don't care if he does. There's absolutely no substance to what you say."

I started to stand up. "Okay. Then I'll go give it to him. Sorry to have taken up your time."

"Wait," he said quickly. "Why are you doing this? What do you want?"

"The answers to a few questions, that's all."

"What questions?"

"We can start with who is putting pressure on the Attorney General to have my investigator's license revoked."

His forehead furrowed with lines and he shook his head. "I haven't the faintest idea what you're talking about."

"Okay." I started to get up again.

"Hold on, hold on. What would make you think I knew anything about it?"

"The pressure is coming from somebody in Sacramento. Somebody with political clout. You've got political clout."

"And that's it? You just picked my name out of a hat? Why would I have your license taken away? I don't even know you." His confusion seemed real, but then he was a politician, which meant he was used to lying with a straight face.

"I thought maybe somebody suggested making some calls about me."

"Who would do a thing like that?"

"Oh, maybe Joe Pallisgaard or Clyde Laughlin or Emma Dysinger."

His eyelid twitched. I'd hit a nerve. "Why would they do that?"

"Maybe because I've been asking some questions about

their Seaview project they'd rather not have asked, and because I've been looking for a man named Hoffman. They might call you to handle the matter because they might figure you owed them a favor or two. After all, they did toss some coins into your campaign coffers." I paused significantly. "And Joe Pallisgaard has had quite a few financial dealings with First City National in the past."

His upper lip tightened visibly. "Look, if you're trying to imply that Joe Pallisgaard arranged for that loan for me, you're off base. I barely know the man. We've met at campaign functions once or twice, but that's it."

"What did you talk about, Seaview?"

"As a matter of fact, yes. I'm interested in Seaview. I'm proud that it's in my district, and I'd like to do everything in my power to make sure it is a success. It is important to the future of this country."

"I know. I've heard the pep talk before. Every time anybody talks about it, they break out the pom-poms. Is that why you and Hoffman argued, because you went into your rah-rah Seaview routine?"

"Hoffman? Hoffman who?"

"Merle Hoffman. He's a county sanitation engineer. Works at Landfill Number Eight."

"I don't know him."

"That's funny, because on February eleventh you met him at a condominium development called Skycrest Estates. From there you followed him to the future site of Seaview Country Club Estates and the two of you argued—"

"Now I know you're crazy."

"I was *there*, Eastland. I saw you."

"You couldn't have," he said, his voice rising in pitch. He picked up a calendar from the desk and ran a finger over its face. "February eleventh. That was a Friday. There, that proves it. I wasn't even in town that day. I was in Sacramento, voting on the tricounty canal bill. You can check that out if you want."

Screech, halt. I sat there idling, then backed up and went around the wall. "Somebody was driving your car that day. Who was it?"

He thought about it and started to say something, but then his eyes flickered up at the pictures on the wall for just a split second, and he shook his head. He rubbed the side of his nose with an index finger and said: "If somebody was using my car, I am not aware of it."

I followed his glance to the pictures. My eyes stopped on one of Eastland and Madden standing, facing one another, and it hit me. Something in the posture, in the way the head was held on the shoulders. "You and Madden are pretty close, aren't you?"

He bit his lip. "Yes, we are."

"Some people think you're too close," I said. "Your opponent in your last campaign—Arnold, I believe his name was—accused you of killing certain bills in Ways and Means to save Madden the political embarrassment of having to veto them."

"That was just political rhetoric."

"But you two are close enough to borrow each other's cars."

"Preston could call up the state motor pool and get a car anytime he wanted it. Why would he use mine?"

"Maybe he didn't want anybody to know he was coming into town. He knew you'd be in Sacramento, so he asked if he could borrow yours."

"That didn't happen." His eyes looked away.

"Of course not. None of this happened. Your mortgage was never paid off, my license is not being taken away, Hoffman hasn't disappeared, nobody has been murdered—"

"Murdered?" The word seemed to startle him, even when it came out of his own mouth.

"Two murders, to be exact. A secretary from Seaview and a friend of Hoffman's. You remember Hoffman, don't you?"

176

Irritated lines crisscrossed his face. "How many times do I have to tell you that I've never heard of any Hoffman?"

"Maybe you didn't meet him at Seaview, but you've heard of him. You talked to him on the phone. He called here a couple of times to bitch about the Seaview project and Burt Casey."

"Wait a minute. The nut case. I remember now. I did talk to him on the phone, but only once. After that, I told Peggy, my secretary, to tell him I was out."

"What did you say when you talked to him?"

He shrugged. "He was nuts. He made wild charges about Burt Casey being paid off by the Seaview people to arrange for the county contract. He said the whole deal was corrupt and demanded to know why I'd lent my support to it."

"Did he say he had proof that Casey took a bribe?"

"He didn't have anything," he said, waving a hand irascibly. "He kept saying that all anyone had to do was look at the contract to know what had gone down."

"What did you tell him?"

"That it wasn't my job. I am not on the Board of Supervisors. I am an assemblyman. But just to get rid of him, I told him I'd look into it."

"Did you?"

"I didn't have to. There was no substance in his charges at all. The man had a personal vendetta with Burt Casey. He just about admitted that on the phone himself."

"When did he call here last?"

"How would I know? I told you, I instructed my secretary to brush him off."

"Can you ask her when was the last time he called?"

He lowered his eyelids and sighed, then picked up the phone and asked the girl to come in. When she appeared in the doorway, he asked: "Remember that nut that kept calling a few weeks back about the Seaview project?"

"Yes?"

"When did he call last?"

She rolled her shoulders and said: "Gee, Mr. Eastland, I don't really know. It's been at least a couple of weeks."

He smiled at her paternally. "Thanks." She left, and his eyes flickered over to me. "Is that all?"

"One more question," I said. "Did you tell anybody about Hoffman calling you?"

He rubbed the side of his nose. "Who would I tell?"

"That's what I'm asking you."

"No," he said, looking straight into my eyes. Very few liars could do it that well. He would probably go a long way. He had more going for him than just his teeth.

I stood up. "Thanks for your time, Mr. Eastland."

"That stuff about my mortgage," he said anxiously. "There's nothing in it, of course, but if the wrong people got hold of it, they would try to make it sound as if there were. The public always wants to believe the worst, even if it isn't true. Where there's smoke, there's fire, and all that."

"I know what you mean," I said, my voice oozing sympathy. "But don't worry, nobody will make anything of it. It'll be our little secret."

I left him with his pictures and a pained expression in his eyes, and went to the car. I was lost in thought, pondering the meaning of Preston Madden's entrance into this whole mess but not so lost that I didn't notice the dark green Ford Fairmont that pulled out behind me as I turned onto Ventura Boulevard.

I speeded up, just to see what it would do. It speeded up, too. I slowed down. It maintained the same distance behind me. I pulled into the first gas station with a pay phone and sat in the car until the Fairmont drove by. There were two men in it, big men, and they didn't even glance at me. The Fairmont turned at the next corner and drove down the street. I jotted down the license number in my notebook and went to the phone booth.

The address in the phone book of the nearest DMV office

was about a mile from where I was. I drove there with my windows rolled up and my doors locked and my eyes glued on the rearview mirror. I didn't figure the boys in the Fairmont would try to get cute in public, but you never could tell.

They reappeared behind me and parked down the block from the DMV office while I went inside. I gave the clerk the old hit-and-run story and she came back with the registration for the plate.

They were sitting in the car, trying not to notice me, when I walked up to the passenger's side and bent down.

The driver was a bullnecked, red-faced man, and the one sitting shotgun had a close-cropped bullet head. Neither of them said anything when I said, "Hi," so I tried another tack. "I'm going home now, but I'm going to stop at the market first. You guys like any particular kind of dip, or is bean okay?"

The driver was not going to give up that easily. He tried to look at me as if he thought I'd just graduated from the Laughing Academy and said: "What are you, buddy, some kind of nut? Get outta here."

"Sure," I said. "Just one question before I do, though: Does everybody who didn't vote for our illustrious attorney general get a tail, or am I a special case?"

The man's face reddened even more. "I don't know what the fuck you're talking about. Shove off, chum."

"On your way over to the apartment, pick up a *TV Guide*, will you? Maybe there's a good episode of 'The FBI' on tonight."

Bullet-head sneered and flapped a hand at me. "I said, shove off."

I laughed and waved as I walked away. "My regards to the A.G. when you call in."

I didn't stop at the market on the way home. If they didn't like bean, to hell with them.

Twenty-two

A thick beach fog had rolled in during the night, but I could see the dim outline of the Ford parked across the street when I stepped onto my porch to retrieve the morning paper. I took mild satisfaction in the thought that they had spent a thoroughly damp and miserable night in the Hotel Fairmont. I found more satisfaction, however, thinking about the Just Married sign and the string of tin cans I'd snuck down last night and attached to their tail.

I was on my third cup of coffee, scanning the paper to see if there was anything new on Dunland's murder, when the phone rang.

"Mr. Asch?" It was a woman.

"Yes?"

"This is Sarita Thomas, Mr. Joseph Pallisgaard's personal secretary. Mr. Pallisgaard would like to know if you could come to his office this morning to talk to him." Her voice was grave, like one of those lady political reporters on CBS who stand outside the White House in snowstorms with microphones in their hands.

"Would eleven o'clock be satisfactory?" she asked in the same solemn tone.

"Eleven o'clock is fine."

"Fifty-eight hundred Wilshire Boulevard, Suite Fourteen-oh-one. Across from the La Brea Tar Pits."

"Very symbolic," I said.

"Pardon me?"

"The tar pits. That's where all the animals came to get a drink of water and wound up stuck in the tar."

"I'm afraid I don't understand," she said.

"Eleven o'clock is fine," I repeated, and hung up.

I had on a three-piece, beige pin-striped suit, a brown shirt, and a brown-and-yellow-striped tie. All I would have needed was a briefcase to look like a high-priced criminal attorney. I wasn't sure what you were supposed to look like when you talked to a hundred and fifty million dollars, but I figured that was as good a come-on as any.

The front office was full of soothing Muzak and architectural renderings of various Pallisgaard projects. The receptionist took my name and relayed it by phone to the back, and momentarily a tall, stiff blonde in a severely cut blue dress and large, bone-rimmed glasses appeared in the doorway. She was a poor man's Leslie Stahl, although she did not look quite right without the blizzard. She confirmed my expectations when she said: "Mr. Asch, I'm Sarita Thomas. Mr. Pallisgaard will see you now."

I nodded and followed her past a series of open doors to a closed one at the end of the hall. She opened it without knocking and announced: "Mr. Asch is here, Mr. Pallisgaard."

The room was very large, almost large enough for the furniture in it to get lost. The spongy carpeting was gold, the walls pale yellow and lined with gilt-framed paintings of eighteenth-century English landscapes. I could not tell if the paintings were valuable, but I did know the furniture was.

There was a long maroon couch covered in velvet, two plump chairs covered in rough chocolaty cloth, and another chair that could have been a real Charles Eames. The center of the cluster and what gave it weight was the desk. It was huge and old, made of polished mahogany, and had an aura of solid solemnity about it.

The man standing behind it gave off the same aura. He was a big man, tall and very wide across the shoulders. He wore a conservative, charcoal-gray suit, a mistake because it showed off the dandruff liberally sprinkled across his shoulders. Maybe he was not aware of it. I guess when you control a hundred and fifty million dollars, you don't have people running up to you telling you about your dandruff.

He had brown hair that was turning gray and a long, almost horsey face that was going soft under the chin. That was about the only soft thing about his face. His massive jaw looked like a curbstone, his mouth was stern and tight-lipped, and his gray eyes were cold and totally devoid of humor.

There were two other people in the room. Clyde Laughlin sat on the couch, watching me with a sour expression. And in a chair nearby, with her legs crossed, was a middle-aged woman with dyed red hair and a smooth, shiny face that had been lifted so many times it should have had dotted lines on it, like around one of those masks on the back of a cereal box, showing you where to cut.

"I'm Joseph Pallisgaard," the man behind the desk said. He came around and thrust out an enormous, big-knuckled hand that belonged more on the end of a farmer's arm than a business tycoon's. I made the mistake of accepting it. He had a grip like a potato masher. He waved at the other two and said: "Emma Dysinger, and I believe you've met Mr. Laughlin."

The woman gave me a small, tight smile, which was probably all she could manage without splitting a seam. Laughlin looked at me distastefully and said: "You had a different name then."

"I was just evening things up. The last time I talked to your secretary, she used one on me."

Pallisgaard frowned at Laughlin, then said to me: "Sit down, Mr. Asch."

I chose the Eames chair. Pallisgaard remained standing, probably to remind me of the difference in our social status. He looked down on me and inserted his hand into the outside pocket of his jacket, leaving the thumb sticking out. "You're probably wondering why I asked you here today. Or maybe you've already guessed."

"I'm a terrible guesser."

"That's very apparent. You've been making some terrible guesses about all of us, I'm afraid. And our project."

"I'm afraid I don't follow you, Mr. Pallisgaard."

"Come now, you're an intelligent man. Give us credit for some intelligence, also. I have a very low tolerance for cat-and-mouse games. We know you've been looking into our business affairs. Particularly Seaview. You were doing that first on your own, then for Jerry Maher. And you have continued your prying after Mr. Maher let you go. What we don't know is *why*."

"It's my rising sign," I said. "My chart says I'm supposed to be naturally inquisitive."

"I'm afraid that's not good enough."

"Mr. Pallisgaard, if you didn't want me poking around in your business transactions, you never should have sent somebody to ask me to do just that."

"Me?" He put his hand on his chest. "I never asked anyone to do any such thing."

"Not specifically, no. But you should have known that sending Laughlin's secretary to me with a cock-and-bull story was going to get me curious."

"I have no idea what you're talking about."

183

"Okay, I'll lay it out for you. Act One, scene one. Nina Rivera, Clyde Laughlin's devoted and impressionable secretary, comes to me with a phony name and an equally phony story that her fiancé is cheating on her. She hires me to shadow the guy. Act One, scene two. The fiancé turns out to be a bit of a pederast and I take some pictures of him in flagrante delicto, or close enough to convince her, and she pays me in cash and says ta-ta. Only that isn't the end of it. A week later, she calls me, very edgy, and asks for a meeting, saying she is in some kind of trouble. On the way to said meeting, Nina Rivera is run down by a fast-moving car and is killed."

"A tragic accident," said Pallisgaard, shaking his head sorrowfully.

"And a convenient one. Because in Act Two, we find that her homosexual fiancé is not her fiancé at all but a county sanitation engineer named Hoffman who has been spending a lot of time making waves for Seaview. Miss Rivera did not have a fiancé at all, but she was quite smitten by her boss, Mr. Laughlin, with whom she had been spending a lot of free time lately. You're quite a ladykiller, Clyde."

Laughlin's face had reddened and his lip curled under, but I went on before he could say anything. "Now, here is where the plot really starts to get heavy. The money Nina Rivera paid me did not come from any of her bank accounts, which means that she had to have gotten it from another source. What source could that be? That becomes clear when we find that shortly before she came to me, Nina Rivera was given a check for five hundred dollars from the Eldorado account." I did not know that for sure, but I wanted to see what kind of a reaction it got. Laughlin started to say something, but Pallisgaard cut him off with a glance. It was enough to keep me going. "Deduction: the money she paid me was also from Eldorado."

Pallisgaard said: "I don't see the logic of the deduction."

"Number one, where else would she get thirteen hundred

dollars? Number two, why would Eldorado pay her an extra five hundred? She received a paycheck that week. It wasn't salary. Answer: she was paid by you people to play Sylvia Calabrese to get me to tail Hoffman."

"Now why would we do that? Are you implying we are in the blackmail business?"

"It probably didn't start that way. I doubt when Nina hired me that she or anybody else had any idea that Hoffman was a chickenhawk. What you probably wanted was a log of Hoffman's movements—who he was talking to, where he was going. After all, he had been making nuisance calls to political people about Seaview. But when the pictures fell into old Clyde's hands, I think he figured what the hell, might as well use them to try to shut Hoffman up."

Pallisgaard looked over to Laughlin, who was looking at me with a bored expression. "You know anything about this, Clyde?"

"The whole thing is ridiculous. That check I gave Nina was a bonus. She'd been a loyal employee and she needed the money. Her father was out of work. We certainly were not seeing each other socially, and as far as her hiring Mr. Asch here, I don't know a thing about it. This man is suffering from delusions or else he is lying, for some reason I can't fathom."

"Leaving both of those aside for a minute, why would your secretary hire me to get information on Hoffman?"

"I wouldn't know. Nina was a very loyal girl. Maybe she thought she would be doing the firm a favor by taking it upon herself to do such a thing. She was devoted to Eldorado."

"Even more devoted than she was to you?"

His face colored. "What do you mean by that?"

"Both her parents and one of your own employees confirmed that you and Nina had gone out several times after work for cocktails—"

"We were discussing office business," he said in a tired voice.

"Like the special hush-hush project you'd just put her in charge of?"

He leaned back and shook his head. "I don't know what you're talking about. What's your motive in all this, Asch? Money? You trying to work some kind of a shakedown?"

"If I were, I wouldn't have waited for you to get in touch with me. No, I'm just trying to find a way out of a hole I'm in. See, I haven't finished with my story. We still have Act Three to go. It's a rainy night. I get a call at midnight from someone claiming to be Hoffman, telling me to meet him at Kenneth Dunland's house, that he has things to tell me. Kenneth Dunland, you see, was a homosexual friend of Hoffman's who also happened to be in those pictures that I handed over to Nina Rivera. When I get to Dunland's house, I don't find Hoffman, but I do find Dunland—dead—and someone else who must have been taking those gay rights people much too literally, because he comes out of the closet and hits me over the head. When I wake up, I find I'm a prime suspect for murder. I get fired from my job and suddenly there's a pack of homicide cops snapping at my heels, smelling blood. The attorney general files an action to take away my license and sends a pair of his finest to follow me around and steam up the back of my neck."

Pallisgaard waved a hand at his companions. "You can't be saying that any of us has had anything to do with your problems?"

"All I know, Mr. Pallisgaard, is that I was doing just fine until I started looking into your deal with the county. Now suddenly my life reads like the Book of Job. But I guess that's just coincidence, huh? Just like it's a coincidence that the pressure on the A.G. to pull my license is coming out of Sacramento and that less than twenty-four hours after I go see Ron Eastland about that, I get a call from your secretary requesting my presence here."

"What are you trying to imply?"

"If you wanted me to stop poking around, one way would be to take away my right to ask questions. You and your partners made sizable contributions to Eastland's last campaign. If you wanted to stay removed from the situation, you could have called him up and asked him for a favor."

He smiled sardonically. "I don't know anything about your license or your conflict with the attorney general, Mr. Asch. And I'm afraid you overestimate both my influence and interest in state politics. It seems to be just one of the many misconceptions under which you are laboring."

"Why don't you straighten me out?"

"That, Mr. Asch, is why you are here." He folded his arms and sat sideways on the edge of the desk. "How much do you know about me?"

"Not much," I said shrugging. "I know you're fifty-four years old and you've been married for twenty-six years to the same woman and that you have a twenty-five-year-old son and a daughter two years younger. I know your great-grandfather came to the U.S. from Sweden in eighteen sixty-seven and settled in Nebraska, where he was a farmer, and that your father came to California in nineteen twenty-three to seek his fortune. He died before he found it, but you took over the dream and made it happen. In the middle of the war, you made your first real estate investment, a ramshackle triplex in Boyle Heights, the down payment for which you made with a fifteen-hundred-dollar nest egg you saved up from your jobs as an office boy and janitor. You fixed the place up with your own hands and four months later turned it over for a ten-thousand-dollar profit.

"You used the ten thousand as a down payment on a run-down office building, and you were off and running. Today, you control a real estate empire worth over one hundred fifty million dollars. You own shopping centers, apartment complexes, hotels, industrial property, office buildings, and a large chain of drugstores. I know you don't drink or smoke, and you don't approve of people who do. Aside from that, I don't know much about you at all, Mr. Pallisgaard."

He turned back to me. "Very thorough."

"Not really. Most of the stuff I got out of a couple of newspaper articles that were in the real estate section of the *Chronicle*. I don't think anyone is ever going to write the definitive bio on you, Mr. Pallisgaard. You keep too low a profile."

"I'm a man who likes his privacy," he said matter-of-factly. "I pay a price for it, of course. Distortions of the truth, wild speculation about what I am and what I'm up to, when I'm really up to nothing at all. You, for example, seem convinced that something nefarious is going on at Seaview. It isn't. You also seem to think that I buy and sell politicians. I don't. I don't have to."

He pushed off the desk and walked a step, then turned back and said in a patient tone: "People rise to positions of power in this life in one of three ways—ability, luck, or treachery—and usually it takes a combination of all three. But treachery has a way of catching you from behind, and luck almost invariably runs out. Only the man with ability stays on top once he gets there, and that is usually because he has the foresight to lay his foundations on the way up. It's like building a house. If you don't pour the foundation properly in the first place, the house will be in constant danger of falling down. You might shore it up by bracing it here and there, but that will take up all your time and a hell of a lot of effort."

"What's your point?"

"Simply this. I don't like politics and I have no great fondness for politicians. They are usually men of limited intelligence and not much vision. But I would be a fool if I ignored the effect political decisions have on my business. To insure that those effects are at least not deleterious, I aid those people that get elected who think along the same lines that I do and will be sympathetic to my interests. That's part of the democratic process. But I don't call up politicians in the middle of the night and tell them what I want them to do. They already know. And the reason they know is that most of the time they think the same way themselves."

"Burt Casey shoved through that contract because he believed in the importance of the Seaview development to the county, is that what you're trying to say?"

"I'm not trying to deny that all of us contributed heavily to Burt Casey's reelection, or that that had nothing to do with his thinking on Seaview. If it didn't, I would have been stupid to give anything, wouldn't I? What I am saying is that Burt was aware of the importance of the project, and he was also keenly aware that we probably wouldn't have gone through with it without the county contract."

His arguments and apparent earnestness were very convincing. I almost believed him. Almost. But half-truths are almost always more believable than out-and-out lies, no matter what Hitler said.

"It probably didn't hurt anything that Mrs. Dysinger was part of your team, either."

"What do you mean by that?" she asked in a combative tone.

"I didn't know you had remarried. Until I did some reading, I never realized you were Emma Wymer, widow of City Councilman Lloyd Wymer."

Her face was a glazed mask. "You make it sound as if I've been trying to conceal the fact."

"I didn't mean to. Your husband and Burt Casey were always great friends, weren't they? Part of the old California Club group?"

"Burt was always a friend of the family, yes."

"I remember when the new baseball stadium was built. I was working at the *Chronicle* then. I knew a man who knew a man, you know how it goes. The man my friend knew was trying to get the food concession at the stadium and he had to go through your late husband. He sold him four pieces of property for about a quarter of their value. But he got his concession." I turned to Pallisgaard. "You're right. You people don't have to buy politicians. You just rent them by the hour."

Mrs. Dysinger started to get up out of her chair, her face twisted with rage. "I don't have to sit here and listen to this—"

Pallisgaard waved her down with his hand and said in a frosty voice: "Don't try to play games with us, Mr. Asch. You'll come out the loser, I guarantee it."

"Maybe I'll be run down on my way to lunch?"

"There are other ways to beat someone without resorting to physical force."

"Like having their right of a livelihood taken away from them?"

"I told you I don't know anything about your license," he said, looking at me squarely. "But that might be one initial step. And things could get a lot worse than that. Your financial condition is not so strong that it could take a lot of shaking, Mr. Asch. I know. I checked."

"Is that a threat?"

"Just advice. Go back to your business and stay out of ours."

I nodded. "One thing I don't understand: If there's nothing going on at Seaview, why are you so concerned about my poking around in it?"

He walked to the windows and looked out. The city spread beyond him like a photograph slightly out of focus. "We're concerned about you, Mr. Asch, but not for the reasons you think. The kinds of business ventures in which we are involved require investments of millions of dollars. A goodly sum of that is not our own, needless to say. When a person is thinking of investing hundreds of thousands of dollars in a business deal, it doesn't take much to frighten him off. He's

190

already half-frightened to begin with. All it would take to put an element of doubt in his mind would be someone like yourself coming around asking the wrong questions at the wrong time."

"I never realized what kind of an effect I was having on the world of finance."

"You'd be surprised. The sort of blind blundering around you have been engaged in could upset some very delicate business deals the three of us are currently trying to put together. The fact that all of us are totally innocent of wrongdoing does not matter. Merely the fact that questions are being asked could be enough to start a stampede. I wanted to explain that to you, before something tragic happened."

"Something already has, in case you've forgotten."

"We are businessmen, Mr. Asch, not gangsters," Pallisgaard said.

"Meyer Lansky always predicted that big business and organized crime would merge until you wouldn't be able to tell them apart."

He turned from the window. With his back to the light, it seemed as if a dark cloud had moved over his face. "My patience is wearing thin, Mr. Asch. I'm going to tell you once and for all: Don't try to spar with us. You're out of your weight class."

I nodded and smiled. "Don't worry. I'm throwing in the towel. You win by default. I'm not about to get rolled on by a hundred and fifty million bucks, especially when I'm not getting paid for it."

"I sincerely hope you're serious about that," he said in a flat tone, "because you would just wind up getting flattened. As you pointed out in your brief character sketch, I came up from nothing—the hard way. You don't come up the hard way, Mr. Asch, without learning how to fight."

"I know," I said agreeably. "It's a dog-eat-dog world out there."

"That's right. It is."

"And it's a lot easier to eat a dead dog than one that's still alive."

His entire face was a curbstone now. "A crude metaphor, but it does get the point across." He smiled, but the smile did not penetrate the hardness. He made a short, abrupt motion to the door with a turned-up palm and said: "Thank you for coming, Mr. Asch."

I left, feeling as I had thought I might feel when I came, like one of those mastodons across the street.

Twenty-three

"This isn't the end of it," Paul said as we came through the doors of the hearing room. He put his hand on my shoulder. "We'll appeal—"

He was trying his best, but I was not in the mood to listen. "Sure."

"That Miller character, it was obvious he had a grudge against you. The judge had to be an idiot not to have seen it. And the fact that the Riveras received a ten-thousand-dollar indemnity from the insurance policy Eldorado carried on their daughter prejudices their testimony—"

"You forget that we have to prove that somebody in Eldorado wanted my ticket yanked."

"So we'll find out. We'll find out who talked to them."

Steuben, the tight-faced A.G. prosecutor, came through the doorway carrying his briefcase. I stepped in front of him. "Happy, asshole?"

The man stopped, seemingly surprised to see me in his way. "You seem to be taking this thing personally, Mr. Asch."

"Fucking A, I'm taking it personally," I snarled.

"Hold on, Jake," Paul said, clamping a restraining hand on my forearm. Steuben took the opportunity to slide past me and escape down the hall.

193

My eyes followed him and lighted on Baatz, who was leaning against a marble wall in the corridor, watching me impassively. "Oh Christ, the hounds of hell—"

Paul's eyes followed my gaze. He said: "Don't worry about him." His voice was a trifle hot. "Listen, don't you know shit like that just makes things look worse for you? You get a guy like Steuben pissed off at you and you'll really know what a hound of hell is like."

"Yeah, yeah." I shrugged and straightened my tie, and we started down the hall. When we got to Baatz, Paul said: "You here on official business, Sergeant?"

Baatz came away from the wall and took the toothpick out of his mouth and smiled. "No. But for a minute I thought I was going to have to arrest your client for assault. I take it it didn't go well in there."

"Oh, it went super," I said.

"What did they hit you with?"

"A little of everything. They dug up an old client of mine who has always hated my guts who said I'd taken his money and sold his industrial secrets to his competition. Then they dug up some old police reports that said I'd done a little breaking and entering while working on a case. I was never charged, but that didn't seem to matter. They had statements from a couple of cops who claimed I'd withheld information on a couple of felony cases. And then the Riveras were claiming I'd tried to unethically solicit business from them. I'm surprised you weren't there. This isn't the NFL. There aren't any rules about piling on."

He looked at the end of the toothpick and said casually: "They asked me. I turned them down."

I watched him curiously. "Why?"

"Let's just say I have an aversion to railroads. I have ever since I was a kid and I got shocked by a Lionel set my father gave me."

"Are you here to question my client about something?" Paul broke in.

194

Baatz shook his head. "I just wanted to see how things turned out. To see how far they'd take it." He turned to me. "And I want you to know, Asch, that I didn't have anything to do with it. We may not get along so well, but I still don't like to see this kind of bullshit. You're getting a raw deal."

I stared at him, trying to figure his angle. I knew he could not be going human on me. The chair and the hot lights had to be waiting around the corner. Paul seemed to be having the same thoughts. He looked at Baatz distrustfully, then said to me: "Jake, I've got to run. You want to go out with me?"

"That's okay, Paul. My car is in the other lot. Go on. I'll be all right."

He hesitated, then nodded, and we shook hands. He started down the shiny waxed floor of the corridor. "Well," I said to Baatz, "see you."

He put the toothpick back into his mouth and stepped in stride with me. "I'm not following you," he said quickly. "I figure you've got enough people following you around as it is. I'm just going out the same way."

I nodded without saying anything. At the end of the corridor, we turned and headed for the front doors, and he said: "I've never seen them go after a case like this this hard before."

"It's understandable. I'm a menace to society."

"Somebody up high really must have a hard-on for you."

"Tell me something I don't know."

"Figure out who yet?"

"No."

"What about your buddy, Maher? Can't he pull some strings for you somewhere?"

"I doubt it. I wouldn't ask him anyway."

"Funny," he said, shaking his head. "I didn't figure him for the type to leave one of his people standing out on the ice like that. He's been a pain in the ass sometimes—he's tied up a lot of Department man-hours running down bullshit charges he's leveled at people—but out of all the people on the board, I always figured he was the only one that was honest."

"You're probably right about that. And in all fairness to Jerry, I'm not one of 'his people.' I was only put on temporarily as a special investigator, and my usefulness on that job was shot. There's no reason he should lie down in front of a moving truck to keep me from getting run over."

He nodded as if he could understand that, then said in a tone that was supposed to be reassuring: "Well, Ellman's a good attorney. I don't care for him much, but he's good. If anybody can get your license back, he can."

"Yeah, sure."

He put his hands in his pockets and watched his feet as he walked. "What are you going to do in the meantime?"

"Oh, I don't know. I thought I might take up acting."

He looked up sharply. "Acting?"

"Sure. Maybe this is a blessing in disguise. I've always wanted to be an actor anyway. I even have my stage name all picked out. Chance Romance. You don't think that's too Hollywood, do you?"

"You're really addicted to the flip lip, aren't you?" He said it without a hint of amusement in his voice.

"Purely a defense mechanism," I said, smiling. "It's the only thing that keeps me from going completely nuts."

He looked back down at his feet and said: "I've done some checking around about Dunland."

I was obviously not supposed to leave it there, so I said: "Find out anything interesting?"

"Yeah, as a matter of fact. Dunland liked them young and tight, all right—he even got a year's probation for it once about eight years back—but he also liked to spice up his sex life with some variety every once in a while. Hard trade. Rough, hairy, truck-driver types." He paused and glanced up at me to see how I was taking it, and when he saw I was taking it just fine he went on: "The guys I've talked to who go in for that kind of stuff all tell me that the thrill is in the knowledge that they're literally sitting on a live volcano that can explode at any minute. We know Dunland went in for those kinds of sports because he'd had a couple of them explode on him. He called the West Hollywood substation twice last year for assistance when things got out of hand. The last time, he got his cheekbone broken and wound up in the hospital."

"So that's what you think happened this time? Dunland went out cruising for some hard trade and brought him back to the house?"

"It's possible."

"You're forgetting about the phone call. Where does Hoffman fit into that little scenario?"

"I'm not forgetting about the phone call," he snapped. "I just don't know yet. We're probably going to have to find Hoffman and ask him before we get an answer."

"Does this mean that you no longer consider me the Closet Queen Killer?"

"I never did, really."

"Then why all the bullshit, holding me for seventy-two hours?"

"What would *you* have done? You were found at the scene without your clothes and covered with blood. I mean, shit, how the hell am I going to explain that to my people, if I turn you loose and find out I'm wrong?"

I smiled. "I would have done the same thing you did," I said. "From what I hear, Hoffman can play rough. He likes to play the macho role around his friends at the landfill, too, which means he could have ambivalent feelings about his homosexuality."

"That's why I got real interested when you said the guy who hit you was wearing a yellow slicker. There's one trouble with it, though. Hoffman wears an eleven shoe."

197

"So?"

"The guy who was standing in the closet was wearing a size twelve."

"You got a print?" I asked, surprised.

"Just a heel, but enough to make the size."

"I wear a ten."

"I know."

"And you still put me through that bullshit for seventy-two hours."

He didn't say anything. We went through the front doors and stopped on the steps. Clerical workers on their lunch breaks sat on the stone wall and dotted the lawn, eating sandwiches they had brought to work in bags or bought from machines in the hallways, or reading paperback books in the sun. White puffs of cloud looked crisply clean floating over the dirty downtown buildings.

"What size did Dunland wear?"

"You thinking the killer got into Dunland's shoes? I already thought the same thing. Dunland had petite feet. Nines." He motioned at the street. "Which way you going?"

"I'm parked in a lot over on First."

"I go the other way."

We both stood there, not saying anything. I was still waiting for the big question, whatever it was going to be. He shifted his weight from one foot to the other and looked out at the street uncomfortably. "Anyway, I just wanted to clear the air. I didn't want you thinking I had anything to do with this."

So he was really going human on me. I didn't know quite how to handle that. "You're sure you don't want to ask me where I was on the night of October third, or what I was working on for Maher?"

"Don't worry," he said, grinning wolfishly. "I'll get around to that another time." He flinched uncertainly, as if trying to decide whether or not to offer his hand, but it never made it out of his pocket. "Take it easy," he said, and walked away quickly across the lawn.

I stood on the steps for a while, watching him get smaller as he headed up the street, trying to figure him out. I was still trying to figure him out when a green county car pulled up at the curb at the end of the walkway and the driver called my name. Marty stuck his head out of the window as I got to the car. "Sorry about your license."

"Word travels fast."

"I was outside the hearing room."

"I didn't see you."

"You were with your attorney, then I saw you talking with that cop. I figured I'd wait until you were alone to talk to you."

"My funeral is really going to be impressive," I said. "I can't wait for it. Everybody will be there."

He cocked his head at the front seat and said: "Why don't you get in?"

"That's all right. I can walk—"

"Jerry wants to talk to you."

I gave him a suspicious look. "What about?"

He cocked his head at the seat again. "Get in."

I sighed and shrugged and got in.

Jerry Maher was in his office, waiting for us. He stood and we shook hands, then he waved me into a chair and said: "I hear you got the big shaft today."

"They probably know about it in Peking by now. The interest seems to be running high."

"Abnormally high," he said. "I also hear you've been over to talk to Ron Eastland."

"I never promised you I wouldn't talk to Eastland."

"No," he said. "You didn't. But you must have made him very nervous. I hear he has been making a lot of phone calls since your visit. The word is that that's why the A.G. went after your license, because you've been making a lot of people nervous." One of his eyebrows curled into a dark question mark. "You want to fill me in on what you've been doing?"

I thought about it and shrugged. Why the hell not? I couldn't go any further with it on my own. Maybe he could. After this morning, I was in the mood to make trouble for anybody I could.

I told him about my meeting with Eastland and my subsequent summons to the high court of Joseph Pallisgaard. He listened intently, poised stiffly over the desk, tapping a pen against his chin. When I was through, he said: "You've scared them. The question is what they're afraid of."

"It could be like they say: loose lips sink financial ships and all that."

"Maybe."

"That stuff about Eastland's loan could be dynamite," Savich said. "Maybe he got scared and called Pallisgaard and told him you'd been around and that if Pallisgaard wanted his continued support on Seaview, he'd have to make sure you were muzzled."

"That's a possibility, too," I said, then stood up and began pacing. "But what bugs me is how the hell Madden figures into the whole thing. And why would he meet Hoffman at Seaview?"

"You're not one hundred percent sure it was Madden you saw," Maher said.

"No, but I'm ninety-five percent sure, and that's enough for me." I turned to both of them and tossed my hands in the air. "The only reason I started digging through Eastland's bank records is that I thought the pressure coming out of Sacramento was his doing. But if the pressure really is coming from Madden, the whole picture changes."

"Pallisgaard is a big Madden backer," Maher said. "So is Emma Dysinger. She helped organize a fifteen-hundred-dollar-a-plate dinner for Madden's campaign when he made a run at the Oregon and Iowa presidential primaries in seventy-six. From what I hear, he's going to run again in 1980, but this time for real. That means he's going to need big bucks."

"I have a feeling you're about to make a point," I said.

"If he really plans on waging a serious campaign, he's going to need Pallisgaard and his friends. And if they called him up and asked him to do something for them, he couldn't very well refuse them."

I was beginning to get his drift. "A favor. Like if they called him up and asked him to meet with some kooky sanitation engineer and give him a big Ann Miller song-and-dance routine that something was being done about Seaview?"

He nodded. "Hoffman had been everywhere trying to get political action. Maybe they figured he would shut up if he could get an audience with the governor and the governor were then to convince him that he was on Hoffman's side." He pursed his lips thoughtfully. "I'm beginning to think you were right about Seaview, Jake. Something smells there. You want to keep digging into it?"

"Sure. Wonderful. All it's gotten me so far is a couple of grand in legal fees, my right to make a living revoked, a murder rap hanging over my head, and the threat of a few hundred million bucks dropping on my back like a pissed-off leopard."

"There seems to be one solution," he said coolly. "Come back to work for me."

I glanced at Savich, who was nodding.

"Are you serious?"

"I wouldn't make the offer unless I was serious," Maher said. The man might make a convert of me yet.

"The media would squeeze it for all it was worth," I said, "and once whoever I've got on the run in Sacramento gets the word that I'm back working for you, they'll try to crucify you."

A small smile tugged at the corners of his mouth. "I don't

201

intend to hold a press conference to tell the world you're back on staff."

"You seem to forget that I've still got those yo-yos from the A.G.'s office looking up my exhaust pipe. They're just waiting for me to ask someone what time it is so they can nail me for operating as a detective without a license. Once they know I'm working for you, whoever sent them is going to know, too."

"We'll just have to cross that bridge when we get to it."

"Isn't that what Ted Kennedy said to Mary Jo Kopechne when she told him she was pregnant?"

His smile grew broader until it filled his whole face. "You know, somehow I get the feeling that you don't look upon our political leaders with the proper degree of reverence."

I shrugged and smiled back. "Yeah, well, if they can't take a joke, fuck 'em."

Twenty-four

I think the first priorities of any government should be the preservation of the quality of life. We have only so much water, air, and natural resources. Once they are gone, we will follow.
—Preston Madden speech, 1963

I don't believe it is the function of government to unnecessarily restrict economic development. Growth is going to come whether we like it or not. We must just find the most acceptable alternatives through which to channel it.
—Preston Madden speech, 1974

I'm not contradicting myself. My mind has changed. That is how we all develop, isn't it?
—Preston Madden speech, 1976

To be in politics, you have to be more than a little crazy.
—Preston Madden speech, 1978

Preston Madden. Age forty-five. One of the most popular governors in California history, despite frequent criticism for little accomplished in the way of effective legislation and for appointments less than breathtaking.

Graduated UCLA, 1955; served as lieutenant in Army, 1955–58. Graduated Loyola law school, 1962. Worked for law firm of Decker, Decker, and Weiss, 1962–63, until appointed to Air Resources Board, where he acquired a reputation as a rabid environmentalist when he prevented a $500 million oil refinery from being built in Redondo Beach. Resigned the post in 1968 to run for lieutenant governor, and won. Attracting attention for his outspoken views, he barely squeaked by his Republican opponent in the 1972 gubernatorial election, having been put in an alliance of conservationists, consumer groups, and antiwar coalitions. He won some praise from those groups for successfully ramming through a liberal farm-labor bill, but by the next election in 1976 he had fallen out with the environmentalists, who were accusing him of selling out to real estate interests. He opposed the Coastal Initiative and the proposed ban on development around state parks, but none of that seemed to hurt his public image. Was reelected by a landslide, in spite of the fact that he did it with one hand tied behind his back. The other hand was busy making a token run in three presidential primaries—California, Oregon, and Iowa. He shocked political analysts by winning all three handily.

The experts were all quick to ascribe certain reasons for his growing popularity: youth, a certain indifference he seemed to exude toward public office, a sense of mystery and aloofness that lent him a charismatic aura. But one thing was sure: if the source of his popularity was hard to pin down, it was nonetheless very, very real.

I started about where I'd left off, at the office of the secretary of state. Since I already had a list of names to work from, tracing the cash flow from Pallisgaard and company to the campaign coffers of Preston Madden was a lot easier than the Eastland effort. It only took a day and a half, and after I was through the only thing I could say was that for people who disliked politics and politicians, Pallisgaard and his partners were certainly generous with their money. In the

1978 gubernatorial campaign, they had donated a minimum of $122,000 to Madden's reelection; and to his 1976 token presidential bid, in which Madden had surprised everyone by winning the three primaries, they had chipped in another $62,000.

Next, I combed through the files in the State Corporation Commission of all the corporations in which I knew the Unholy Three were officers, but I could not find any record of the huge transactions Pallisgaard had hinted about. That did not mean that he had no big business deals on the stove, it just meant that no solid contract negotiations were going on with the corporations whose names I had.

I also made a call to a friend of mine at the telephone company who was working on stealing me copies of the bills for Pallisgaard's personal and business phones, as well as Eldorado's and Eastland's. I wanted to know who had been calling Sacramento lately, and when.

My A.G. bird dogs stuck with me through all this (after they'd taken the cans off their tail), but I had no idea if they guessed what I was doing. I worked out of my house, restricting my contact with Maher to the phone, and if anyone had caught on that I was back on the county payroll, he was not mentioning it.

It was Wednesday night, about 9:00. As I stepped out to get something to eat, I noticed that the Hotel Fairmont was gone from its usual parking space across the street. I shrugged it off, figuring they'd probably ducked out to get something to eat, too, and went downstairs trying to guess where they might have gone to so that I wouldn't find myself at the same place.

I went down the sloping driveway to the underground garage. I unlocked the car and opened the door, and there was a rustling sound behind me. I started to turn, but something cold and hard jammed against my cheek and a voice said: "The keys."

I could make out a vague shape in the dim light, but my

peripheral vision didn't extend far enough to get a good look. "Is that a gun?"

"It ain't chopped liver." Fingers snapped. "C'mon. The keys."

I held out the keys, and they were snatched out of my hand. "Okay. Now move around to the other side of the car."

I did as I was told, and he said to step back while he unlocked the other door. I got my first real look at him then. A big, thick-necked man, dressed in jeans and a down jacket. The big head and sloping shoulders, the bushy dark hair and the simian upper lip, made the gun in his hand look incongruous. A spear would have looked better. He could have used it to protect Carole Landis from dinosaurs. His small, squinty eyes burned brightly with something—some kind of speed, maybe—and he exuded the rank, sour smell of cheap wine.

"Hands up on the roof of the car," he said.

I put my hands on the roof, and he kept the gun in the back of my neck while he patted me down. Then he said: "Okay. You drive."

"Forget it."

"Don't try to get cute with me, sport, or I'll pop you right here. The only chance you got is following directions. You'll come out of this okay if you do that. Piss me off and you've had it."

"This is a residential neighborhood. A gun going off would attract attention—"

"You know anything about guns, sport? What I got in my hand is a .22 magnum target pistol with a silencer on it. It don't make a hell of a lot of noise, just a good pop. Even if it did make noise, it wouldn't make much difference. It's a shame, but people nowadays just don't like to get involved. Y'know what I mean, sport?"

I got in the car and slid across the seat to the wheel. He got in after me.

"Where to?"

"Santa Monica Freeway first. I'll tell you where after that. And remember, the only thing you gotta be concerned about is that you're still breathing. You wanna keep up the habit, just do what I say. You got it, sport?"

"Sure do, sport."

I drove out of the garage and down the street. My eyes searched the cars parked on both sides for a blue Fairmont, but couldn't find one. Maybe it was behind us, I thought as I turned on Pacific. I kept glancing at the rearview mirror trying to pick out headlights following us, but traffic was too heavy.

He caught me looking in the mirror and said: "What are you looking at?"

"Nothing."

I forced my eyes straight ahead to keep him from getting suspicious. I turned on Pico and drove to Lincoln and hung a left. My eyes kept scanning the street for a cop. Nothing. It figured. If I'd had a sixteen-year-old girl in the car, there would have been ten of them attached to my bumper. Until I saw one, I planned to drive carefully, signaling for every turn and lane change, trying to make it as easy as I could to be followed. Those two in the Fairmont were not finalists on the "$25,000 Pyramid," and I didn't want to confuse them with any unnecessarily fast moves.

I thought about the flatiron. It was in easy reach, on the floor by my left side, between the door and the seat. I had put it there last year when the governor had instituted odd-even gas rationing and people had started going crazy in the gas lines and attacking one another. After that, I'd gotten used to having it there and just left it. With the world going screaming yellow bonkers, you never knew when a five-pound piece of cast iron could come in handy. I mean, when James Garner—Rockford the Great—gets pulled from his car and has the shit kicked out of him, it is time to give yourself a little edge. The only trouble was, I had no idea how the hell

207

I was going to get to it, never mind use it, without the Neanderthaler pulling my act.

We sailed through a series of green lights, then hit a red. As the car slowed, my mind speeded up. It felt like a 33 record on 78. The sign for the freeway was two blocks ahead of the light. This would be the last chance before we really started rolling.

Hell, I would just open the door and step out. What the hell could he do? We were not in any subterranean garage. He wouldn't dare try anything. My stomach bucked as I thought about it, willing my hand toward the door handle, but I couldn't get it to move. I couldn't get it to move because I thought about what he said about people, and I knew he was right. He could pop me before I got one foot out the door, then just step out and walk away calm as he pleased, and eyewitnesses would be describing a tall, short, skinny, fat man to the cops.

No, it was better to wait. Stay calm and bide my time. After all, I didn't know what this was all about yet. He did say he wouldn't hurt me if I behaved. Sure. And the Ayatollah Assahollah was coming to the Shah's birthday party this year.

Who was I kidding? My mind was playing tricks. I was filling myself with false hopes in order to shut out the inevitable. Those A.G. assholes might not be behind us at all. They might be at Shakey's eating greasy pizza, for all I knew. I had to formulate some kind of a plan, and I had to do it now.

Before I could, the Neanderthaler stuck the gun into my neck under the jawbone and growled: "Move this fucking tub."

I realized then that the light had changed. I stepped on the gas and we took off. I signaled and turned onto the freeway on ramp, and he said: "Go to the San Diego Freeway northbound."

I nodded, but my mind was on the flatiron. I was tempted to reach down and touch it, just to be reassured it was still there, but stopped myself. If I blew it and he caught me, that would be that. There wouldn't be any second chances. If and when I moved, I wanted to do it when I was ready and not before.

I turned up the long cement ramp that swept over the San Diego Freeway and headed north. The black sky was starless, a halfhearted half-moon hovered faintly over the lighted office towers of Westwood, as if knowing it could not compete with the cold glow of the city. I watched regretfully as the checkerboard lights of the buildings slipped by. It seemed like a good time to get a job in one of them.

At Montana, he told me to get off, and I signaled and pulled off the freeway. I got to the bottom of the off ramp and stopped, trying not to show any exhilaration when I noticed the set of headlights pulling up directly behind us. I glanced over quickly at my passenger, but he never turned to look. He told me to go under the overpass and then to turn onto Sepulveda, and I knew where we were going. He confirmed it when I approached the road that led to Landfill Number Eight and he told me to turn.

The white gate was closed in front of us, and I pulled up and stopped. The headlights pulled in behind us, hemming us in, and I heard a car door slam and gravelly footsteps crunch behind us. Thank God, I said to myself, and pledged my lifetime vote to Attorney General Battersea, regardless of what office he decided to run for.

"Okay," I said, turning to the Neanderthaler. "This is it. That happens to be the attorney general's office behind us. I suggest you put away the piece and give yourself up. The worst they can pin on you is a CCW, and they probably won't even be able to make that stick."

The footsteps were crunching up along his side of the car, but he didn't seem too worried about it. A man I'd never

209

seen before, wearing a leather jacket, stuck his head in the Neanderthaler's window and said: "Everything okay?"

"Yeah, fine," the Neanderthaler said, then smiled at him. "Tell your boss, the attorney general, I'm sorry we're late, but we got hung up in traffic."

The man at the window looked confused. "Huh?"

"Open the fucking gate," the Neanderthaler said.

I watched the man open the gate, spotlighted in the car's headlights, and my stomach felt like a wheel in a mouse cage being turned by a mouse on speed. The man swung the gate open and waved at us, and my friend poked the gun into my neck again and said: "Drive."

The kiosk and the trailer were both dark. A sign on the front of the kiosk read:

Refuse $3.50 per ton
Solid Inert Material $3.00
Hard-to-Handle Bulky Material $4.50

I wondered what classification I would fall under.

We cut up the steep dirt face of the garbage slope. Below, far below, the red taillights coursed up the freeway pass like electrified corpuscles along a concrete artery, bypassing the dark and lifeless mountain. We leveled off and passed between two rocky outcrops, and the plain opened up in front of us as heavy and still as a dead ocean. It seemed to give off an unearthly, blue-gray glow in the moonlight.

We started down and over it. He pointed across the spectral sea to the cluster of earthmovers that squatted silently at the foot of the cutfill. "Stop up there."

I pulled up and stopped, but left the headlights on.

"Keys," he said.

I killed the engine and handed him the keys. He opened the door and started around the front of the car. I knew this was it. While he was in the glare of the headlights, I quickly dipped my left hand down and felt for the iron. For a second, I could not find it. My heart jumped, but then my fingers touched it and I snatched it up and stuck it under my jacket. I didn't have time to conceal it well before he was by my door, pulling it open. "Okay. Out."

My right elbow was pinning the flatiron to my side and I stepped out awkwardly. To cover, I said: "I don't feel so good."

"You won't feel a thing pretty soon, don't worry."

"You said you weren't going to do anything—" I said, trying to sound panicked. I didn't have to try hard.

He prodded me with the gun and told me to walk toward the tractors.

The headlights of the other car swept across the plain and pulled up ahead of my car. He left his lights on, too. It was a dark-colored Monte Carlo. The man with the leather jacket got out and, without saying anything, climbed up one of the bulldozers and fired up the engine. The great beast coughed and then roared, and the man in the leather jacket gave my guardian a thumbs-up and began expertly working the levers. The yellow monster backed up and the big steel blade in front lowered and started forward, cutting a slice out of the hard ground at the base of the cutfill.

Carruthers and his men had done their job today. There was not a piece of paper showing on the twenty-foot-high muddy face of the fill. There was no smell, either, except a faint, sweet smell of sage from the hills. I expected the smell of corruption, of flesh coming away from bone. I told myself not to rush things.

"You're going to kill me," I said, trembling.

"That's the general idea, sport."

"But why?"

"For money. That's what makes the world go round, right?"

211

"I'll give you double what you're getting," I pleaded. "Nobody will know."

He shook his head and smiled. He was enjoying this. "Sorry."

"But who would want me dead? I have a right to know before I die, don't I?"

"I don't know and I don't give a shit, sport. On your knees."

I began blubbering. "PLEASE!"

He laughed. "Hey, Bo, we got a real wailer here! Turn around, sport." When I didn't turn around, he said angrily: "Now I can make this quick or I can make it painful, it's up to you."

I sank to my knees and sobbed loudly. I reached inside my jacket with my left hand and bent over to get more weight behind it. I had to force myself to wait. The silencer was still on the gun and I knew he would probably take it off before he used it. There was no need up here for silencers, which have a tendency to make guns jam. I kept my back to him as I slipped the flatiron out of my jacket, then turned slightly toward him.

He was unscrewing the silencer when I uncoiled like a spring and brought the iron around backhanded. He shrieked as it splintered his shinbone into forty pieces, and involuntarily he squeezed the trigger on the .22 as he fell.

I rolled and scrambled to my feet, and the one called Bo stood up on the cat and saw what was happening and drew his gun. I was off like I was on starting blocks as he squeezed off two rounds. I didn't look to see by how far he missed me, but ducked behind the Monte Carlo for cover.

The Neanderthaler was still writhing around on the ground, screaming. "That motherfucker! I'll kill him! He broke my fucking leg!"

My head bobbed up above the window of the Monte Carlo, but there were no keys in the ignition.

"Go get him, Bo!" the Neanderthaler bellowed. "GET HIM!"

They were confused now, and I did not want to wait around until they regrouped. The road leading up to the embankment was thirty yards to my left. The scraper sat at the top of it—huge, still. I broke for it.

"There he goes!" one of them yelled, and two bullets whanged by my head.

I ran an erratic pattern up the hill, trying not to give him a target. I made it to the top and squatted down behind the front tires of the scraper. Bo was coming up the hill, grunting. He was probably out of shape, but the gun in his hand compensated for whatever edge I had in that department.

My hand was starting to cramp from holding the iron so tightly, and I relaxed my grip. I moved behind the tire and under the belly of the scraper.

Bo puffed up to the top of the slope, then slowed, approaching the scraper warily. The moonlight threw anemic shadows on the ground in front of him. I edged around the tire, keeping it between us. He couldn't see me. He was making a wide circle around the gigantic machine, making sure I wouldn't be able to jump out at him.

He was circling clockwise, toward the back of the scraper, and I moved underneath it, like a crab, toward the front. I reached a front tire and ducked behind it just as he crouched down and fired. The bullet kicked up some dirt by the tire, and I heard him pant as he ran around the front, toward me. I started back in the direction I'd come, and he charged around the tire and squeezed off another round under the scraper. I dove behind another one of the five-thousand-dollar tires for cover.

That made six for him, if I was counting right. He might have reloaded after the first two. He might even have had a nine-shot automatic for all I knew. I decided to chance it. He was getting wild, out of control, and likely wouldn't be able

213

to hit anything even if he got a clear shot. Hitting something when you're excited isn't that easy, no matter what they do in the movies. I stepped out in front of the machine and yelled: "Asshole! Over here!"

He raised his gun and fired, but the hammer fell on an empty chamber. He was maybe forty feet away. I ran for him.

His eyes grew wild, not believing what was happening, and he took the time to squeeze the trigger a few more times before taking off. That hesitation and my speed allowed me to catch him halfway down the slope. I brought the flatiron across the back of his head full-stride. It made a sickening *whap* sound, and he went down hard and skidded along on his face and lay still.

I stopped and looked below. The Neanderthaler was up and hobbling frantically toward the Monte Carlo. I slid down the embankment on my ass and sprinted to the cat, which was still running. I jumped aboard, put in the clutch, and began jerking on gears and levers. The beast lurched and started forward.

He was in the Monte Carlo, hitting the ignition, but he had flooded it in his panic and pain and it wouldn't start. The zinc lights on top of the cab of the cat froze him in their icy-white glare, and his mouth opened as he saw the mountain of dirt moving toward the car.

He pulled the trigger of his .22 rapid-fire, but the angle was all wrong, and then he hit the door handle and tried to get out of the car, but he had waited too long. The dirt being pushed by the dozer blade caught the rocker panel underneath the car and tipped it. Metal creaked and groaned as the Monte Carlo turned in slow motion on its side, then onto its top. I heard him scream, and I stopped.

I stood up in my seat and took a look. Dirt had poured through the open windows of the car, filling it.

I grabbed the flatiron and jumped down from the cat and

ran around to the other side of the car. He was buried to the waist, trying to crawl out of the driver's window as if he were trying to get out of a very tight pair of pants. He must have lost his gun because he didn't have it in his hand. He saw me and stopped squirming.

I squatted down beside him and smiled. "Well, hello there, *sport.*" I smacked the flatiron in my palm a few times, just to let him hear the sound. "Now. The answers to a few questions."

His mouth became a mean line. "Fuck you."

I nodded and picked up a handful of dirt with my free hand.

"You were the one who killed Nina Rivera, weren't you?"

"Fuck you."

I hit him in the sternum with the iron, and as he opened his mouth to scream I packed the dirt into it. He gagged and spat up the dirt all over himself. "One more time," I said.

He spat some more and snarled: "Fuck you."

"Okay." I hit him in the sternum again, and again he yelled and I shoveled another handful of dirt into his mouth. He choked and sputtered and spat. "Eat up all your dirt like a good boy, otherwise you don't get any dessert."

I hit him again and he screamed again, and began bucking and thrashing, but it didn't do him any good. What didn't go into his mouth went into his eyes.

"Now, I can keep this up all night, *sport*, until you drown in dirt or choke on your own vomit. One more time: You killed Nina Rivera, didn't you?"

He tried to blink away the dirt that stung his eyes, then turned his head wildly from side to side. "You're crazy! You're fucking nuts!"

I hit him in the sternum again, harder, and he screamed: "YES! YES! I stole the car and ran her down! I had to get her before she got to you!"

"And Dunland?"

215

"Yes! Yes!"

"You're the one who called me?"

"I was supposed to get you up to the house! I was supposed to make you look good for it! When I found out the guy was a fag, I made it look like you and he had been partying—"

"Who hired you?"

He coughed and spat again. His lips were covered with spittle-made mud. He shook his head. I hit him on the forearm this time, not hard enough to break a bone, but hard enough to give him something to think about. He thought about it by screaming, and not wanting him to go hungry I packed another mouthful of dirt into his mouth.

He vomited on himself, and I jumped back to get out of the way. He retched twice more, then his head dropped back exhausted onto its pillow of dirt. He smelled rank, acidic. It was ironic that in a place that got rid of 2,800 tons of garbage a day, he was the worst smelling thing around.

"Who hired you, goddamnit?"

I waited for the answer, knowing what it was going to be.

"Riccio!" he said, coughing. "Frank Riccio!"

I looked down at him and blinked in confusion. "Who the fuck is Frank Riccio?"

Twenty-five

I was staring at the grimy walls of the squad room, wondering what was the attraction cops felt for algae green, when Baatz came back and plopped down at his desk. "I just got off the phone to the A.G.'s office. They pulled off their surveillance team this afternoon."

"That's great. Who told the two gorillas?"

"We don't know anybody did."

"Hey, they might not be intellectual giants, but nobody is going to convince me that they'd be stupid enough to hang around the neighborhood with the cops baby-sitting outside. Come on, Sergeant."

He stroked his black mustache and stared at me darkly.

"You get names from them yet?" I asked.

"That's about all we've got from them. The one whose skull you played squash with is still out. Concussion, maybe a skull fracture. He's a peanut grifter named—get this—Beauregard Longstreet."

"You gotta be kidding."

"Cute, huh? He's from Mississippi and I guess his mother likes Confederate generals. She probably should've named him Quantrill. Beauregard just got through pulling a bullet at Tehachapi for boosting TVs out of motel room windows.

"The one who will be shitting rocks for the next five days

is a puke named Scott Zouganelis, aka Scott Meeker, aka John Zukor, aka John Scott. You could paper a ten-room house with his rap sheet. Everything from armed robbery to mayhem. He just got out of Tehachapi a year ago and I'd bet that's where he met Longstreet. He's been working for Riccio for the past three months."

"Doing what?"

"Sandblasting," he said. "Riccio owns a small home-improvement company over in Glendale called FR Home Developers. Aluminum siding, textured coatings, shit like that. At least that's what it is on the surface. Sheriff's Intelligence has always thought it's a front to launder the bread he pulls in from other business ventures—like coke peddling and porno and dealing stolen merchandise. He's been busted twice, for porno and gambling, but nothing has ever stuck on him. I just talked to Intelligence. This is the first time they've ever heard of him handling a contract, but it didn't seem to surprise them much. He's got a couple of cousins in one of the New York families."

"Well, it sure surprises the hell out of me. I don't even know him."

"Riccio was probably just brokering it for somebody."

"Who?"

"That's what I intend to ask Mr. Riccio. When I'm ready."

"Ready? Ready for what?"

"When I pick up Riccio, I want to read him his rights. Right now, I haven't got dick to hold him on."

I waved a hand in the air. "What do you mean you haven't got dick? What about this Zouganelis's statement?"

He ran a hand over his smooth head. "You can wipe your ass with that statement. It was made under duress. He's changed his tune now. He's saying that he only came up with Riccio's name because it was the first one that popped into his head."

"What about the other murders he confessed to?"

"He claims he's never heard of either of them. Says he confessed to them only because he thought you were going to kill him if he didn't."

My mouth dropped open a little. "Bullshit."

"Sure it's bullshit. And after he sees what we're booking him on, he might agree that it was bullshit. But right now, the only thing he's talking about is seeing his attorney, which means, for the time being at least, we're going to have to pull some answers from other sources. You, for instance."

I put my hand on my chest. "Me?"

"Yeah, you," he said in a voice about as tender as a shrike's. "Why would somebody want you dead?"

"For the same reason they would want me framed or would want my license taken away. To stop me from asking questions."

"About what?"

I looked at the clock on the wall. Eleven-twelve. Time to talk. What the hell, I was tired of playing superstar. It was time to try to get some other players on my side. "Can I use your phone? I want to call my client."

Consternation stiffened his jaw muscles. "You can't have a client. You don't have a goddamn license."

I winked at him and grinned. "I won't tell anybody if you won't." He looked around the room and flung his arm out in a hopeless shrug, and I said: "Don't worry, Sergeant, it's all perfectly legal, I assure you."

"I'm sure it is," he said sarcastically. "Everything you do is perfectly legal. Like pounding sand down a suspect's throat—"

I picked up the receiver from the phone on the desk and cupped my hand over the mouthpiece. "Would you mind?" I said to him. "I'd like to talk to my client privately."

He stood up. "No, not at all. Would you like me to arrange for a private room or anything? Maybe a fresh cup of coffee while you're talking?"

219

"That's not necessary. Thanks anyway for your thoughtfulness."

He walked to the other side of the room, muttering, and I dialed Maher's home number. Maher picked up the phone immediately. "Hello?"

"Jerry, this is Jake. I'm sorry for disturbing you at home at this hour, but this can't wait until morning. Two men tried to kill me tonight. It looks like a contract hit, and the cops want some answers. Now."

"A contract hit? Are you all right? Where are you?"

"I'm at Sheriff's Homicide. I'm fine. They've got the two men in custody. One of them told me that they were hired by a man named Frank Riccio. He owns a home-improvement business in Glendale. He also seems to have some ties to organized crime. You know him?"

"No," he said. "You think it's tied in with our investigation?"

"I don't know. That would be my guess."

"What do you suggest we do?"

"I think I should fill in Baatz about what we've been doing. It's getting too hot to handle by ourselves. Somebody is going to get hurt. I'd hate for it to be me."

The receiver was filled with thoughtful silence. "Think you can trust him?"

I looked over at Baatz who was impatiently tapping his toe and giving me the Evil Eye. "I think so."

"Do it then. Just impress upon him the need for confidentiality. I wouldn't want Sheriff Rayburn to get hold of the Eastland thing."

"I really don't know how he could help it at this stage."

"Maybe he could keep it off his reports for the time being."

"I doubt it," I said.

"Well, whatever he can do. I'll talk to you in the morning."

"Right," I said, and hung up.

Baatz came back over and sat down. "What's the deal?"

"That was Jerry Maher. He gave me the green light to tell you what we've been working on."

His eyebrows arched. "Maher? I thought you were canned."

"I got rehired. He'd like you to keep this off your reports, if possible."

"I can't do that and you know it," he said, frowning.

"That's what I told him."

"Let's hear it."

He heard it. While he did, his bottom teeth kept scraping his upper lip and his eyes grew nasty. After I'd finished, he looked at me with mild surprise and said: "That's it?"

"That's it."

He tossed a hand at me. "Shit, you've only mentioned the governor and a county supervisor and a state assemblyman and a multimillionaire and the attorney general. Sure you don't want to add the president or the secretary of defense?"

"You wanted to know what I've been working on. I told you. Whatever you want to do with it is up to you. At least now that you've heard it, you can appreciate the need for discretion."

"Discretion?" His eyebrows took off toward his shaved pate and he leaned across the desk. "You got all the discretion you could want. You know what would happen to me if I started running around questioning the governor and the attorney general and state assemblyman about a fag killing and an attempt on the life of one of Jerry Maher's deputies? Rayburn would have me driving black-and-whites in the north end of the Valley. I don't want to drive black-and-whites in the north end of the Valley, Asch. I like working downtown in my street clothes. So I'll tell you what: I'll just forget we ever had this conversation."

"If I were you, I'd start digging into Pallisgaard and his group first," I said. "They warned me off. Pallisgaard came

221

close to threatening me. And his lines of influence have to flow into the A.G.'s office. Whoever tipped Riccio that those men were being pulled off me tonight has to be plugged into the A.G."

"I don't know what I'd do without your great ideas, Asch."

"Who knows? Maybe have one of your own."

He glared at me hotly. "Yeah? Well, I have a couple and they're a hell of a lot better than yours. One, bust Riccio. Two, squeeze a name out of him."

"Terrific. Only bust him on what? Your canaries aren't singing."

"They'll sing, don't worry. I'm going to talk to the D.A. I'm going to have them charged with ADW and kidnap and CCW and GTA and attempted murder and whatever else I can dig up that will get them fifty to life, and they'll be screaming for a deal. That's how I'll get a name, Asch, not by calling up the governor or any state assemblyman or the attorney general and accusing them of conspiracy to get Jacob Asch."

"Just check out Riccio's connections, at least—"

The muscle on his jaw bulged like an egg under the skin, and he leaned toward me. "Don't tell me my fucking job. I'm not going to tell you that again." His anger was more a reaction to the situation he found himself being sucked into than to anything specific I had done, but he was aiming it at the most convenient target.

"Look, Sergeant, I'm sorry it—"

He cut me off in a tired voice: "Why don't you just get the hell out of here and go home?"

Twenty-six

I was on number forty-two of my second set of one hundred sit-ups when there was a knock at the door. I got up off the floor and picked up the Colt .45 Commander automatic from the coffee table and padded in my bare feet to the door. "Who is it?"

"Baatz."

I cracked the door and peeked out, then pulled it open, keeping the gun out of sight behind it. He gave my sweatsuit the once-over and asked: "I interrupt something?"

"Sit-ups," I said, huffing.

"I tried calling you at Maher's. They said you hadn't been in in a couple of days."

"I've been working out of the house."

"Can I come in?"

I shrugged and stepped aside. His eyes grew sharp when he walked by and saw the big .45 dangling at my side. "Can't be too careful nowadays," I explained.

I shut the door and put the gun back on the coffee table. "I've only got another fifty-eight to go. Sit down and watch a little of *God Is My Co-Pilot*." I pointed at Raymond Massey, who was having a conversation with Dennis Morgan on the tube. "Did you know that Fernando DePlancy, the famous microbiologist, was killed watching this very movie on VE

Day when a victory celebrant ripped a toilet off the wall of the theater's men's room and threw it off the balcony? That's true, I swear."

"No shit," he said disinterestedly.

"Not in the account I read." He sat on the couch, and I adjusted my ass on the pillow on the floor and put my legs up in the seat of the chair and went back to work. He stared at the television for a while, then looked around the room in that same old cop way and said: "Where's your maid? The cop hater?"

"She doesn't come today . . . fifty-one, fifty-two . . . Is that why you're here, to see Mary Kay? I *knew* it was love at first sight."

"I just wanted to be sure we're alone."

"We're alone. Sixty-one . . ."

He watched me do a few repetitions, then asked non-chalantly: "You done any more work on your Seaview angle?"

He was trying to be coy. He was about as coy as a bear looking for food in a campground trash can.

"Some."

"Come up with anything?"

"Yeah, but you wouldn't be interested. Seventy-two, seventy-three . . ."

"Why not?" His voice had an edge on it now.

"You don't want to end up driving a black-and-white around the north end of the Valley, remember?"

"Well, maybe I've changed my mind. What'd you find out?"

"You tell me what you found out first."

"What makes you think I've found out something?" he asked sharply.

"Because you wouldn't be here if you hadn't. One hundred. There."

I got up off the floor and sat in the chair and looked at him. His face squirmed with irritation. "Oh, all right, damnit.

I went over Pallisgaard's phone records."

"And?"

"On February 23, the same afternoon you were picked up by those gorillas, a call was placed from Pallisgaard's office to a number in Sacramento. The number is an apartment in the Sunset Towers being leased by Gary Ormansky. Ormansky is Preston Madden's executive assistant. Anybody who gets to the governor has to go through him. It doesn't prove anything. Anybody in Pallisgaard's office could have made the call, and there's nothing to say what it was about. But it ties together, because on February 12—just a couple of days before Hoffman disappeared—somebody from FR Developers in Glendale also called Pallisgaard's office."

"The day after I spotted Hoffman and Madden together."

He shook his head somberly. "I just have trouble putting a millionaire like Pallisgaard together with a two-bit aluminum siding salesman who does hits on the side."

"Have you checked the County Assessor's files to see who owns the industrial complex FR Home Developers is in?"

"No."

"I did," I said, grinning.

"Pallisgaard?"

"The one and only."

Baatz smacked a fist into his palm. "So *that's* the connection."

I nodded. "Did you check out the prints at Dunland's against Quantrill's raiders?"

He stared at me. "It looks like Zouganelis is our boy. He wears size twelve shoes."

"You charge him with the murder yet?"

"He's going to be arraigned tomorrow. He's still not talking, though. Neither of them is. But if everything works out, we may not need them." He took a breath and said: "We got a break.

"A few days ago, Metro busted a puke named Danny Kramer for burglary. They caught him and a puke friend of

225

his in an alley behind an office supply warehouse loading up a van with adding machines and typewriters and calculators. Metro had had a rash of burglaries with the same M.O. in the past couple of months, so they get a warrant and mosey on over to Kramer's house and, lo and behold, they find his old lady and stuff from at least four other burglaries, plus some smack and about a thousand whites I don't have to tell you he didn't have a prescription for. They bust the old lady—who happens to be six months pregnant—and charge both her and Kramer with receiving stolen merchandise and possession of drugs for resale, in addition to the burglary charge.

"Now this is where it gets interesting. Kramer is already a three-time loser, and he knows what they're laying on him could put him back in the slammer for five or six years, and if his old lady goes, the state will pull their kid and put him in a foster home. So right away, he sends word to the detectives on the case that he wants to deal. He wants to talk about a murder."

"Dunland," I said.

He shook his head. "Hoffman."

I sat up and stared at him blankly. He smiled a little, then went on: "The detectives check it out and find out that Hoffman is a missing person, so they tell Kramer that a deal might be possible if they like his story, so he gives them one. He says that a couple of weeks before the adding-machine job, he was approached by Frank Riccio, who wanted to know if he would be interested in making twenty-five hundred bucks for helping to hit a guy. Kramer knew Riccio because Riccio fenced a lot of the stuff Kramer ripped off. Riccio told Kramer he wouldn't have to be in on any rough stuff, that all he would have to do would be operate some heavy equipment to plant the guy after it was done—Kramer drives a cat when he isn't boosting typewriters—but Kramer turns down the job because he doesn't have the stomach for that kind of work. After they hear him out, the detectives call

226

Sheriff's Intelligence to see what the hell they've got on Riccio, and the guy they talk to there tells them to call me. So I go talk to Kramer."

I got up and sat in the chair. "Did Riccio tell him why he wanted Hoffman hit?"

He shook his head. "But he did tell him that Zouganelis was going to do the actual killing. Anyway, after I talk to Kramer, I go to the D.A. and he agrees to drop the charges on the girl—he probably couldn't get a conviction anyway—and the narcotics and merchandise raps on Kramer, which means he'd probably only pull two, three years in state prison, and with good behavior he'd get a third of that knocked off. Kramer is happy about that, until he hears the rest of it. I tell him that the only way we deal is if we get something concrete on Riccio. He says that's up to us, he gave us the information and what we do with it is our business, and I say, uh-uh, that's not the way it works, and unless he wants to pull some heavy time he's going to have to talk his old lady into setting up a meet with Riccio. He screams bloody murder, but after he sees he's got no other way out, he agrees."

"What kind of a meet?"

"She's going to tell Riccio that Kramer needs help with his bail, that he's going nuts in jail. She's going to tell him that unless he gets it, Kramer says he's going to start talking about the hit. We'll wire her up before she goes to see him. Maybe he'll say something we'll be able to use to nail his ass with."

"Does she know Riccio?"

"Yeah, she knows him."

"Think Riccio will go for it?"

"We'll find out tonight," he said, then paused thoughtfully. "You want to go along?"

"Does a chicken have lips? When and where?"

He stood up. "There's a Pioneer takeout on Western, just north of Hollywood Boulevard. Meet us in the parking lot at

227

eight-thirty. We'll be in a gray Dodge." He took a parting glance at Raymond Massey. "And we won't wait around for you, so don't be late."

I smiled. "Not unless I get hit by a low-flying toilet."

It was raining again. The front of a storm had just dumped two inches in Northern California, and it was supposed to come down heavy in L.A. by tonight, but right now my wipers had to work only lazily to keep the light spray off the windshield. I spotted the Pioneer Chicken covered wagon ahead on the right and turned into the lot.

They were parked on the side, in a gray Marauder. I pulled in next to them and killed my motor. Baatz was sitting shotgun, Walker was behind the wheel. Baatz said hello and told me to get in the back with a Chicano girl with cropped black hair. I thought she was Kramer's girl friend, until Baatz introduced her as Deputy Vargas.

Vargas and I shook hands, and I said hi to Walker, who looked as if he didn't think I had any business being there.

"She should be here any minute," Baatz said, consulting his watch.

The counter inside was crowded with customers, mostly blacks and Chicanos, waiting for their plastic buckets of fried chicken. We watched the people pass in and out of the building for a few minutes, then Baatz said, "There she is," and our eyes turned collectively to see a canary-yellow Capri with a primer-gray front end pull into the lot and park a few slots away.

The girl got out of the car and started over. She was small and her skinny, stick legs looked like they were having a little trouble supporting the swelling under her white maternity dress. She walked splayfooted, leaning backward in a concentrated effort to compensate for the extra weight. I got out of the car, and she got into the back seat between me and Deputy Vargas.

She was pale and had stringy red hair, and the thick layer of makeup she wore did little to conceal the fact that she was not attractive. If anything it gave her an emaciated, hollow-eyed look. "How about a cigarette?" was the first thing she said.

Baatz gave her one, and she took it greedily.

"You shouldn't smoke when you're pregnant," Walker admonished her. "It's not good for the baby."

She glared at him and inhaled deeply. "Yeah? Well, I guess that's tough shit, because I *need* a cigarette. I'm scared shitless, I don't mind telling you."

"Don't worry about a thing, Lois," Baatz reassured her. "We'll be right on top of the whole thing. We'll be hearing everything both of you will be saying, and if anything looks like it's going to come down, we'll be on top of it in a matter of seconds."

"I'm not worried about that. I'm worried about Danny."

"Look, it's going to be okay. Danny told you to do it himself, didn't he?"

"It'd better be okay," she whined. "Because I can't make it without him, y'know? I'm due in three months and I've got to go through it alone, but I can't go through the rest of it alone. . . ."

Her eyes dropped to her lap and her voice faded out. I felt sorry for her. She was trying to be tough, but that was just an act. She was really frightened and fragile, trapped by circumstances and her own emotions. She was in the wrong place at the wrong time and in love with the wrong guy. I just hoped her hands didn't shake as badly when she was with Riccio as when she was with us.

"It's going to be fine, Lois, I'm telling you," Baatz said, then handed the recorder-transmitter over the back seat to Vargas. It was about the size of a pack of cigarettes and had a tiny wire protruding from it.

"You want to lift up your blouse?" Vargas asked Lois. I turned my head and watched the comings and goings outside as adhesive tape was torn and the transmitter attached to the girl's stomach.

229

"Good job," Baatz said after it was done. "You can't see it at all. Now, we've gone over the questions, Lois. You remember what you're supposed to ask him?"

"Yeah, yeah," she said, sucking nervously on her cigarette. "Come on, let's get this fucking thing over with."

I got out again to let her out, and she waddled back over to her car and got in.

"She shouldn't be smoking when she's pregnant," Walker said again.

Nobody looked at him. She left the lot, and we gave her a minute or two before following her down Western.

Young blacks and old winos coagulated in sparse groups on corners, their collars turned up against the mist that leaked from the sky. An occasional burst of neon stained the night, advertising pinball or a porno movie arcade. We drove past a dance studio with age-yellowed photographs in its front windows of its hoofer dance-team instructors whose last big gig had been at the Palladium in 1934, past a series of dingy brick flophouses with rusted fire escapes running drunkenly up their fronts and painted signs on their sides advertising rooms by the month, week, and day. They did not mention by the hour, but you could probably get those, too. The neighborhood was discount everything, discount life.

We crossed Sunset, and then Baatz pointed to a bar in a section of brick storefront that looked as if it might have once been yellow, but was now soot-black. "That's it."

Walker slowed. It was called the Safari Club. The name was spelled out above the door in red neon along with a red neon martini glass, complete with olive.

"Nice place," Walker said.

Baatz shrugged. "Yeah, well, he hasn't forgotten his roots, at least."

He spotted a space about half a block down and pulled in. I could see the door of the place clearly through the back window.

Lois was already inside and transmitting. She seemed to be talking to somebody, but the only other voice, a man's voice, was being drowned out by the sounds of laughter and loud conversation and soul music that was blaring from a jukebox.

"Great," Baatz said worriedly. "I hope to hell she remembers what I told her and gets him out of there. Otherwise, we ain't gonna get shit."

It went on like that for a while, with only occasional snatches of conversation coming through, then Lois was telling the man that the noise was giving her a headache and she had to go outside.

"Good girl," Baatz said.

Chairs scraped, and soon there was nothing but the sounds of the music and tinkling glasses and raucous shouts. Then the noise and music subsided and Lois came through the door of the bar with a lanky, dark-haired man dressed in a leather car coat.

"Thanks," Lois said clearly. "I couldn't stand any more of that. My head feels like it's gonna explode."

The man didn't say anything. He stopped to light a cigarette. The streets glistened wetly and the red from the sign gathered in angry puddles at their feet. The man bent over the cupped flame in his hand and said: "Okay, so what the hell is so urgent that you hadda talk to me?"

"Danny needs a little help from his friends, Mr. Riccio. He sent me to talk to you."

"We all need help, baby." His voice was cold, brittle.

"You gotta help us," she said, her voice full of emotion. "Danny's gonna go crazy, I swear to God. Not only did they nail him cold on the burglary, they found all sorts of shit at the house, from some other jobs. And some dope. That's what they busted me for."

"So? What am I supposed to do about it?"

"We blew everything raising my bail. Now they've set

231

Danny's bail at fifty K and the bondsman won't go for it. We ain't got that kind of collateral."

"Let me tell you something, Lois. As far as I'm concerned, your boyfriend has got nobody to blame for the shit he's in but himself. So go tell him to forget it."

He started to walk away, but she grabbed his arm. "Mr. Riccio, Danny says that if you don't help him out, he's gonna start talking."

"What's he gonna talk about?"

"The hit you wanted him to do. That Hoffman guy."

There was silence. Then: "You wanna talk, let's talk in my car. I'm getting fucking soaked out here."

Walker hunkered forward and said in a worried tone: "I hope she doesn't let him drive her anywhere."

"He wouldn't do anything to her," Baatz said. "He knows Kramer would really start screaming then."

We watched them walk to a white Cadillac Seville parked at the curb a few cars from the entrance to the bar. Over the body of the car, the red sign was broken up into a series of parallel wavy lines. Considering the neighborhood, I was surprised that the car was not already up on blocks, its tires gone. Riccio unlocked the door for her, then went around to the driver's side and got in. There was a closing of car doors from our receiver and a momentary silence, then Riccio said: "Listen, Lois, I got enough to worry about with those other two fucking red-freaks sitting in the Hall of Justice. You tell your boyfriend that if he keeps his mouth shut, everything will work out for him. If he opens it, he won't live out his sentence, I don't give a fuck how short it is."

"Danny's not trying to burn nobody," she said. "He just wants a fair shake, that's all. He says if he doesn't get bail, he'll talk about the man who hired out the hit on the engineer."

"How the hell would he know who hired out the hit on the engineer?" he said angrily. "I don't really think they run in the same social circles."

232

Walker glanced at Baatz and smiled. "That's it. He just admitted it. Shall we pick him up?"

"Wait," Baatz said. "Maybe she can get the name of the money man out of him."

"I'm just telling you what he said," Lois said.

"And I'm telling you what I'm saying. Danny had better keep his mouth shut." There was another gap, then Riccio said, softer: "Look, let me consult with my people, see what I can do. We'll probably be able to work something out with the bail. But if he talks, tell him he won't be the only one to suffer. Other people, innocent people, could get hurt. You getting where I'm coming from?"

"Yeah, sure, Mr. Riccio. I'll tell him." She sounded frightened.

"Now get out of here."

There was a rustling sound and then the sound of a door handle being opened and then the ignition of a car turning over and then our car was rocked by a concussive blast as the night turned into day and the Seville disappeared into a yellow-orange ball of fire.

"Jesus Christ," I heard myself say as pieces of car fell from the night sky like a flaming meteor shower.

Twenty-seven

The bomb squad came and went, the coroner came and went, the charred debris—human and metal—was cleared away, delivered to various laboratories for inspection and study, but the debris that littered my mind refused to be cleaned up.

Riccio was a firebreak. He had been cut down to keep the fire from spreading, and whoever had done it had not left an ax behind.

The cops had enough physical evidence on Zouganelis to make the Dunland killing stick, and his partner, General Longstreet, was taking requests and singing like Bette Midler, but it would not make much difference. He had agreed to be a witness for the state and testify that Riccio had used Zouganelis for the Hoffman and Rivera hits, but he didn't know why or who was paying for it.

The county spent $140,000 of the taxpayers' money digging up Landfill Number Eight looking for Hoffman's body, but they could not find it. Carruthers did not seem to think that was unusual, saying the task was analogous to finding "the perennial needle in a haystack," but the D.A.'s office was undeterred, saying they would try the case without a corpse. In the meantime, all the boys in Sheriff's Homicide had taken to wearing T-shirts that some enterprising detective with a sense of humor had made up, saying:

MERLE
We dig you.

That was where things stood six days later when Baatz called me at the office and said he wanted to see me. When I told him to come over, he said, no, he would meet me at the Triforium in twenty minutes. It was important, he said.

The Triforium was just a couple of blocks away, and as I hoofed it I wondered about the strange tone in Baatz's voice and the reasons for picking the Triforium as a meeting spot. Maybe he was trying to tell me something. The Triforium had long been maligned as an example of how the taxpayers' money was typically wasted by stupid governmental decisions. A "three-million-dollar jukebox," it was called by its detractors. And that was one of the nicer things they said about it. Myself, I could not think of a better way the county could have spent three million bucks. At least the people could get some enjoyment out of it and it wasn't going as graft into some cement contractor's pocket.

I went up the stairs that led to the elevated platform above the street. Bums, county clerks, even a couple of priests sat in the warm sunshine on the benches around the sculptured tower, brown-bagging it and listening to Paul Simon. At night, different-colored lights moved in the tower to the frequencies of the music, and you could sit for hours, hypnotized by the light show. But now, the daylight was killing the magic and it was just a piece of sculpture.

Paul Simon's voice died, replaced by Rachmaninoff's *Second Piano Concerto*. I sat down next to a pretty black girl who was eating a carton of yogurt with a plastic spoon, and looked at my watch. Baatz was late. Then I saw him coming across the pedestrian bridge that spanned the street, and I stood up.

235

We shook hands and he said: "Thanks for coming. I didn't want to be seen talking to you at your office."

"Why not?"

He didn't answer, but walked away a few steps. I followed. He picked an unoccupied bench and sat down. "Have you come up with anything?" he asked.

There was something different about him—his carriage, the slope of his shoulders. His posture was tired, defeated. Dark glasses covered his eyes, but I would have bet they were smudged by dark circles.

"Nothing worth much," I said. "We're looking into Seaview's funding. It looks okay on the surface, but there might be something. How about you?"

He stared at the tower and smiled mirthlessly. "I'm off the case."

"What? Why?"

"They're closing it out. As far as Dunland is concerned, it's officially solved. We're turning over what we have to the D.A. and that's it."

I stood up and said loudly: "But it's not solved."

He looked around quickly as if afraid someone might have heard that, then said quietly: "Tell Rayburn."

"Somebody got to somebody. What about Riccio's statement to Lois that somebody hired him to do the hit? What about the phone call from Riccio's office to Pallisgaard?"

"I talked to Pallisgaard a few days ago. He claims the phone conversation was about the rent. As for Riccio's comment to Lois, it doesn't mean shit."

I sat down on the bench, hard, and exhaled in disgust. "It sucks."

"How do you think I feel about it?" he asked, resentment clogging his voice. "I've been sleeping four hours a fucking night for the past week, trying to break this fucking case. I've probably seen my wife and kid a total of five hours since Riccio got blown away." He stared reflectively at the colored tower, and his voice grew quiet. "I really wanted it, Asch.

236

For Lois and her baby. I've been carrying both of them around with me."

"You can't blame yourself for that," I said.

"I just wanted to nail the asshole that did it."

"There aren't any clues who set the bomb?"

He shook his head and leaned over and began rubbing his hands together. "Nothing. The position of the department is that Riccio's death was unrelated to the other three hits. It's going on the books as a gangland killing. The case will stay open, but unless the puke who wired up the car starts shooting his mouth off in a bar somewhere or somebody turns him over, it'll never get solved." He paused, then said: "That's why I called you, Asch. I'm going to give you something. Maybe your boss will find a way to use it. He's probably the only one around who'd have the balls to do it. I've been trying to figure a way, but that's all I can come up with."

"What is it?"

He sat up and looked at me. His face was pasty, colorless like a waxen mask. "You didn't get this from me."

"Sure."

"I mean it. I don't even want Maher knowing where you got it."

"I give you my word. I protect my sources. I even went to jail for it once."

He nodded. "That's one reason I'm telling you. I trust you to keep your mouth shut." He leaned forward again, resting his elbows on his knees. "When you brought up Madden's name, I got curious. There have been rumors floating around the department for a long time, you know? Mostly jokes about why Madden is a bachelor and why he's such a big supporter of gay rights, shit like that. So when you put him talking to Hoffman, I started checking with some people I know in the S.O. and on LAPD Vice, and one of them puts me in touch with a friend of his from the Hollywood Division. I'll call him Flaherty. That isn't his real name."

Pigeons patrolled the cement around our feet, looking for

237

stray bits of bread dropped by lunchers. He kicked at one, but it barely speeded up to get away from his shoe. "Flaherty was the watch commander one night two years ago when a call comes in from the chief. Flaherty is kind of surprised, y'know, because it's not often the chief calls the division personally. Anyway, the chief tells him that Governor Madden is going to be flying into L.A. to spend the weekend with Lola Sheldon—"

"The actress?"

"Right. They're supposed to be having this hot thing going. Madden and her. The chief tells Flaherty that the governor wants to make sure that if any LAPD units happen to be cruising by the Sheldon house and see anything, to keep their mouths shut about it. Flaherty asks the chief if Madden is going to have any security, and the chief tells him no, he offered it, but the governor was adamant about it. No security.

"All this got Flaherty curious. He was especially curious because he'd just recently busted a dyke script girl on Sheldon's new movie for coke and the dyke told him that Lola gave really good head. So being the curious guy he is, Flaherty goes by Ms. Sheldon's house and finds it all dark. The neighbor next door tells him Lola hasn't been home in two days. Things are getting curiouser and curiouser and the wheels are starting to turn in old Flaherty's head real good now, so he drives out to the airport and waits around for the plane to come in, and sure enough, it does and Madden gets off. He's met by a car—Eastland's car—and Flaherty tags along behind, just to see where they're going to go. They go over to Lola Sheldon's house, all right, but Eastland or whoever is driving doesn't stick around. Just drops Madden off and splits."

"But what—"

He killed what I was going to ask by holding up a hand. "Flaherty decides he's got nothing else to do, so he sits on the house. He's got this gut feeling something is happening, y'know? And about an hour later, something does. Another car pulls up with two guys in it and pulls into the garage. Now Flaherty knows it's not Sheldon's car because he has her plate number in front of him, so he runs a make on it and guess who he comes up with?"

I shook my head.

"Dunland."

The name shook me. "Did Flaherty identify anybody in the car?"

"I'll get to that. Anyway, the pair didn't leave the house until the following morning. Flaherty is just about dead by this time—he's been sitting on the house all night—but he follows the car into Hollywood where the driver drops off the passenger at an old apartment building on Yucca. It's a kid. Flaherty figures he knows where to get Dunland, so he takes the kid. The kid is named Jaime Ramirez and he's been living at that address with two other kids for the past three months. Flaherty runs a make on him, just for fun, and finds that little sweet-ass Jaime is a sixteen-year-old runaway who's been picked up twice in the past year on the Boulevard for hustling. Like it so far?"

"Lovely," I said.

"It gets better. Flaherty then checks out Dunland. He finds out that not only is the guy a chickenhawk, he also knows some very influential people who share the same tastes. A year before, in fact, he threw a party on a rented yacht in the Marina that got busted. He had naked teenage boys serving the guests, from drinks and hors d'oeuvres to anything else they wanted. When the smoke cleared, Vice found two state senators and three superior court judges among the guests."

"You never mentioned that before."

"I never knew about it before. It got buried. There are no reports in existence about the bust."

"Politics in America," I said, shaking my head.

239

His upper lip tightened and curled under. "Yeah. Those two senators and three judges owed somebody in the D.A.'s office, and I guarantee they paid off later."

"So what happened? What did Flaherty do?"

He shrugged. "The same thing I'm going to do. Nothing. Look, he starts making noise about it and all he'd succeed in doing would be blow his pension. Besides, what's he going to prove? Maybe Madden and Jaime and Dunland played canasta in that house all night. Flaherty didn't see anything. He maybe could have shaken Jaime down, but even if he had, what kind of a witness do you think he'd make? Flaherty talked to a couple of people he trusted in the PD. They told him to forget about it. He never forgot, but he never said anything to anybody, either."

"Just like they're telling you to forget about this one?"

He gave me a look that was not quite sinister.

"What about Eastland?" I asked.

"I don't know. He seems to be okay in that department. I haven't heard anything about him, anyway. He just seems to be a friend of Madden's. I don't even know if he knows Madden likes to pack sixteen-year-old poopers."

I shook my head. "Here all the time I thought it was Seaview, when what they were trying to keep the lid on was the fact that the governor is a chickenhawk."

"Hoffman must have known Madden through Dunland, and when Pallisgaard's people tried to pressure him to drop his anti-Seaview campaign, he must have called him up. Threatened to expose him unless he did something about Seaview."

I nodded. "Madden gets scared and calls Pallisgaard, and Pallisgaard calls up Riccio to take care of the situation. Nina Rivera finds out about Hoffman and gets scared, and she has to go. Dunland must have guessed it. They were afraid I would eventually, too, so I had to be eliminated. It's like a line of dominoes."

Rachmaninoff finished and Ferlin Husky came on. That

was too much for one of the gray-haired priests. He got up and started shuffling off. "Some people think Madden has a damn good chance to be our next president," I said.

"That'd be nice. We could have naked dancing boys on the White House lawn."

"I wonder if Pallisgaard and his people realized that when they bankrolled his campaign. Probably not. They probably just thought they were buying a governor. When he won those primaries going away, they realized what they had in their pockets. The next president. The whole country. It would be something to kill for, wouldn't it?"

He rubbed the back of his neck. "What do you figure to do with it?"

"I don't know. I'll have to consult with Jerry."

He sighed and stood up. "Whatever you do, you'd better cover your ass with both hands. A lot of people will be trying to kick it."

We shook hands again. "Thanks for everything," I said. "And don't lose any sleep about your name being drawn into it."

He smiled bravely as if trying to buck himself up like Lucifer after the Fall. "I couldn't lose much more than I already have."

He walked away briskly, and I watched him until he had disappeared over the bridge, then walked back to the Hall of Administration.

Jerry was in his office, getting ready to leave for a meeting with the RTD people about the new rapid-transit proposals, but I told him he'd better hear what I had to say first. As I relayed Baatz's story, dark frown lines gathered at the corners of his mouth, and when it was over he said: "Where did you get this?"

"I promised I wouldn't tell anyone. Even you."

He nodded as if he understood. "But it's a reliable source?"

"Yes."

"Can it be documented?"

"I doubt it."

He bit the inside of his lip and turned his chair to look out the window. After letting him think about it for a couple of minutes, I said: "What do you think we should do about it?"

He swiveled back to face me, then picked up the phone. "Jenny? Get me Governor Madden's office in Sacramento." He cupped a hand over the receiver and waited.

"What are you going to say to him?" I asked.

His mouth turned into a nasty grin, and there was a predatory glint in his eye. "I'm going to tell him that he'd better get his ass down here. Otherwise, he'll never be president."

Twenty-eight

The entire office was astir—especially the female secretaries—when Preston Madden strode into the office the following afternoon. It was funny, but he had that kind of effect on women.

He was tall and thin with pale, thin skin that made him look delicate, almost feverish. His hair was brown, and only the touch of gray at each temple lent his boyish good looks an air of maturity they might otherwise have lacked. All the planes of the face were sharply cut, from the jutting cheekbones that sloped cleanly down to the straight jaw to the long, turned-down nose to the deep cleft in the precise center of the chin. The mouth was thin, controlled, and the brown eyes sparkled with intelligence, or at least looked as if they did. Everything about him seemed self-assured and knowing.

He was accompanied by Gary Ormansky, who looked like the Yale grad he was. He had an Ivy League haircut that emphasized his receding reddish hairline and was dressed like a Botany 500 ad. He was dressed, in fact, better than the governor, who himself wore a crisp blue suit and white shirt, blue tie.

After Madden had done his thing, shaking the hands of all the weak-kneed secretaries, I escorted him and Ormansky

243

back to Jerry's office. Marty was waiting there. They shook hands politely all around, and Madden and his aide sat down while Savich and I remained standing.

"Do you want Mr. Ormansky here?" Maher asked.

"He stays," Madden said firmly.

I looked at the two of them and wondered if they had something going.

"Now what's this all about?" Madden began with an air of impatience. "On the phone, you mentioned Seaview. And Joseph Pallisgaard."

Maher put his hands on the desk. "Mr. Pallisgaard was invited to attend this meeting, but he refused." My head snapped around. That was the first I'd heard that Maher had talked to Pallisgaard. He did not look at me, but went on: "Mr. Pallisgaard and his business partners are big backers of yours."

Madden's eyes were fixed on the supervisor's. "So what?"

Maher put his fist in front of his mouth and cleared his throat. "On February twenty-third, at two twenty-five P.M., a telephone call was placed from Mr. Pallisgaard's office to an apartment in Sacramento leased by Mr. Ormansky. The call lasted for two and one-half minutes. Shortly thereafter, the attorney general called off a surveillance team that he had following my deputy here, Mr. Asch. That night, two hired assassins kidnapped Mr. Asch and attempted to kill him. They were hired by a man named Frank Riccio, who since then has himself been murdered. Mr. Riccio had organized-crime contacts and was a business associate of Mr. Pallisgaard. He has been linked by the Sheriff's Department with three other contract murders—one, a secretary of one of Mr. Pallisgaard's partners at Eldorado, Clyde Laughlin; two, a county sanitation engineer named Merle Hoffman who was opposed to Eldorado's contract with the county; and three, an Art Deco dealer friend of Hoffman's named Kenneth Dunland. You knew the latter two, I believe."

244

Madden stirred in his seat. He tried on several expressions before settling for caution. "I'm sorry, but the names don't sound familiar."

"I'll try to jog your memory a little," Maher said almost nastily. "You met Hoffman at least once, on February eleven, at the Seaview site. You were driving Eastland's car, which you borrowed when you flew into town. Mr. Asch saw you. He was following Hoffman at the time."

Madden's face grew taut. He threw a glance at Ormansky, then tried on a tight smile that failed. "There must be some mistake—"

"No mistake," Maher went on. "Hoffman got word to you that you'd better come down and talk to him if you wanted to save your political career, isn't that right?"

"I have no idea what you're talking about," Madden said, but there was no conviction in his voice, as if he were one jump ahead of himself, trying to anticipate the rebuttal that was coming.

Maher leaned toward him. "We have photographs, governor. Photographs of you and Hoffman."

I was looking at Maher now. Unlike Madden, his voice was full of diamond-hard certainty. He was a very good liar.

"Look here—" Ormansky started to say.

Maher ignored him. "You're sure you want him to hear this?" he asked Madden.

"Hear what? You haven't said anything." He was still trying the big bluff. He looked truly feverish now.

"Hoffman knew about your, shall we say, 'affliction'? He knew about it because his lover Dunland told him about it. Dunland knew about it because he supplied boys for you every now and then when you came into town—"

"Let's get out of here," Ormansky said, and stood up.

Savich stepped up behind him and clamped a hand on his shoulder.

"Get your hands off me!" the aide shouted, shaking off the

grip. "Come on, Preston, let's get out of here." He sighted Maher down his out-pointed finger. "In case you didn't know it, Mr. Maher, you just cooked your own goose. What you just indulged in happens to be slander, as defined under Section Two Fifty-eight of the California Criminal Code."

"Maybe," Maher said. "But you aren't going to do anything about it. To do that, you'd have to file charges with the D.A., and then there'd be a trial and I'd have to get the cop on the stand who happened to follow Mr. Madden here from the airport one night over to Lola Sheldon's house where he was joined by Mr. Dunland and a sixteen-year-old street hustler named Jaime Ramirez."

"This is outrageous!" Ormansky snarled.

Maher's eyes bored holes into the aide's face. "You're right, Mr. Ormansky. Murder is outrageous."

Madden looked around blankly, as if the room was doing a fast-fade on him. "I . . . I don't know anything about any murders."

"Are you denying that you knew Kenneth Dunland?"

Madden said nothing.

"I can prove you knew Dunland, Mr. Madden, and once I do that you are dropped right in the middle of it."

Madden sat very still. His eyes cleared a bit, and he said in a steady voice: "I'd like to talk to you alone for a few minutes."

Maher looked at us and cocked his head toward the door, and Savich and I went out. Ormansky stayed. We went into Marty's office and sat down.

"What do you think he's saying?" I asked Marty.

"Madden's a smooth politician. If we had him dead to rights, he'd confess just enough to make his story plausible, but he knows a lot of what we have is flimsy and that the papers wouldn't be likely to touch it."

"You think Ormansky knows about it?"

"He must, otherwise Madden would have wanted him out of there with us."

I nodded, then sat rubbing my knuckles. Twenty minutes later, we heard Jerry's door open. We stepped out into the hallway. Madden and Ormansky came out of the door. Madden's face was white and drawn. He looked shaken. He stared at me glassily and walked past me like one of Bela Lugosi's house servants in *White Zombie*. Ormansky looked at us both like a spitting cobra.

Marty and I went into Maher's office and shut the door. "Well?"

Maher loosened his tie and unbuttoned the top button of his shirt as if he were choking. "He admitted knowing Dunland and he admitted having stayed at Lola Sheldon's house, but he denied being a homosexual."

Marty glanced at me triumphantly, then turned to Maher and said: "You didn't expect him to, did you?"

"Not really."

"What about Hoffman?" I asked.

"He admitted meeting him at Seaview. Dunland called him, he said, and told him he had a friend who was really concerned about what was going on at Seaview. He asked him to meet with the man as a personal favor. Madden came to L.A. and borrowed Eastland's car and met him at Skycrest. He said Hoffman showed him what had happened to the landfill there and then said that he didn't like what was going on between Pallisgaard's people and the county, and that he was afraid that once Eastland was appointed to the Board of Supervisors any action that might be taken about it would be permanently stifled. Madden said he told Hoffman that he couldn't do anything about it, that he had the welfare of the entire state to think about and he considered Seaview important to that welfare. He said Hoffman couldn't understand that he had to make certain compromises as governor he wouldn't normally make, and they argued. He claims that was the sum total of it. He went back to Sacramento. End of story."

"Did Pallisgaard know about the meeting?"

"According to him, not then. He says that Pallisgaard called him up a few days later, wanting to know about it. After you gave your report to Nina Rivera, she told Laughlin, and I guess Pallisgaard called up Eastland and wanted to know why he was meeting Hoffman. That's when Eastland told him that Madden had borrowed his car."

"And Hoffman?"

"He claims he knew nothing about Hoffman being killed until now. I don't think he was lying about that. He really looked shocked when I told him. He said Pallisgaard said he would take care of Hoffman, but he had no idea he meant to do anything drastic."

"It doesn't wash," I said. "Hoffman knew Madden was a chickenhawk, and Madden must have been worried about it and called Pallisgaard—"

"Maybe it happened that way, but we'd never be able to prove it."

"Did he deny knowing anything about Dunland's murder, too?"

Maher nodded. "He says he thought it was a sex killing. He knew Dunland went in for certain types. When he heard about it, he says he was naturally worried that it might come out that he and Dunland were friends, and that people might misinterpret their relationship. That was why he called the attorney general and asked to be kept up-to-date on the case. He denies having put on any pressure to get your license revoked, by the way."

I nodded. "And the cow jumped over the moon."

"That could have been Pallisgaard's doing, you know."

"Maybe," I conceded.

"I'll tell you one thing," Maher said proudly, "we shook his cookies up. I let him know flat out that I didn't believe his denials about being a pederast. I told him I didn't care whether or not he was aware of what his supporters were doing—if he wasn't, then he had just closed his eyes to it, and that made him an accessory. Of course, I didn't let on just

248

how much documentation we had for our charges. That's why he caved in to all my demands."

"What demands?"

"First, that he relay the message to Pallisgaard that there would be no more attempts on anyone's life—yours or anyone's. Second, that he retire at the end of his current term and never run for any public office again, including the presidency. Third, that he not submit Eastland's name for appointment to the board. Fourth, that your license be returned, with an apology."

"I guarantee he'll be running again for something within four years," Savich said.

"Maybe. But I guarantee his campaign will be grossly underfinanced, whatever he runs for. He's too vulnerable to keep in public office now."

Savich looked at him. "That didn't seem to bother his backers before."

"I doubt they knew about his sex life then. All Pallisgaard and his people probably knew was that he had tremendous appeal and that he would be their man. By the time they'd found out he was a chickenhawk, it was too late. He was too damn popular to give up. When he won those three presidential primaries, they must have seen that they had a chance to go all the way. So the lid had to stay on, no matter what the cost. The stakes were too high to let a few lives stand in the way."

I looked at both of them as a strange feeling like a heavy lump of rubber began to settle in my stomach. "Wait a minute. Do you mean you intend to hold this back? You're not going to do anything with it?"

Maher turned to face me, slowly. "What do you propose we do with it? The papers would never handle it. The D.A. would laugh in our faces if we went to him and asked for an indictment. What we've got is a sum total of two phone conversations in which you don't even know who was talking and the statement of a cop whose real name you don't know, a cop who saw Madden, Dunland, and a street hustler together two years ago. Oh, and you placing him at the Seaview site, talking to Hoffman. What does it all add up to?"

I didn't say anything.

"No, I think we've accomplished quite a bit, considering everything."

Savich nodded and said: "Jerry's right, Jake. We accomplished quite a bit."

"What about Seaview?"

"Marty will take over the Seaview investigation."

"Marty?"

He rubbed the side of his nose and rearranged some papers on the desk. "Yes." He looked up and smiled. "I'm letting you go, Jake. As of today."

I gave him a knowing look and began nodding, very slowly.

He stood up and placed his fingertips on the desk top. "Your work is finished, after all. We accomplished what we set out to. Eastland will not be on the board. And you know how county government works, Jake. I would keep you on to continue the Seaview probe, but if I let things go too long, you'd have a civil-service rating and then I'd never be able to get rid of you."

"I couldn't get a civil-service rating for six months."

"That's right," he said, smiling tightly. "But we don't know how long this investigation is going to drag on. Frankly, I'd love to have you on the staff permanently, but with the new budget cuts, I just couldn't justify it. You understand, don't you?"

"Oh, I understand. In a general way. I'm not sure about some of the specifics, though."

"Like what?"

"You never mentioned you'd talked to Pallisgaard."

"No?"

"No," I said. "You invited him to the meeting?"

"That's right."

I nodded. "And you two decided it would be better for him not to be here, is that it?"

He frowned. "I'm not sure I get your meaning."

"Simple. If Pallisgaard knew what you had, he would know Madden is no longer a viable candidate. Since he knows that, it would be smart for him to stay away from the meeting today. It would serve as a message to Madden that he was being sandbagged."

"I'm still not sure what your point is," he said, his voice cautious.

I shrugged. "I'm just sort of thinking out loud. You call up Pallisgaard and suddenly the Seaview investigation gets scrapped, Pallisgaard's connections with Riccio get buried, and his connections to Madden and Eastland are hushed up."

He leaned forward. "See here—"

"What did he promise you, Maher? What kind of a deal did you make with him?"

His eyes got dark. "That trade with Madden was one of the hardest things I've done in my political career. I don't care for your insinuations, Asch."

"I guess I'm just ungrateful. I guess I should say thanks for getting my license back. I owe you. Really. You taught me a lot. I don't think I'll ever get suckered again." He stared at me icily as I stood up. "How about my check?"

"It'll be mailed to you."

I nodded and walked out. Savich caught up with me in the hall and grabbed my arm. He spun me around and I could see the pain in his eyes. "Why did you do that to him, Jake?"

"I really think you can't see it, Marty."

He shook his head violently. "You've got him all wrong—"

"You were right before, Marty. When we worked at the paper. You were right then."

His grip tightened on my arm. "He wouldn't do anything like that. Go back and apologize to him—"

I grabbed his wrist and yanked it off my arm. "You go

back and apologize for me, Marty. I think that's what you're going to be doing for a long time anyway. You might as well get in the practice."

I walked away from him and went down the hall and cleaned out my desk for the second time. I said good-bye to everybody. Then I drove over to the offices of the *Chronicle* and gave the whole story to Mike Sangster, not because I expected him to print it, but just because I wanted someone else to know about it in case something happened to me.

A major storm was on its way from the north and the gray sky was pregnant as I drove the freeway home. It was going to be the wettest February in the history of Los Angeles, the man on the radio was saying, and as if to back him up the rain was already starting to fall. It came down in a soft, gentle baptism, but there did not seem to be anything redeeming in it at all.

As I expected, the story was never printed in the *Chronicle*, or anywhere else.

My license was returned to me by mail, with a note from the head of the Bureau of Consumer Affairs saying that a mistake had been made, and that after further deliberation the decision of the administrative judge who had heard my case had been overturned.

Burt Casey retired from the Board of Supervisors four weeks after I left Maher's employ. Preston Madden appointed Stephen Canby, a state senator from Saugus, to take his place, with the unanimous approval of the board. At the same time, Madden surprised everyone by announcing that he intended to retire from political life at the end of his current term and practice law. He cited exhaustion and finances as his reasons.

Three weeks later, I picked up the morning paper and saw the story I'd been looking for. At a press conference, Jerry

Maher announced that with the backing of the Madden machine he was throwing his hat into the gubernatorial ring. He was expected to be the front runner.

In April, Mary Kay broke all my crockery and left me, leaving behind only a note saying that she would not work for a fascist.

I never talked to any of them again.